Someone else's Summer

····· **PRAISE** *for* ·····
RACHEL BATEMAN and
SOMEONE ELSE'S SUMMER:

"Equally heartbreaking and inspiring,
Rachel Bateman's *Someone Else's Summer*
is a journey of love and healing that
examines the true meaning of bravery."
—Kristina McBride,
author of *A Million Times Goodnight* and *One Moment*

"Plenty of romantic moments
will make starry-eyed readers swoon."

—*Kirkus Reviews*

"[W]ill appeal to fans of contemporary
novels in the vein of Jessi Kirby and
Morgan Matson."
—*Booklist*

"The perfect summer novel."
—YA Books Central

Someone else's Summer

Rachel Bateman

RP|TEENS
PHILADELPHIA

Running Press Teens
Hachette Book Group
1290 Avenue of the Americas, New York, NY 10104
www.runningpress.com/rpkids
@RP_Kids

Printed in the United States of America

First Trade Paperback Edition: May 2018

Published by Running Press Teens, an imprint of Perseus Books, LLC, a subsidiary of Hachette Book Group, Inc. The Running Press Teens name and logo is a trademark of the Hachette Book Group.

The Hachette Speakers Bureau provides a wide range of authors for speaking events. To find out more, go to www.hachettespeakersbureau.com or call (866) 376-6591.

The publisher is not responsible for websites (or their content) that are not owned by the publisher.

Print book cover and interior design by T.L. Bonaddio

Library of Congress Control Number: 2017964015

ISBNs: 978-0-7624-6505-7 (paperback), 978-0-7624-6219-3 (hardcover), 978-0-7624-6221-6 (ebook)

LSC-C

10 9 8 7 6 5 4 3 2 1

to Rani

who got the cooler name
and the cooler sister.

No thanks for the sushi that time, though.

I remember the rain most of all. The day had been beautiful, the sun just peeking through the clouds and falling across the grass where the graduates sat on metal folding chairs. A light breeze played with tassels hanging from mortarboards and fluttered cheap polyester robes as the speakers passed token words of wisdom from the podium.

Suddenly, just as hundreds of maroon caps took to the sky, the clouds opened up and rain washed the earth.

It was just a sprinkling at first, enough to scatter dark spots across shoulders and cool sunburned skin. As the day wore on, the skies darkened more, until it looked like dusk at midafternoon. By the time the all-night party started, the gutters had filled with small rivers and our backyard was a swamp.

Hours later, the rain still pattered a steady rhythm on the roof as a shrill ring pulled me from sleep. Mom and Dad insisted on keeping a landline with receivers throughout the house, even though we rarely used it. The ancient, corded phone blaring just outside my bedroom door should have been my first indication something was wrong; I should have known right away. That's the way it always happens in movies—there's intuition, a feeling deep in the gut. I had none of that, just a mild irritation at whoever was calling. And the constant, insistent rain.

Then my world ended with Mom's ear-breaking scream.

Chapter 1

People stream past photo collages and an overgrown collection of sickly sweet flowers, passing me on the way to their seats. They try not to stare, but how can they not? I sit, not in customary black, but in intense blue, a bright star blinding them in the darkest night. The little sister, left behind. Pretty soon, I'll be the big sister. The only sister.

The church is packed. Television screens have been set up in the auxiliary rooms to broadcast the service to people who can't fit in the chapel. When I arrived this morning, ushered in by Aunt Morgan, the church staff was erecting a projection screen on the front lawn, anticipating more people than will fit in the tiny building. They're apparently preparing for all of Muscatine to show up.

Because that's what happens when someone so young dies tragically. The whole town was rocked when the news hit—Storm Holloway, shining star of Muscatine High School, dies in a one-car accident on her way home from an all-night graduation party held at the Civic Center. Storm, who was heading to UNCW in the fall on academic scholarships. Storm, who the town remembers as the spunky little girl they rallied behind a decade earlier as she fought cancer and won.

Jovani tenses, his arm tightening around me, and Aunt Morgan squeezes my hand so hard the bones grind against each other. I force my gaze to the front of the chapel. A boy is standing in front of a collage filled with pictures of the three of us as kids, and even from behind, I can tell how broken he is. His body is all sharp corners and acute angles, pieced together with tape and a child's glue stick. Nothing fits together; he clutches his lanky arms around his midsection so tightly it looks like he's afraid he'll fall apart if he lets go. His shoulders shake, threatening to vibrate his whole body to pieces.

Cameron Andrews: the boy who was supposed to drive her home.

I sneak a glance at Mom and Dad. I don't know if they blame Cam—I don't know anything about what they think or feel anymore. It's like the phone call that early morning didn't just pull my parents from their sleep, but from their entire lives. The daughter they'd fought so hard to protect, to heal. The daughter they'd beaten the odds with was gone. Now they didn't talk to me or anyone, only to each other. Aunt Morgan had to plan the service when they refused to make any decisions. They completely shut down, and I have no idea how to bring them back.

When Cameron turns from the pictures and his eyes lock with mine—his bloodshot and wet, framed by splotchy skin and pure devastation; mine clear and steely—I can see the fear on his face. He thinks I hate him, that everyone hates him. It hits me as he passes our row, hesitating briefly, that he blames himself.

"I . . ." I don't know what to say, so I gesture vaguely toward the aisle Cameron just vacated.

Aunt Morgan lets my hand go for the first time since we arrived at the church. "Hurry back," she whispers. "I think it's about to start."

Shrugging Jovani's arm from around me, I stand, and my back is bombarded with stares. I can feel the eyes of everyone in the room turning in my direction, watching, waiting for me to make a scene. But I won't give them that. Instead, I square my shoulders, set my gaze straight ahead, and make my way toward the aisle, stepping over Jovani and my best friend, Piper. I pull in a deep breath and turn to face the room, forcing back the panic rising in me, threatening tears. These people don't deserve my tears, don't get to see me break down. They aren't here to support me or my family; they aren't here to grieve.

No, when this many people come to the funeral of a teenage girl they don't really know, they do it for one reason only: to celebrate their own lives. To remind them how short life can be and how lucky they are to have made it past eighteen.

A movement to the right catches my attention, and my eyes flick toward it before I can stop myself. Taylor sits at the far end of the row, surrounded by the rest of the cheerleaders. They are here for me, the logical part of my brain reminds me. Piper and me, we're part of them. We go to the parties, eat together at lunch. We sleep at one another's houses and share secrets. But when I see Taylor now, all I can think of is how heartless she can be. How she'll make fun of anyone who isn't just like the rest of us.

Did Storm know back then? Did she know my friends mocked her? That I was too weak, too insecure, to stop them?

Anger licks my skin, and my hands clench into fists at my sides. Taylor smiles sadly and offers a small wave, but I turn away from her and continue down the aisle.

Cameron startles when I squeeze myself between him and the middle-aged woman sitting beside him near the back. He stares with open shock for a moment before finding his voice.

"Nice dress," he says, his words falling flat.

"Thanks." I finger the white and hot pink tulle sticking out from the bottom of the blue skirt. The dress is almost comically bright. "It was—"

"Her favorite. I know. I was there when she bought it."

I don't know why this surprises me. They were always together. Cameron and Storm. Storm and Cameron. A package deal. It'd been that way since we were kids. But somehow, I never imagined what that meant. That if she bought a dress, Cam would be there, waiting outside the fitting room until she found the perfect one. Since I joined the squad and started going out with my own friends instead of tagging along with them, I guess I forgot what it was like between Storm and Cameron.

"It looks nice on you," he says.

A small laugh barks from my mouth, and I clamp a hand over my lips. A few people in the row ahead of us turn to glare.

"This thing barely covers my butt," I whisper. "I feel like some perv's happy-gram in it." Guess that's what happens when I put my five-foot-ten body into a dress made for my five-foot-zero sister.

"It can't be any shorter than your cheerleading skirt," Cameron says. His face breaks into a lopsided grin, still with a twinge of sadness, but he's clearly trying for lighthearted. "Besides, you've got great legs. She always said she wished she had your legs. She's probably thrilled to see one of her crazy dresses on you finally." He shakes his head. "Sorry. That was so—"

"No, it's good. I'm so sick of people treating me like I might explode at any second if they mention her."

He shrugs, dropping his head to stare at his hands, where they hang between his knees. His thick-framed glasses slip down his nose. I reach over and grab his hand. "Come on."

Cameron gives me a confused look, and I give a little tug. "You're family, always have been. Come sit with us."

Staring at our clasped hands, he says, "I don't know, Anna. Your parents . . ."

"My parents are in such a daze they don't even know what's happening right now. But if they did, they would want you with us."

"Are you sure?" His voice breaks on the last word and a shudder works its way through his body, down his arm, and into my hand. "I should have—why did I let her go by herself?"

A fissure breaks in my heart, and I swallow back my tears before they appear. I wrap my other hand around his. "I love

Storm more than anything in the world, Cameron. You know that. But she is . . . was"—a tiny sob sounds like a hiccup in my throat—"the most stubborn person in the history of stubborn people. If she didn't want you to come with her, you would have had to knock her out to get into that car."

"Maybe I should have."

"And then what, Cam?" I'm aware that my voice is rising to near hysteria. People are staring out right now, not bothering to be discreet. The pastor stands just to the left of the pulpit, watching us. The ornate clock behind him tells me the service was supposed to start three minutes ago. I lower my voice, slightly. "And then what? You would both be up there on the altar? Should we have gotten you matching urns? You had no way to know what was going to happen."

He squeezes his eyes shut tight, shakes his head slowly as if trying to shake off the deluge of emotions washing over him. "I still should have . . ."

"Enough," I say. "The service is going to start. Please, come sit with us. Storm would have wanted it." I stand, pulling his hand softly. "I want it."

"Okay," he says so softly the word barely makes it to my ears. He stands and we make our way back to sit with my broken family.

I clutch his hand the whole way, as if he's the only thing keeping me from floating away.

Chapter 2

At Muscatine High School, I'm not queen bee, but I'm close enough. I know how people see me: cocaptain of the cheer squad, popular, pretty. They don't see the girl I was—the one I still am, somewhere deep down. The girl who idolized her older sister, who wanted to be just like her and do everything she did. No, they see what I want them to see. And so girls want to be me, and guys want to be with me. My best friend is the hottest girl in school, and my sometimes-boyfriend is on the football team. Since freshman year, when Piper and I were the only new girls on Varsity, I've had it made.

Storm was an outcast, a geek. She was the girl who dressed weird and always carried an old camera around and took five AP classes her senior year. She listened to bands nobody had ever heard of and spent lunch breaks leaned against a pillar in the middle of the quad with oversize headphones on her ears and equally oversize Russian novels in her lap. Everyone knew her—by her loud outfits and whispers about her cancer and oft-told stories of revolts she led in classes, pressing her teachers until she got her way. But nobody really knew her the way I did.

We were born only eleven months apart. Irish twins, Mom loved to call us, even though there was nothing Irish about our family. When Storm and I were kids, Mom and Dad would joke that I was so eager to follow Storm that I couldn't even wait to join the family.

And follow her I did. All my earliest memories are of the two of us, her always leading the way. With Storm, the backyard wasn't just the backyard. It was an enchanted forest and a medieval battlefield and a haunted fortress. We spent our days building faerie traps under the oak tree and collecting ingredients for witches' brews. Being with Storm was everything, and I wanted to be just like her. Our days were filled with make-believe and magic, just the two of us in a world of our own.

Then one day, a new car pulled into the driveway next door, and a boy Storm's age stumbled out of the backseat. He was tall and gawky; his hair stuck up at an odd angle on the side of his head, and the glasses that wrapped around the backs of his ears overpowered his face. His pants were a full inch too short, and he scratched the toe of one scuffed tennis shoe across the exposed ankle of the opposite leg. When he saw us watching him, he raised a tentative hand. I mimicked his shy wave; Storm ran across the driveways to meet him.

Two grew to three. From then on, Cameron was a part of our world, right beside us every day. The two of them would be going to kindergarten that fall, and we did everything we could to prolong the summer. We were up before the sun and begged the parentals every night to let us stay outside way later than our normal bedtimes. It was a summer of Popsicles and swimming pools and sleeping in tents. We wore the mothers out during the days and dragged the fathers, in their suits and ties, to the small wood at the edge of our yards right after work to help us search for faerie rings.

The day school started, I stood and watched Storm and Cameron settle into their new classroom, seated side by side at their table, knees and shoulders touching. I swallowed the lump in my throat and waved good-bye to them, trying to smile.

I cried the whole way home, begging the mothers to turn back and let me go to school, too. When we arrived home, I ran straight through the backyard to the big oak tree to check our faerie trap. But without Storm there, the tree was just a tree. The magic wasn't in the woods or the yard or anywhere; the magic was in my sister, and she wasn't there. Lost, I went inside.

That school year, I spent my days hovering over Mom, trying to learn everything she was doing, finding someone else to follow. I learned how to can peaches and make ice cream and how to perfectly fold a fitted sheet. We played Trouble for hours and read Nancy Drew and the Little House books and watched *The NeverEnding Story* on repeat. Until three thirty came, and the squeak of the school bus's brakes sounded Storm and Cameron's return. Then the magic came back for the evening.

Storm's diagnosis came just before my seventh birthday. Non-Hodgkin Burkitt lymphoma. It sounded like a foreign language. I had no idea what it meant or why Mom and Dad were so scared. All I knew was that, with those words, everything changed.

Our days morphed from soccer games and tree climbing to doctor visits and obsessive house cleaning. I got in trouble for doing the exact same things nobody cared about just a month before, and Mom was constantly shushing me, pushing me out the door so I wouldn't interrupt Storm's rest. Cameron was in Nevada with his nana and papa for the summer, so it was just me in the backyard, separated from my sister and a whole world.

Then she went to the hospital, and I was really alone. Aunt Morgan came to watch me, feeding me frozen pizza and letting me stay up late to watch *Law & Order* with her. The summer blew by in a haze of murder mysteries, pepperoni, and visits to the pediatric cancer ward, where Mom made me dress in a full paper gown and mask, even when the doctors said the risk of infection wasn't that high anymore. Cameron came home at the end of the summer, but it wasn't the same without Storm there. Cam and I rode the school bus together and played outside when we got home. We had fun, but my sister's absence always hung over us.

When she came back home, her hair was nothing more than soft black fuzz on her head, and her eyebrows were gone. But her smile was just the same: bigger than big and so bright it made me grin every time I saw it. I moved into her room then, sneaking in every night after bedtime to curl up next to her and share the bed.

My eighth-grade year was the worst. We all went to private school from kindergarten through eighth grade, so I'd been with Storm and Cameron since I started school. But that year, they'd moved to the public school, Muscatine High, leaving me all alone. With them gone, I finally realized how much they were the center of my life. I had no other friends; I knew the kids in my classes and was friendly with them, but I'd never tried to become close with them, and by eighth grade, everyone already had a group to hang out with. I ended up eating lunch with some girls from my social studies class, but I was decidedly "other." I didn't get invited out bowling or to birthday parties. I was lonely.

During the last month of school, the Muscatine High cheerleaders came to our school to recruit for tryouts. They held a small assembly in the auditorium where they showed off some of their routines and told us all about how wonderful cheerleading was. I don't really remember what all they said. I sat there, bored, with the rest of my classmates, watching the clock tick by to the final bell. What I do remember is one of the cheerleaders running up to me at the end of the assembly. She was all wild red hair and sparkly eye shadow, a ball of energy in a neon tank top.

"Hey," she said breathlessly.

"Um. Hi?"

She shoved a stick of gum into her mouth and held the pack out, offering me a piece. I waved it away, and she slipped it back into her pocket with a shrug. "Are you gonna try out?"

"Um . . ."

"Because you totally should. I'm only on JV this year, but I think I'll make Varsity next year." She laughed, throwing her hair over her shoulders. "Oh, sorry." She giggled. "I'm Piper."

"Anna," I said with a weak smile.

"So, will you? Our coach really wants us to each bring someone, and I just moved here halfway through the year so I don't really know any eighth graders to ask."

I must've looked as hesitant as I felt, because she grabbed my hand and her voice took on a pleading tone. "Please? I think you'd be great—no, really! I can just tell. Please?"

The bleachers were emptying now, some of my classmates lingering behind to talk to the other cheerleaders and take fliers. I found the girls I'd been eating lunch with that year; they stood in a small clump at the edge of the gym rolling their eyes whenever someone walked past them with a tryout form in hand. I looked back to Piper and shrugged. "Okay."

Visibly excited, she looped her arm through mine and led me toward the sign-up table. "'Louis,'" she said, "'I think this is the beginning of a beautiful friendship.'"

And it was. From the first night of tryouts on, Piper and I were inseparable. Before long, I had a new group of friends and parties to go to and games to cheer at. I spent fewer and fewer evenings with Storm and Cameron until one day they stopped asking me to hang out. It wasn't a big deal at the time—I had my own friends to hang out with—but now? Now I felt the distance like a chasm in my heart, and it was too late to close the gap.

Chapter 3

Mom and Dad rise, and I realize the service is over and the crowd is waiting for the family to exit before standing. Just another chance for our grief to be paraded before them. My parents hug, clinging desperately to each other. Tears stream down Dad's face, and Mom's small frame shakes with her sobs. She sounds like an animal, feral and injured.

We stand as a unit, Aunt Morgan, Cameron, and me. Piper and Jovani follow suit, and the two of them quietly make their way out to the aisle to let us pass. Still, I refuse to let go of my anchors, so we make our way past my friends' vacant seats, an awkward, six-legged creature, followed closely by my shaking parents. An old man—the funeral director, maybe?—leads us from the chapel via a small door behind a curtain, and then we are alone. Finally, I release my grip on Cameron's and Aunt Morgan's hands. I flex and stretch my fingers, coaxing blood back to the tips.

Piper makes her way past Cameron and wraps her arms around me, tight. My face disappears into her hair, and I inhale, her familiar scent of vanilla and cinnamon grounding me.

"Thank you so much for coming," I say.

She squeezes even tighter. "Don't be stupid," she says. "Where else would I be?"

"I don't know," I say, and I feel a laugh working its way into my voice. It feels foreign. "Maybe anywhere in the world other than a church."

She lets go and backs up just enough to look at me. "Not just any church, either," she says. "This is, like, the most uptight, conservative church ever."

Cameron chuckles, and I realize how close he's stayed by my side, as if I never let go of his hand.

"That's the Holloways," he tells Piper. "Go big, or go home. If you're going to church, you better *really* go to church."

Dad makes his way across the room now and wraps one arm around my shoulder and pulls me into his side. I melt into place there, and finally the dam breaks. Tears flood from my eyes so fast I don't even know how they got there, and pretty soon, I'm a mess of sobs and snot and tears. All the sadness, anger, fear—everything I've forced down for the past ninety minutes—rushes to the surface, fighting to be the first out of me. I gasp for air, my lungs screaming. Black spots prickle the edges of my vision.

"Bring her here," Aunt Morgan says. She sounds far away, her voice muffled. It's like when Storm and I used to play in the pool during the summer, talking to each other under water, telling secrets and jokes, never really sure if we heard things right. Suddenly, hands are on my upper arms, guiding me across the room. I can't see through the tears.

Something pushes against the back of my knees. I fight it for a moment, but finally allow them to bend, and I crash down onto the couch. A hand presses my back, forcing me forward. I don't fight it. I can't—I can't focus on anything but trying to pull air into my lungs. They burn. My head throbs. The room spins around me.

The hand forces my head between my knees then starts tracing soft circles across my back.

"Breathe," the voice whispers into my ear. "Just take a breath, Anna."

I reach my hand out and grasp at the air for a moment before he realizes what I'm doing. Jovani takes my hand in his, continuing the circles with his other. "Come on, Anna," he says, his voice as calm and steady as always. "We're here. Just take a breath."

He talks to me like that, his voice soft and soothing, until my sobs have turned into quiet, erratic hiccups. When I pull myself back up to sitting, my head protesting the movement violently, he's there beside me, waiting. My parents are huddled together at the edge of the couch, Aunt Morgan holding Mom's arm, and Cameron and Piper stand just behind Jovani.

"Sorry," I say shakily. "I don't know—"

"Don't be sorry," Jovani says. "You're allowed to fall apart, you know."

I nod. Focusing on my breathing for a couple minutes, feeling my heart slow back to a normal cadence, I look up at everyone assembled in the room. "I'm better." I turn to Mom and Dad. "I'm sorry if I scared you."

Mom still looks shaken, but Dad smiles softly. "It's okay, pumpkin. It's okay." He glances at his watch. "We need to get back to the house. Cameron?"

"Yes, sir?" Cameron pulls at the collar of his shirt. As far as I remember, he's never called my dad *sir*. Ever. Red blotches climb up Cam's neck and into his cheeks.

Dad doesn't seem to notice Cameron's nerves. "Pastor Willitz is going to drive us home. Can you take Anna with you, please?"

The room is a vacuum—I'm not sure anyone even breathes. Cam's face crumples, and he makes his way to the couch to sit next to me, silent tears hanging on the edges of his eyelashes. I watch as the realization hits Dad.

Just days before, after the graduation ceremony, Dad clapped Cam on the shoulder. "Congratulations," he said jovially.

"Thanks, Roger." Cam waved his diploma cover in front of his face. "Of course this thing is empty, so maybe they aren't going to let me out of here after all."

Dad laughed his bellowing Dad laugh. "Hey," he whisper-shouted conspiratorially, "I'm taking Storm's car back home to detail it. We're getting her that paint job she's been so subtly hinting at for graduation. Can you take her with you to the party, please?"

That was the last time we saw her, as she left the gymnasium with Cam in their polyester robes. When did she convince him to come get my car? Why couldn't she just ride with him like Dad asked?

Now, finally, a noise breaks the silence of the room. Mom pulls in a shaky, shuddering breath, then speaks the first words I've heard from her in days. "You know we don't blame you, Cam. You're still our favorite." She forces a caricature of a smile onto her face.

Cameron slumps farther into the couch, his whole body relaxing beside me until our arms are pressed together.

"Told you nobody blames you," I whisper. Then I look up at my parents. "We'll be fine," I say.

"You can come with us, baby," Mom says. "We just thought..."

"No," I interrupt. "You're right. I would rather Cam just take me home." I force a pathetic smile and stand to hug my parents. Mom feels like she might break under the pressure of my arms, but Dad is strong and solid. I pull him tighter. "I love you."

"I love you, too." He kisses my head then lets me go before grabbing Mom's hand, leading her out of the room. Pastor Willitz is waiting on the other side as they swing the heavy door open, and he looks past them at me, his eyes full of pity. Aunt Morgan gives one last look over her shoulder, too, searching my face for any indication she should stay, but I wave her away.

As soon as the door shuts, Piper starts, "We got Mama Mae's soccer mobile, so there's room for you with us, Anna." Jovani drives an old Civic Del Sol, so whenever there are more than two people, he charms his mom into giving him the keys to her minivan. Piper looks at me expectantly, waiting for me to jump up and go with them. Which I would, any other time.

Today, with the warmth of Cameron's arm pressed against mine, instead of leaving with my best friends, I look at Piper and say, "That's okay. I'll see you guys there, all right?"

"Sure. Give me a call if you need me to grab you anything. I should probably go give the Mom Mobile back," Jovani says. On the surface, he's completely calm, but I know him and know that, underneath, he's hurt. But he won't show that—not in front of Cameron. Piper, though, stares at me, fire sparking in her eyes. She swears the stereotypes about redheads—that they have fiery tempers, that they are heart-breakers—are completely false, but she pretty much embodies them both. She glares at Cameron then looks at me, disbelief painted across her face.

"Seriously?"

I nod.

"Fine," she snaps, softer than her normal lashing, but still. "I'll see you there, I guess." She follows Jovani out the door.

Cam and I continue to sit. Neither of us makes a move toward the door. "You could have gone with them," he says after a minute passes.

"I know."

"Why didn't you?"

Why didn't I? I could tell him it's because Dad asked him to drive me, but we'd both know that's a lie. It's not that I'm a complete rebel—I typically stay in line—but Dad asking Cameron to drive me is definitely not enough to stop me from riding with my friends, and we both know it. I'm not sure I can fully explain why, but I try.

"You get it," I say. He doesn't respond, so I continue. "I love Jo and Piper, but they will never get it the way you do."

"Get what?"

"Storm. They are part of my world, not hers. They never knew her the way you do. They just . . . they can't get it. They don't know what it's like to lose her."

He nods, but he doesn't speak. He doesn't need to. We sit as the clock on the wall clicks away the seconds. Then Cameron holds his hand out to me.

"Okay," he says. "Let's go face this."

Chapter 4

Cars line both sides of our street for as far as I can see. Cameron pulls the truck into his driveway, blocking his mom's car. Not that it matters—she's probably at my house anyway. The rest of the town certainly is.

I don't want to go in; I want to sit here in Cameron's truck, listening to the radio, to silence, anything other than the soft chatter inside my home. But he's already opening his door, so I do the same.

The walk from his driveway to my front door is only about forty yards cut across my lawn, but it seems to stretch for eternity. Each step closer, my anxiety ratchets up, and the urge to turn and run the other direction grows stronger.

We reach the porch. Climb the three steps to the front door. I stare at the door, willing it to open. Automatically, I grasp Cam's hand in mine. *Don't let go of me*, I tell him through my grip. *Don't let me face them alone.*

We enter.

The house is crammed with people. Some I recognize from school—Taylor is talking to Piper in the corner of the living room, the other cheerleaders buzzing around them in a frenzy of nervous energy. Jovani is nowhere to be seen. He probably dropped Piper off before taking his mom's car back home. Or he's up hiding from the crowd in my room. He's never been much for the crowds and crush of bodies. The rest of the living room is filled with faces I barely recognize—people from church, Dad's coworkers, Storm's old teachers. I recognize some doctors from the cancer ward. How did they react when they heard the news? Such a fight to beat cancer only to lose Storm to an old oak tree on Rock Hill Road.

"I can't," I say through clenched jaws. "I don't want to talk to all those people."

Cameron's grip on my hand tightens. "Let's make it to the kitchen," he says. "Get something to drink, get away from the crowd. We'll figure it out." He leads me through the door and past the featureless faces, slowing for nobody until we pass through the dining room and make it to the kitchen.

Thankfully, there are only a few people here, dropping off casseroles and filling plates with the generic funeral spread. We scoot around the island toward the fridge, and, with cans of Dr Pepper in hand, lean against the long buffet, waiting until the people leave and we are alone.

"Thank you," I say.

"Anytime."

He cracks his can open, and I'm brought back to a million afternoons as a kid, the three of us drinking Dr Pepper out of chilled metallic cups while watching cartoons. I wish we could've stayed like that forever, just three kids splayed out on the living room floor, not a worry in the world.

I wonder if Cameron is thinking the same thing, if the smell of Dr Pepper brings him back the way it does me.

Aunt Morgan breezes into the kitchen. "Oh thank goodness," she says. She smiles sadly—is there any other way to smile today?—and turns to Cameron. "Your mom just got called to the hospital. Apparently Sarah is at home puking—you know what, it doesn't matter. She has to go in, but your truck . . ." She trails off and looks at the two of us, then down at our hands, still clasped between our bodies. I grip him tighter.

"I'll go move it," he says as he sets his can on the counter. To me, he says, "Just hang out in here. I'll be back as soon as I can find a place to park the truck, okay?"

I nod and force myself to let go of his hand. Cameron rushes out the side door.

"Hey," Aunt Morgan says, "I'm supposed to be, you know, making sure everything is okay out there?" She has a bad habit of making nonquestions sound like questions, something Mom says she picked up from her sorority sisters. "But I can hang out in here if you want?"

"No," I say, shaking my head for emphasis. "I'm fine. I kinda want to just chill alone anyway."

"Okay. I'll be out there if you need me."

"Seriously, go." I wave her out of the room. "I'll be fine."

As the minutes tick by, though, I begin to realize how not fine I really am. I watch the clock above the range as it clicks by four, five, six minutes since Cameron left. How long does it take to move a truck, really? Anxiety crawls under my skin, tingling, and I want to claw my way out of my own body. I feel another panic attack creeping its way to the surface, but I can't let it break free this time. Not with all these people to hear me. I need to find another way to disperse this energy.

The side door swings open, blowing a warm breeze through the kitchen, and relief washes over me. But it's not Cameron, like I expect. Instead, Jovani enters and quietly latches the door behind him. He's changed out of his suit into khakis and a fitted polo. His long, black hair is loose around his face instead of in the clean ponytail he wore to the funeral.

Heat blooms low in my stomach, and suddenly I know how to release this pent-up anxiety. My can drops onto the kitchen counter, almost tipping over, and I make a beeline across the kitchen to Jo, grabbing him by the hand and pulling him behind me.

"What—"

"I gotta get out of here," I say over my shoulder. "Come with me."

Pulling him behind me a bit too harshly, I make my way up the kitchen stairs—they are dark and narrow, built as servants' stairs when the house was new. I push the door at the top open slowly, peeking out to make sure the hallway is empty, then dart across to my bedroom door.

Once we're inside and I've closed the door with a soft click, I drop Jovani's hand, and he says, "What do you want—"

I don't let him finish. Instead, I push him up against the wall, hard, and press my lips to his. They are warm and soft, as familiar as anything. And when he opens his mouth—out of surprise or lust, I'm not sure—I open mine, too, letting our tongues mingle together.

My body is flush against his, so I can feel as he begins to respond to my kiss. He presses back against me and groans softly into my mouth. He tastes like he always does, like he just ate a piece of bitter dark chocolate. His hands tangle in my hair, run over my shoulders and upper arms. I press myself tighter to him. I need to feel him. I need to feel anything other than this emptiness Storm's death has left me with.

My fingers grasp at his pants, fumbling to get his belt unbuckled, desperate to remove the layers between us. He gasps a sharp breath and moves to help me. His hands wrap around mine, big and warm, and—

The door swings open next to us, bouncing off Jo's shoulder, and Cameron steps into the room. "Hey, Anna. You in—oh!" He spots us and forces his gaze to the floor, his face growing bright red.

My hands jerk back from Jovani's pants straight to my hair, trying to smooth it back down. I twist it into a quick braid and let it hang over one shoulder. Jo keeps angled toward me, refusing to turn and look at Cameron. We all stand there, three awkward statues, everyone afraid to make the first move. Finally, Cameron clears his throat. "Uh, sorry. I didn't . . ."

Someone Else's Summer

And still he's standing there. I can feel my eyes growing bigger, bugging out of my head. He shuffles his feet a bit, pushes a toe against the melted piece of carpet Piper burned with her curling iron two years ago. Back and forth, back and forth. This day can't get any longer, but somehow it is anyway.

"Well," he says quietly, "I guess I'll just . . ."

"Go!" I scream, my anger so sudden it scares even me. "Just go, Cam. Get out!"

I catch one last glimpse of his face before he leaves, the shock clear for only a moment before his eyes go hard and flinty. He backs into the hallway, pulling the door behind him so softly it barely clicks as it latches. All my breath rushes out of me in a huff, leaving a void in my lungs. Deep in my soul. It's the emptiness more than anything that I can't stand. I'm not ready. Will never be ready.

I turn and kiss Jovani again, fiercely, trying to bring us back to where we were before Cam's interruption. My hands find his still at the front of his pants, and I grab to find his belt again. But then, instead of undoing his belt, he grips my wrists, pulling my hands up between our chests, pushing me back. "Hold on," he gasps.

I lean in to kiss him again, but he pushes me back farther. "I can't."

"What?" It's not like we've not been here before. Quickly, I push back to him. "Sure feels like you can," I say.

Jovani drops my hands and crosses the room to sit on my

bed, just as calm as he always is. "You don't want this, Anna."

"You don't know what I want," I snap.

"Do you?" His dark eyes pierce mine. "You know I love you, Anna. Always. But really, think about this, okay?"

The anger rising in me falls back down almost immediately. I drop onto the bed next to him, lying on my back with my legs hanging over the edge. "What if I don't want to think about it? What if I just want to feel . . . something?"

The bed bounces as Jovani drops next to me. "Come here," he whispers, pulling me into him, giving me his bicep as a pillow. "If you want to feel something, you have to let yourself feel it. I'm here for you as long as you want me to be. But I can't let you use me to try to ignore your pain. Just feel it."

Tears come again now, quietly this time, as I allow myself to miss Storm, really miss her for the first time since the accident. I cry in Jovani's arms until my head hurts and my eyes are so puffy I can barely open them. After my sobs subside, I yawn, and he hugs me tight.

"Go ahead and sleep. I'm not going anywhere."

"Thank you," I say. "For not, you know . . ."

"No problem," he says.

"Really?"

He laughs, a deep rumble in his chest. "Well, no, I think I deserve a medal for that, actually."

"I'll make sure to get you one in the morning," I say, just before drifting to sleep.

Chapter 5

My tank top is wrinkled, but I don't care. I pull it over my suit and step into a pair of soft shorts. I work my hair into a braid without brushing it. It's a mess, but hopefully the good kind of mess, not the I-couldn't-care-less-about-life kind of mess. Even if I couldn't care less about life right now.

It's been three weeks. Three weeks since graduation, since that night, since that tree, since my whole world fell out from under me.

Three weeks since she left me.

I gave myself a week. I could have taken more time. Gillian would have given me as much time off as I needed, but I couldn't be in the house with Mom and Dad's grief anymore. Pastor Willitz came by every afternoon to counsel them. The day after the funeral, after he witnessed Jovani leaving my room, he invited me to join them, no doubt trying to save my soul, but I declined. That's their thing, not mine. They seem to be doing better, but not at the same time. They are responsive now; the haze they broke through at the funeral hasn't come back, thankfully. But I've never felt so distant from them, so separate. It's like I wasn't even there all those days, but just a ghost making my way through the house that's way too big for only the three of us. Funny, me being the ghost when she's the one who's gone.

On day eight, I pulled my swimsuit on followed by a pair of soft shorts and my official lifeguard tank top, and I rode my bike to the city pool. Gillian was shocked to see me and tried to send me back home, but I insisted I was ready to work. She must've sensed my desperation to be doing something normal, because she worked me into the rotation, even though the pool was fully staffed that day.

That was two weeks ago. I've been going through the motions ever since. Maybe if I do the things I've always done, I'll eventually make my way back to feeling like myself again. I get up, ride my bike to work, and watch the kids of Muscatine practice their cannonballs and their flirting. I take breaks when scheduled, and I make sure nobody drowns. After work, Piper waits for me. We throw my bike into the back of her stepdad's truck and go to a party. Every night, a different party at a different house, but they are all the same to me. Sometimes, I'm still stung by that bitter anger that grabbed me at the funeral. I remember their mocking attitudes, their seeming hatred for anything *other*—for Storm—and it makes me want to hate them, too. But, I remind myself time and time again, they are my friends. They aren't perfect, but they are here for me, to support me.

So I let Piper whisk me away to the parties. I smile, because people don't know how to handle sad at a party. And I drink what Piper gives me, because that's what I've always done. My skin gets darker, my hair gets lighter, and it's just like any other summer. Except, this summer, she isn't here.

Today is supposed to be the hottest day of the year so far, so we are gearing up for the pool to hit capacity. Hot days are always the most dangerous—more people come to swim, making it harder to see what's going on in the water. Gillian posts extra lifeguards on duty just in case.

"Anna," she says, "are you good to share point with Kurt?" Kurt is a middle-aged high school math teacher and the closest thing to a beach bum you can find in Iowa.

"Of course," I say. Point is technically the hardest job of the day, but I love it. The position in the tower gives a better view of the pool, so it's up to me to see past the chaos if anything happens, but it also means if I see something that's not life-threatening, I can dispatch one of the other guards to take care of it rather than dealing with the swimmers myself. I can't think of a better way to spend the day.

After all the lifeguards know where to spend our first rotation, we make our way to the back room for a quick snack and break before the gates open.

I'm not on the tower long when they come in. The pool is already crowded, but somehow, I notice the second they walk out of the locker room and onto the lawn. They are talking to each other, animated, hands flying with their words. Their smiles are genuine, and they seem so carefree, like they didn't just lose their friend a month ago. How can her friends come here like nothing happened, move on, and not notice the huge Storm-shaped hole following them around?

The girls find a spot on the grass to lay out their towels then they set to work applying sunscreen. I'm still watching them, and I have to force myself to look away and watch the pool instead. Kurt stares at me from the other tower, wondering what has my attention so shattered.

I have no idea how long he has been sitting there when I notice him, but when I climb down from the tower to take my break halfway through my shift, my eyes make my way back toward the pack of girls on the grass, and there he is.

Cameron looks uncomfortable sitting there as they talk and laugh and snack on cheese fries from the concession stand. My eye catches his for a moment, and he offers me a small grimace and a quick wave. We've not talked since that day at my house, when I screamed at him.

I've seen him since, of course. It's hard not to—he's my next-door neighbor. Cam works for his uncle every summer, doing cleanup on construction sites. I notice him in the mornings when he leaves for work and, if I'm home, again in the evenings when he comes back, dusty and sweaty and worn-out looking.

The first day I saw him, two mornings after the funeral, I didn't know what to do. We hadn't been close since freshman year, but all that disappeared as soon as I grabbed his hand and pulled him to sit with the family at the service. Removed from the immediacy and panic of that day, I didn't know how to handle being around him. So I avoided him—have been

avoiding him for weeks, slipping back into my house whenever he happens to be outside his.

I should go talk to him. I almost do, almost go sit on his
towel with him, spend my entire thirty-minute lunch break
there, but then it hits me: maybe it's not just me. We didn't
exactly part on the best terms last time. He was hurting, too,
probably the only person other than my parents who was
feeling the pain as intensely as I was. And I yelled at him.
Kicked him out so I could throw myself at my ex-boyfriend.
It's been easy to avoid him these past weeks, almost too easy,
like maybe he's avoiding me, too?

I change course, tearing my gaze from his, and rush to
the break room. Gillian always gets pizza delivered on busy
days—partly to be nice, partly so nobody has to leave the
pool for lunch. I grab a couple slices and fall onto the couch.

When I come back out to finish my shift half an hour later,
Cameron is nowhere to be seen.

Chapter 6

I should have called Piper. The realization smacks me in the face the second I walk out of the pool office. She's in the parking lot, as always, sitting on the tailgate of her stepdad's rusty old truck. My bike is already in the truck bed, ready to be hauled home.

"About time, chickadee!" Piper jumps down from the truck and dance-walks over to me, her flip-flops slapping the asphalt.

"Hey," I say in a lackluster voice. I've been in a funk ever since my nonencounter with Cameron, and I just want to go home and crawl into bed.

"Guess what?" she says as she turns to walk back to the truck, her arm linking into mine.

"I have no idea."

"Spoilsport." She skips alongside me. "Whatever. Taylor called me, and she got us invited to the most awesome party tonight!" My body tenses at the mention of Taylor, but she doesn't seem to notice.

Suddenly, I'm exhausted. Just the idea of going out makes me want to take a nap. "I don't know, Pip. That shift sucked—"

"All the more reason to get our party on!" She shakes her hips, bumping mine.

"—and I kinda just want to go home."

We are at the truck now, but she hasn't let go of me. "Anna, please come. Jo finally got the night off, so he'll be there.

Who knows, maybe tonight will be the night you two get back together. Again." She laughs—not her real laugh, the one where she really loses control and snorts, but the little bell-tinkle laugh she uses when she wants to draw attention.

I never told Piper what happened between me and Jovani after the funeral, and I know he won't say anything, either. But she isn't stupid. She knows the two of us disappeared for the rest of the day, and, considering our history together, she assumed what she wanted. I never bothered correcting her. Ever since, Piper has been set on the idea of me and Jo getting back together, and if he is going to be at this party tonight, it'll be easier to just go than to try to talk her into taking me home instead.

"Okay," I say, "but I have to shower first. I'm disgusting."

"No prob, Bob!" She lets go of me and dances around the front of the truck to the driver's side door. "Just shower at my house. You can borrow some of my clothes."

"Whatever," I mutter as I climb into the truck, but she either doesn't hear or decides to ignore me.

. . . . . .

Piper's room looks like a magazine puked all over it. Not in the pristine, this-belongs-in-*Better-Homes-and-Gardens* way, either, but in a this-magazine-got-sick-and-now-its-pages-are-stuck-to-the-walls way. Her walls are plastered with pictures she's found throughout the years, first in *Seventeen* and

YM, more recently in *Cosmopolitan* and *Glamour*. She swears there is a method to the display, but in all our time being best friends, I've never been able to figure it out. An ad for the new (three albums ago) We the Me CD is next to a full-page spread of the couple from her favorite soap opera is next to a flier advertising a display board for quarters depicting each of the states. The whole room is wallpapered like this—glossy magazine page after glossy magazine page. If you look closely, you can see other things pinned up, too: concert tickets and stubs from the dollar theater downtown. A receipt from when she bought her first snowboard. Anything that has ever meant something to Piper—or that happened to catch her eye at the right time—is on her walls.

Piper shuts herself in the bathroom to take a shower. I lie down on her bed and am immediately swallowed by her eight pillows and enormous down comforter. She keeps the air-conditioning unit in her window cranked to subarctic year round, just so she never has to take this fluffy beast off her bed. Above my head, a We the Me concert ticket is tacked to the wall with two sparkly, star-shaped thumbtacks. Predictably, this is nowhere near the CD ad page—or any of the three other pictures of the band I can see from here. Instead, the ticket is attached to the bottom of a poster for an old Sega Genesis game, *Earthworm Jim*. I asked Piper about the poster once, and she just shrugged and said, "I don't know, but isn't it funny?"

My phone buzzes with a new text.

AUNT MORGAN: Hey, banana, wanna do lunch sometime this week?

ME: Dude. I thought I told you to stop calling me that when I was twelve.

AUNT MORGAN: Huh, I guess I must've missed that conversation, ANNA BANANA FACE.

ME: You're lucky I love you.

AUNT MORGAN: It's true.

AUNT MORGAN: So, lunch? It's my off week.

ME: Sure. I can't remember my schedule. I'll let you know when I'm off.

AUNT MORGAN: Awesome possum.

ME: I can't believe I used to think you were the coolest person ever.

AUNT MORGAN: Whatever. You still think that. Don't lie.

ME: If you say so.

The shower shuts off, and Piper starts belting out some country song. She never sings in the shower, but as soon as the water stops, all bets are off. My phone buzzes again.

AUNT MORGAN: You okay, banana?

ME: Yeah. Just at Piper's getting ready for some party.

AUNT MORGAN: Okay. But for serious now, are you OKAY?

ME: Yes, I promise. ☺

It's the first time I've ever lied to Aunt Morgan.

Piper bursts into the room, wearing a tiny bathrobe and a towel perched on her head with tendrils of hair falling out of it. When her hair's wet, the color is so dark, it almost looks like blood trailing across her collar bones. "Holy crap! How did it get so late?"

I roll my eyes. "Maybe it got so late because you are the slowest showerer known to mankind."

"Whatever. Go hop in. Now!" She's tearing through her closet, throwing clothes and hangers onto the chair in front of her vanity. "Leave the door unlocked, 'kay? I need to dry my hair."

The shower actually improves my mood somewhat. I'm still not excited about the party, but my muscles have loosened up, and I'm feeling considerably better. I flip through the clothes left hanging in Piper's closet, looking for something light enough not to make me roast tonight. Hot as it was today, it won't cool down much after the sun sets.

With Piper occupied once again in the bathroom, I find a short gauzy dress and pull it over my head. Piper is curvier than I am, but she also likes to wear her clothes tighter than I do, so the dress fits well enough. The straps slip across my shoulders. I do a quick jump test, making sure everything will stay in if I dance. Satisfied, I slip into a pair of rope wedge sandals. Piper will complain that they make me too tall—I'm over six feet in these shoes—but they are my favorites of hers, so I don't care. I shake my hair out over my shoulders and drop back onto the bed.

Piper rushes back out of the bathroom, still in her bathrobe, but now in full hair and makeup. Her hair is curled and pulled up into a bun at the top of her head that is meant to look messy, but that I know took hours of practice to perfect. She's left her bangs down tonight, blunt and straight across her forehead. Her eyes are lined with thick cat eyeliner, and a dusting of shimmer highlights her cheekbones. She holds up two lipsticks. "Red or peach?"

"Peach, for sure."

"Sweet, thanks." She looks at me then, appraising my outfit no doubt. Her gaze falls to my shoes, and I brace myself for the argument for taking them off. Instead, she says, "I hate you, you know that? I wish I could just air-dry my hair and go without makeup."

"You could, you know. There's no rule saying you have to spend an hour in the bathroom before each party."

She drops her robe and stands, completely naked, in front of the pile of clothes she threw onto the chair. Piper has no shame. "Shut up. I know I could, but it's not the same. On you, it looks breezy and beachy. On me, it looks homeless. What should I wear?"

"Your ripped light capris and that flowy purple tank top you love so much," I say without looking up.

She throws a rolled-up ball of socks at me. "I wore that shirt, like, three days ago. Besides, I gotta look hot tonight."

I join her at the chair and dig through the clothes. Piper doesn't so much have a style of dress as she has every style of dress. Shiny minidresses and prim cardigans and faded band

T-shirts. I pull one of these out of the pile now—soft, faded black with NIRVANA stenciled on the front in orangey bleach spray.

"Anna—"

"I know, hot. But look, it's summer. It's already hot out there. You want to look good, not sweaty, right?"

"I guess."

Throwing the shirt at her, I say, "Then put this on. We can cut the neck out of it if you want. Wear it loose over a cami, and it'll hang off your shoulder." I dig a little deeper in the pile until I find a pair of light denim cutoffs. "There, wear these with it. You can glitz up your shoes."

She puts the outfit on, taking my advice on both the neckline and the shoes, choosing to wear shiny gold gladiator sandals. Like her hair, the outfit looks like she just threw it together, that she never has to try to look hot. I give her an I-told-you-so look, and we finally head to the party.

Chapter 7

"Where are we?" I ask when Piper pulls the truck to a stop at the side of the road. There are no sidewalks, no houses in view, but I can see a long driveway lined with cars, a single, crooked mailbox standing guard at the end—4597 SPRINGTREE scrawled in faded paint on the side of the dented white box.

Piper pushes her door open, and the truck's old hinges groan in protest. "Um, I'm not really sure," she says around a giggle. "Taylor met these guys at some party with her cousin last week. I guess they all go to college and live here together. Let's go."

I'm beginning to remember how badly I did not want to party tonight and regretting my choice to wear these shoes. They aren't normally wobbly, but I'm also not normally bushwhacking my way down a potholed dirt road to get to where I'm going.

We walk right down the middle of the driveway; we can't see well enough to work our way around the edges of the cars without tripping. I hear the party long before I see the house, the steady thrum of bass vibrating its way through the woods. Light from the windows breaks past the tree line about the same time the haze of skunky smoke hits my nose.

I raise an eyebrow at Piper. We go to a lot of parties, so it's not like I'm naïve. I've been around pot, even tried it once or twice, though it never did anything for me, so I don't see the point in trying it again. But this is different. A couple people smoking a bowl in the basement of a house party is one thing. Enough pot to permeate the air all the way around a house? That's not the kind of party we go to.

"Did Taylor tell you anything else about these guys?"

"Not really," Piper says. "Just that they are—and I quote—hotter than hot, and they throw the greatest parties, but super exclusive. We're lucky we got invited. I got the impression that they don't normally let high schoolers come."

"Sure," I say. "Lucky us."

Linking her arm with mine, Piper says, "Come on, don't be like that. This is going to be fun. You'll see."

"I dunno. I'm just not feeling it."

She stops, turns to stare flat at me. "Seriously? You're not feeling it? Are you ever going to be feeling it again? Where have you been this summer, Anna?"

She could have slapped me and I wouldn't have been more shocked. I know I've been distant, just going through the motions, but Piper understands. She has to understand. She was there, the first person I called after my parents told me what happened. She rushed right over, in the middle of the night, just to sit with me. She was next to me when I broke down after the funeral. Through everything, she was there, so how can she be asking this now?

"Whatever," I say, shaking my hair over my back. "Let's just go." I march toward the open front door, and Piper falls into step beside me, the moment past.

The inside of the house is no better than the outside. The pot haze is stronger in here, and there are bodies draped over half a dozen mismatched, seventies-style couches, everyone in various stages of undress. I squint to see in the darkness. If I had to guess, nobody here is under twenty-five.

"Um, where do you think Taylor is?" I ask.

Piper's already tapping out a message on her phone. "I'm on it," she says. "Let's go get some drinks."

A man directly across the room is staring at us, his gaze penetrating my skin. He looks to be in his late twenties maybe. He wears his dark hair slicked back in what I imagine is supposed to be a James Dean pompadour, but looks more like just-got-out-of-prison. A tattoo curls up one side of his neck and disappears into his hair behind his ear. He hooks the index finger of one hand at me, calling me over.

"Um"—I grab Piper's hand and try to force a fun, light smile onto my face—"why don't you grab me something. I'm, uh, gonna go look for Jo, okay?"

Her face lights up at this, and she waves me away. "I've got my phone if you get lost," she teases.

I can't get through the house fast enough. It's a maze of rooms, each one leading to another with no hallway, no real division. There are couches everywhere, old, brown tweed ones that you see on the side of the road at the end of a semester—a FREE sign tacked to one of the cushions. There are no beds, no chairs, no decorations of any kind. Just dark paneled walls and dozens of couches. I focus my eyes straight ahead, trying to ignore the activity happening around me—the deeper into the house I go, the darker it gets, and pretty soon I'm surrounded by couples making out, some two or three to a couch. I have to get out of here.

Finally, I stumble into the kitchen. The bright light burns my eyes after all the darkness, and I have to squeeze them shut against it. Opening them slowly, I spot a door, and I run to it, knocking into a girl leaning against the fridge.

"Hey!" she yells.

"Sorry," I mutter. Or try to mutter—I'm not sure I actually say anything. I push out the door and onto a wide deck looking out over a tree-covered lawn. I gulp in air, not caring about the marijuana smell. Anything is better than the stagnant, sweaty air of that house. I pull my phone from my bra and send Piper a text: BACK DECK.

A couple comes outside, and I press myself against the wooden trellis to let them pass. Maybe I shouldn't have messaged Piper yet. I could ride the party out back here, sitting in the dark by myself until she's ready to go.

But here she is now, stumbling through the door. The drinks she's holding slosh over, splashing sweet, fruity something onto my shoes. She looks wasted already.

"Are you high?" I ask her.

She pushes one of the cups into my hand. "I took a couple hits with this guy Trevor. I'm fine." As if to prove her point, she stands up straighter, pushing her shoulders back. "What are you doing back here, girl? Party's inside."

I set my drink on the porch rail. The odor makes my stomach roll. "I thought maybe I'd find Jo out here," I lie. "You know he hates a big crowd."

"Did you try his phone? It'd be faster, and I know you want to get to him fast," she singsongs.

She's right about the phone. I send him a message.

ME: Where are you?

JOVANI: At Luke's shooting some pool. Why? Wanna come over?

ME: I thought you were coming to the party?

JOVANI: What party?

My throat tightens, and the tips of my fingers grow tingly. I wave my phone at Piper, who struggles to focus on the moving screen. "Jovani doesn't even know about the party, Pip. I thought you said he'd be here!"

"Chill, lady. Taylor said she was inviting him. She must've forgotten. Oh well. Let's just go inside. We'll hang out with him tomorrow, I promise."

"Go ahead," I tell her. "I think I'm going to stay out here a bit."

Her eyes flash, and I brace myself for the tirade that's coming. But she surprises me, shrugging and throwing her arms around me in a hug. Her drink sloshes again, and I shudder as the sticky liquid slides down my back. "Whatever, girl. I've got my phone."

Then she's gone, breezing back into the house. This whole place grosses me out. I cross the deck and drop into the single plastic chair sitting watch over an empty hot tub. Pulling Facebook up on my phone, I hope I can entertain myself until she's ready to leave. A message pops up.

JOVANI: Anna? What party?

ME: Never mind. I thought you were coming, but I guess not.

JOVANI: I can probably come now if you don't mind me bringing Luke.

ME: Don't bother. It's lame.

JOVANI: K. Talk later?

ME: Sure.

A giggle sounds shockingly close to my ear, and I jump. I squint in the direction of the noise. There, in the hot tub, is a couple. I don't know how I didn't see them before, because they aren't trying to hide at all. The girl is straddling the guy's lap, her arms wrapped around his head, pushing his mouth down to her chest. She bobs in the water, fast enough now to make waves splash against the side of the tub, her head thrown back, lips parted slightly. She groans, loud.

I jump out of my chair. I have to get out of here. My phone is pressed to my ear before I'm even to the bottom of the porch steps, dialing Jovani. Voice mail picks up, and I mash the END button. Dial again. As it rings, I make my way toward the front of the house. "Come on," I mutter. "I was just talking to you. Pick up." Voice mail again. I try a third time.

The side door cracks open, spilling light across the lawn. I try to duck away from it, to avoid being seen, but it's too late. The light from the kitchen hits me square in the face, and I hear a gravelly voice say, "There you are. I's wondering where you ran off to." It's the guy from the living room, the one with the greasy prison hair, and the way he leers at me makes the hair on my arms stand on end.

My phone hangs in my hand at my side; I can hear the tinny ringing and beg silently for Jovani to pick up. His voice drifts through the putrid air to my ears: "Hi, it's Jo. I probably lost my phone, so—" I end the call with a swipe of my thumb. Crap. Ignoring Jailbird, I keep walking to the driveway.

Suddenly a sweaty hand wraps around my upper arm, pulling me to a stop.

"Hey now," he says, right in my face. He's standing too close; I can smell his sweat mixing with stale smoke and sour beer on his breath. "Where you going in such a hurry, cutie?"

My stomach rolls, and I try to pull away from his grip, but his hand holds tight. I jerk my arm, wincing when his fingers bite into my bicep. He steps even closer, pressing his hot chest up against me while he wraps his other arm around my waist. His hand presses flat against the small of my back, burning me through Piper's dress. Acid bites the back of my throat. I push against his chest.

"Aw, why you gotta be like that, sweetie?" His face is right in mine. Hot breath on my skin about makes me puke. This guy is seriously like a walking stereotype. I push his chest again, and when he doesn't loosen his grip, I throw my elbow into his jaw. Followed immediately by my knee to his crotch.

He curses, and for a second I think he's going to hit me, but instead he lets me go so quickly I stumble and almost fall. The man doubles forward. "You dumb bi—"

My phone trills, cutting through his words. About time. "Jo, what happened? Can you—"

"Anna?" Dad's voice interrupts. "Are you okay?"

I walk away from the man as fast as I can, wobbling on these tall shoes. Forcing my voice not to shake, I say, "Yeah. I'm fine. What's up?"

"Just making sure you have your keys. Your mom and I are going to bed."

"Yeah," I say, then, "wait. No, I don't." They are in my bag stuffed in Piper's trunk. And there's no way I'm going back in that house for her car keys. "Sorry."

"It's okay. I'll leave the side door open."

"Thanks, Dad. Love you."

"Love you, too, sweetie."

I press the END button then immediately dial Jovani again. His voice mail starts to play when I'm halfway down the driveway. Then, "Jo, it's me. Can you—this party isn't lame, it's awful. Can you come get me?" I'm surprised to find tears streaming down my face. My voice shakes. "Piper doesn't want to leave, and I just can't . . . I don't want to be here anymore. I'm at"—I'm halfway to the road now—"crap, I can't remember the address. I'm gonna start walking. Please call me back."

I hang up and shoot a quick text to Piper.

ME: I'm leaving, so don't freak when you can't find me.

PIPER: what the eff?

ME: I'm just not in the mood tonight. Sorry.

PIPER: just stay another hour, K?

ME: Don't worry about it. Jovani's coming to get me. ☺

I hate lying to her, but it's easy when I know she'll let me go without argument for this. Sure enough, another message comes in almost immediately.

PIPER: ooo la la. don't do anything i wouldn't do. and tell me EVERYTHING.

At the end of the driveway, I read the address on the mailbox, committing it to memory in case Jovani calls back. Then I pull up my phone's GPS service and type in my address: 4.3 miles. I dial Jovani again. Nothing.

I shove my phone into my bra and start walking.

Chapter 8

When I get home an hour and a half later, I'm a complete mess. My feet are killing me—blisters have grown, popped, and regrown where the straps of my shoes lay. I tried taking the shoes off and walking barefoot for a while, but the first jagged rock I hit ended that experiment. The bottom of my left foot now sticks to the sole of Piper's shoe where my blood has dried, fusing the two together.

I stink. I'm sticky and sweaty and need a shower. The top of my dress is soaked, though I can't tell if it's more sweat or tears. As I turn up the front walk, I check my phone for the hundredth time. Still nothing from Jovani.

I round the house to the side door, turning the knob slowly then swinging the door as fast as I can control it, forcing it to breeze past the squeaky spot. I creep up the back staircase so I don't have to cross by Mom and Dad's bedroom. If they wake up now and see me like this, they'll freak. I can still smell the faintest hint of pot clinging to my dress. When I make it to the bathroom, I peel off the fabric and shove it deep in my hamper. I can't take a shower—the groan of the pipes might wake Mom, the world's lightest sleeper—so I wet a washcloth instead, wiping the cool water across my face and chest. Once I'm cleaned off as much as possible, I wrap myself in my bathrobe and head to my room.

I don't know what makes me stop. I pass the door every day, every time I walk between the bathroom and my bedroom. I've avoided this room since the accident—we all have. As far as I know, the door hasn't been opened since we left the house that morning. But now, as if I'm being sucked in, I turn the knob.

Even in the dark, the room looks exactly how I remember it—neat and orderly, with dozens of Polaroids tacked up in a precise grid on the wall. Faces stare down at me, Storm's messy calligraphy scrawled over each picture, obscuring the images with captions. *We met that night,* reads one. Another says, *I took this on July 4.* I squint against the dark and scan the wall, picking out her face, smiling and bright, in picture after picture. In this room, it's like she's still alive.

I lie on the bed and pull a stuffed bear to my chest. It still smells like Storm. Shoving my face into its soft fur, I breathe her in. Wonder where she is.

My muscles relax, melting into the bed. My feet still tingle, and my legs twitch as they wind down from the walk. Sleep threatens me, my eyelids pulling toward each other. Suddenly, my room, just next door, seems too far away. I stretch my arms and fold my hands behind my head to settle in for the night.

My left hand bumps something under the pillow. I pull it out—some kind of book. It's small and colorful, the kind of notebook I used to find lying around the house with random scribbles in them. I click on the bedside lamp and turn the book over. The cover is one big doodle, black Sharpie against rainbow background. Swirls and dots all spiraling around three words: *My Perfect Summer.*

My heart speeds up, kicking into high gear, and suddenly I'm wide awake. Slowly, hesitating—for a moment, wondering if I'll actually do it—I open the book. The pages, just like the cover, are filled with doodles, different colored markers making beautifully ordered chaos across the paper. On the first page, staring right at me, is the number one.

I flip through a few pages, unable to focus on the words, before it hits me. It's a list—of course it is. How many times over the years would I find a scrap of paper, a shoebox lid, or a napkin with a list scribbled on it? Lists littered our house; they ruled our summers as we rushed to check off one random activity after another before school started in the fall.

When was the last List Summer? After eighth grade, maybe ninth? Looking back now, I realize that the summer lists stopped when I got too busy for them, spending my days with Piper and the squad instead of with Storm and Cam. It never occurred to me that maybe Storm kept writing them.

I flip to the first page and read each item, one at a time.

Someone Else's Summer

1. Watch the sunrise.
2. Take pictures of EVERYTHING.
3. Get a tattoo.
4. Go inside a lighthouse.
5. ~~Meet my soulmate.~~ Fall in love.
6. Go skinny dipping.
7. Kiss in the rain.
8. Put a secret in a balloon & let it fly away.
9. Road trip!
10. Crash a wedding.
11. Go to a dive-in movie.
12. Speak in a British accent all day.
13. Sleep in the UNCW dorms.
14. Go parasailing.
15. Be brave with my life.

When we were kids, our lists were filled with random, silly tasks: sleep in the tent in the backyard, play Frisbee, count all the stars we can see through the kitchen window, eat ice cream for dinner, have a water fight. This list is different. Heavier somehow, more grown-up, almost sad. I run my fingers over the ridges her pen made in the pages, trying to imagine what she was feeling when she wrote this.

Turning back to #11: Go to a dive-in movie, I finger a worn ticket stub glued to the opposite page. *Jaws*, playing at Carolina Beach Lake Park dive-in theater some August night six years ago. How did she get that? She'd never been to the Carolinas—she'd never even seen the ocean, which was part of why her insistence to study marine biology in college was so odd to everyone. But Storm never cared what anyone else thought. Once she got an idea in her head, there was no stopping her. Just like with the lists.

The idea hits me so hard I can't believe it took me this long to realize what I'm holding—the gift Storm left behind. Suddenly, this bed is too small—the room, the whole house, can't contain me. I hug the notebook to my chest and dart out into the hall and down the stairs. I'm loud. Way too loud, I know, but I can't help myself. I don't care. I feel like I'm flying.

Soft grass tickles my tender feet as I race across the backyard, past the garage and Mom's garden. My run barely slows when I reach the old tree, and then I'm climbing the worn ladder, the journal tucked into the edge of my robe. When I make it into the tree house, I collapse against the back wall, pulling the journal back out. Moonlight streams through a missing slat of wood, and I try to read the words in the soft light it provides. I want to soak them in, memorize not just the tasks laid out, but the angle of the pen as they were written down, the curve and slope of each letter. A smile, a foreign feeling after all this time, slips onto my face.

A voice cuts through the silence. "I miss her, too," Cameron whispers from the other side of the tree house.

I stifle a scream. "What are you doing here?" I ask in a cracked whisper.

He shifts closer to me. I can't really see him, but I can feel him, hear his movements. He's silent for too long. I'm suddenly hyperaware that I'm only wearing a robe.

"Cam?"

"I'm always here," he says, and I can tell he's been crying. "This was our spot."

"Yours and Storm's." It's not a question.

"Yeah." He scoots closer, speaks softly. "We started coming sophomore year, about the time your parents were hovering over us every time I came by, like they were terrified I was going to deflower their precious child." He manages a weak laugh, and I join him.

"Well, did you?" I try to keep my voice light, but curiosity pulls at it.

"Anyway . . . we'd come out here and do homework or read books or just talk. Whatever we wanted to do, we'd do it up here, away from everything else. Sometimes when I come now, I . . ." His voice fades away.

"You?" I prompt.

"Nothing. It's stupid."

"Humor me."

He pulls in a deep breath and lets it back out slowly. In the moonlight, I watch as he turns to face me. "It's like she's still here, you know? When I'm up here."

Before I even realize what I'm doing, I'm crawling across the tree-house floor and sitting next to Cameron. I drop the book in his lap.

"What's this?" he asks, holding it into the faint light.

I don't answer right away. Instead, I say, "Remember the summer that Storm made us spend a full week eating only orange foods? Or when we rode our bikes to the library every day searching for information about some old crime she was sure we could solve?"

His shoulders shake beside me, but whether it's because of silent laughter or tears, I'm not sure. "She was a weird one, wasn't she?" he says.

"Always." I think of the book, of all the lists of summers past. If anyone would know the answer to the question nagging my brain, it'd be Cameron. "Hey, Cam?"

He grunts acknowledgment.

"When did she—did she keep making the lists? After we all stopped doing them, I mean?"

"She was always writing lists on something, you know that. She would write lists about the tiniest things. If she could find a way to turn anything into numbers and bullet points she would."

"But you guys never did a Summer List . . . without me?"

"No, we never—once we were in high school, we were just too busy, I guess."

He didn't say it, but I can hear the meaning of his words. It was me who got too busy, and we both know it. As soon as cheer tryouts ended freshman year, my name somehow on the list of new recruits, things weren't the same. Instead of the three of us hanging around on Friday and Saturday nights, making pizzas and watching obscure horror movies, now I was out with Piper. Hitting up parties, cheering at games. I moved into the High School Fast Lane, and things haven't slowed since.

What I never told anyone back then—what I still can't bring myself to tell Cameron now—is that I didn't break up our threesome because I became a cheerleader. I became a cheerleader—I set out for something of my own—in order to split apart our trio. Because, really, we hadn't been a threesome for years by then. Storm and Cameron were a pair, and I was the little sister who tagged along. I spent my whole life running after them, trying to have what they did, but never quite making it. With high school approaching, I realized I couldn't do it anymore. So when Piper ran up to me that day in the gym, I took my chance. And never looked back.

Cameron clears his throat, reminding me that I've not answered his question yet. I gesture lamely toward the notebook "She left one," I say.

"She left one what?"

"A list. 'My Perfect Summer.' That's what's in there—a list of all the things she wanted to do this summer. All the things she'll never . . ." I can't finish.

I hear the rustle of pages and wait as Cameron flips through the book. I close my eyes, imagine him caressing the grooves and ridges on the pages, the same way I did. He takes his time, turning the book over in his hand, holding it into the moonlight.

"I can't read any of this. What"—his voice cracks, and he coughs lightly—"what did she put on it?"

The list's words swirl in my mind, Storm's messy calligraphy filling the space behind my eyelids. The memory of her bedroom pulls at me.

"I can't remember all of the items, but they were different," I tell him.

"Different how?"

"You know how she always had these really weird things on her lists? Like, ridiculous adventures and stuff?"

"Yeah," he whispers.

"Well, this list is really . . . normal. I mean, there're things like crash a wedding and speak in a British accent all day that are completely Storm. But there's also watch the sunrise and take pictures of everything and get a tattoo. And, I don't know, it just seems different."

"I guess that doesn't seem so weird to me," Cameron says. "They seem like pretty normal—"

"Yes!" I yell. "That's the thing—they are *normal*. Like, you'd expect those things to be on a Summer Bucket List for a typical eighteen-year-old girl, wouldn't you?"

"I suppose so." His tone tells me he's not following my logic.

"Well, when have you ever known Storm to be a typical girl?"

"Never."

"Exactly."

Cameron scoots even closer; our knees are touching now, skin to skin. I adjust my robe. "Anna, do you remember the other stuff she used to have on her lists?" I don't answer, and he takes my silence as a cue to continue. "Sleep on the trampoline, watch all of the Halloween movies, learn calligraphy—I hated that one."

"What's your point?"

"My point"—he leans toward me, close enough that I can finally make out his features in the dim light, his eyes locked on mine—"is that she put normal things on the list back then, too. But she was older when she wrote this list, and her normal was different."

When I was six, I was climbing up on the bathroom counter so I could sit next to Mom while she did her makeup. I'd just hoisted my knee over the edge when I slipped and fell, catching my ribs on the counter on the way down. It was the first time I'd experienced knocking my wind out, that helpless feeling of not being able to pull breath in, and I was sure I was going to suffocate right there on the bathroom floor.

This realization now hits me that hard, and I'm afraid I won't be able to breathe again. When did she grow up and stop writing simple childhood lists? How did I miss it?

Just as jarring is my next realization: this is the *last* list. The end of growth. Storm will never be older, more mature. I'll never get to see what the lists look like once she is married and has kids.

The tears start again in full force, rolling down my cheeks. I knew the truth. Of course I knew. I didn't spend the past twenty-three days missing her, feeling the hole she left behind, not to know the truth. But that's the thing about truth—even when you think you know it, it can still sneak up behind you and knock you down.

"It's okay," Cameron whispers.

"No, it isn't."

"You're right. It's not okay, and you know what? Her death

will never be okay. But we will. Not now, not tomorrow. Probably not for a long time. But we will be."

"How do you know?" I sniffle, wiping my nose, then eyes on the sleeve of my robe.

"Because we have to be," he says. "This isn't something you get over, Anna. You will never get over Storm dying. But you'll figure it out—how to live your life and be happy, even with this. I promise."

His words wash over me, settle into my pores. He's right. Absolutely. For the first time since she's been gone, I think maybe I can do this. I can figure out how to live my life. Because I don't have to leave her behind or try to get rid of the pain of missing her. I just have to figure out how to experience the loss but still live. That, I just might be able to do.

"I want to do it," I blurt out before I even consider what the words really mean.

"Do what?"

"The list. Storm's list. I want to do it. For her."

I hear a deep click as Cameron swallows. He fidgets in place, his knees rubbing against mine. "I think you should," he says, his voice thick.

"Do it with me."

"Anna, I don't—"

"You have to," I plead. "That's what she would've wanted, and you know it. That's how it always was. Us, doing her lists. Together."

He's crying now, not trying to hide it anymore. His breath hitches, and his body shakes with the silent sobs. I hadn't intended to ask Cameron to do the list with me—until I found him up here, I hadn't even thought to tell him about the list— but now I can't imagine it any other way. It's like Storm meant for it to happen like this, as if she left the list just for the two of us to complete together. And in leaving the list, maybe she left us a way to figure out how to live without her.

Cameron grows still, his tears under control. He doesn't answer me, but I can feel it. We are doing this, finishing her list.

Just me and the boy next door.

Chapter 9

"What is up with you today?" Dani asks as I flop onto the break-room couch next to her and spin the top off a bottle of water.

I take a long drink before answering. "Nothing. Why?"

"You're different. I don't know, happier?"

I shrug, but she's right. I was up before my alarm this morning, my whole body buzzing with excitement. The list was sitting on my bedside table, the first thing I saw when I opened my eyes. I brought it with me to the bathroom, where I left it on the counter while I showered. I kept it with me all morning, moving it from room to room as I got dressed, ate breakfast, and watered Mom's plants for her.

Just before I left for my shift at the pool, I copied the list onto a piece of paper and shoved it into my shorts pocket. I've checked it on and off all day. I don't know where to start—I have no idea *how* to start—but it's kept me motivated. Work has flown by in a haze of whistles, splashes, and daydreams.

Gillian enters the room and eyes the two of us sitting on the couch. "Which of you got here first today?"

"I opened," I say.

She nods slowly. "Brianne just got here," she says. "She wrote her schedule down wrong and thought she had to work today instead of tomorrow. She's begging for the extra hours, but I can't keep you both on. You want to go home early? I told her it's up to you."

I check the clock: 3:45—still more than two hours of my shift left. But the list is burning a hole in my pocket. I can't wait to get home, to talk to Cameron and plan things out.

"Yeah," I say. "She can have it. Thanks!"

"Don't thank me," Gillian says dryly. "Thank Bri's inability to copy dates and the pool's inability to pay every lifeguard in Muscatine to be here today."

"Well," I say, "then, thank you, Bri, and extraspecial thanks to the city of Muscatine for having so very little money in the bank."

Gillian tilts her face down and stares at me from over her glasses. "Okay, what is up with you?"

"I don't know," I say, shooting Dani a grin. "I guess I'm just happy."

. . . . . .

Sweat tickles the skin between my shoulder blades and drips into my eyes. I pedal harder. I can't get home fast enough. My lungs are burning and my legs are protesting, but I see the house now and force myself to pedal even more vigorously. When I reach the driveway, I cruise up it, dismount, and prop my bike against the side gate in one movement. Cameron's truck is parked in his driveway. I pull the list from my back pocket and scan over it again, as if I don't already have it memorized. But this won't do; I need the book before I go next door.

My phone buzzes as I climb the front steps. I stop on the porch to read the message.

PIPER: taylor's parents have some big event tonight. left her money for food. pick you up at 6!

ME: I'm home. Gillian let me leave early.

PIPER: awesome possum! i'll come now. mall?

For some reason, the idea of spending the next few hours at the mall with Piper is more exhausting than my break-neck bike ride home. Piper is a marathon shopper, and normally I'm game to keep up with her, but all I want to do is climb up that tree-house ladder with Cameron and figure out the list.

ME: Ugh. I can't. Sick. It's not pretty.

PIPER: gross. no more. see you tom!

There's nothing that makes Piper stop pushing faster than a hint of any kind of bodily fluid. Guilt tugs at me—I hate lying to my best friend, and it seems I've been doing it more and more these days—but stronger than that guilt right now is excitement.

I push my way through the front door, practically floating across the foyer and into the living room—where I stop dead in my tracks. Mom and Dad are sitting together on the love seat, both looking weepy, and Pastor Willitz is propped on the wingback chair in the corner. I completely missed his car parked out front.

"Oh, Anna," Mom says, bursting the growing bubble of hope that they hadn't seen me, "we didn't realize you'd be home so early."

"Yeah . . ." I back slowly toward the dining room. "Gillian sent me home early. Slow day."

"Come on in," the pastor calls to me. I groan, hopefully too softly for them to hear. How could I have forgotten? He is here every day at the exact same time. And I walked right into his session. I cross the room and perch on the edge of the couch, my back ramrod straight.

"How have you been, Anna?" Pastor Willitz asks.

"I'm fine."

"And work? Your father tells me you're working at the pool, Anna. How's that going?"

I dig my fingernails into my palms, remind myself that him being here comforts the parentals. But seriously, does he have to use my name every time he talks to me?

"It's good," I grit out, forcing a smile.

"So, Jerry," Dad says, and I smile at him, thanking him silently for taking the attention off me. "How old is this kid?"

"Seventeen. He'll go to school with Anna, I believe."

"And he's responsible?"

Pastor Willitz guffaws. "Well, he's seventeen, Roger. But, yeah, I think he's a good choice. It's a good family."

I can't help myself. "A good choice for what?" I ask.

"Sweetie . . ." Crap. Mom is using her trying-not-to-upset-me voice, soft and too sweet. "We've decided it's time to sell Storm's car."

The room grows cold. My hands shake. "What?" My voice

is too loud, echoing in my head.

"It's just sitting there," she says stiffly.

"I'll drive it," I say. "It's not like I'll be getting my car back." There wasn't much car to get back after they pried it from around the tree.

"Honey, you don't know how to drive it," Dad says.

"I'll learn. People learn to drive stick shift every day."

"And we think," Mom starts, talking over my argument, "that it'd be best if you weren't driving for a while."

I stare at her blankly. "You want me to stop driving? What about practice? Games?"

"One of the other girls can give you a ride. And if not, we'll work something out."

"Besides," Dad interjects, "you've been doing just fine this summer. You don't need a car."

"Dad! The pool is a mile away. Do you really want me to ride my bike the ten miles to school in the middle of winter?"

"Piper can——"

"Piper graduated! You were there!" My yell echoes through the house.

Mom stifles a sob, and I realize what I just said. Graduation was the last happy moment, the last time we saw Storm before . . . before it happened. Dad stares at me like he doesn't know who I am.

"I'm sorry," I say lamely.

Pastor Willitz jumps in, trying to smooth things over in his

Pastor Willitz way. "Anna, I know this is hard, but think about your mama and daddy. They are understandably nervous to have you driving after what happened. Can you blame them?"

I'm shaking my head, wanting to agree with him, but I can't help saying, "I'm not her. She got in an accident, and it sucks, and I wish it never happened. That doesn't mean the same thing will happen to me."

"We know," the pastor says, "but—"

"But it's time we start moving on," Mom finishes.

My heart stops then kick-starts again, punching against my rib cage. Each beat tears into me. "Move on?" My voice is barely a whisper.

"Sweetie," Mom starts.

Heat rises in my neck. I jump off the couch. "Move on?" I scream. "How are we supposed to move on? She's dead, Mom. *Dead.* What? Should we just wipe memories of her away, too? Pretend she never existed?" I'm panting for breath.

Mom turns her face into Dad's chest, her sobs sounding more like howls. Her whole body quakes. The heat drains back from my face, and an icy chill settles in its place.

"Anna," Dad says. His voice is calm, cold. "Please, go to your room."

I want to argue, apologize, yell. I don't know what I want, but I know I can't fix what I just said. I lift myself from the couch and walk stiffly to the stairs. As I climb toward my bedroom, I can hear Pastor Willitz's voice behind me, trying to calm my hysterical mother.

I throw myself onto my bed and grab Storm's book. Flipping through the pages, seeing the familiar words, the letters and shapes that have become so much a part of my life since last night, dread settles over me. How could I have been so naïve? I can't do this, will never be able to complete the list. I look at #9: Road Trip! I don't have a car, and I can't drive Storm's old Monte Carlo, if it will even still be there when I go back downstairs. There is no way Mom and Dad will let me take a road trip. They don't even trust me to drive to and from school.

#11: Go to a dive-in movie. The ticket is pasted there, mocking me. Carolina Beach, North Carolina. It may as well be on Jupiter—my chances of getting there would be about the same. I've never heard of a dive-in movie before. I could probably find one closer, not have to drive all the way to the coast. But it wouldn't be the same. I know that it isn't just *a* dive-in movie, but *this* particular one. Why else would the ticket be there?

#13: Sleep in the UNCW dorms. There's no way.

#3: Get a tattoo.

#4: Go inside a lighthouse.

How did I not see this last night? So many of these things I won't be able to do. Not in Muscatine, not without my parents letting me go.

I hear the front door shut, followed by soft footsteps on the stairs. A knock on my bedroom door. I brace myself for the fight—now that Pastor Willitz is gone, the parentals are free to tell me exactly how much trouble I'm in.

"Come in," I call. I try to make myself look apologetic.

The door creaks open and a head peeks in. I jump off the bed. "Cameron! I thought you were my mom."

He laughs and shakes his head. "Sorry to disappoint."

"I'm surprised they let you in."

He looks at me, confusion painted clearly on his face. "They aren't home. But why wouldn't they let me in?"

I stare at the door in disbelief. They just *left*? I'd been ready for a lecture, yelling, fighting, sure that as soon as Pastor Willitz left, the parentals would be in my room to discuss what happened. But for them to just leave? I have no idea what that means and it scares me more than any punishment they would've given.

"No reason," I lie. "What's up?" I try to sound casual, but my voice betrays my nerves.

He has a goofy, crooked smile plastered on his face and a shiny, wrapped box in his hands. He presents it to me with a flourish.

"What's this?" I ask.

"Open and find out."

I slide my finger under the tape and pry the paper open, taking care not to rip it only because I know it drives Cameron crazy that I'm taking so long. The box beneath the paper is plain brown, giving no indication of its contents. I pop the lid off.

Inside, lined up neatly, are three plastic-wrapped packages. Pulling one out, I say, "What's this?"

"Number two. Take pictures of everything. If we're going to do it, we gotta do it her way."

Polaroid film. Of course. My mind fills with all the pictures on Storm's bedroom wall.

"Cam," I say. I can't explain it, not really, so I just tell him flat out, "We can't do the list."

"What? Why?"

Tossing the notebook at him, I say, "Look at it. Get a tattoo? I'm only seventeen. How many tattoo artists in town do you think will work on me? And half those things I can't even do in Muscatine."

"And?"

"And . . . my parents won't even let me drive around town. You really think they'll let me drive a thousand miles to the coast?"

"Probably not." He crosses the room and sits next to me, almost too close. "So?"

"So what?"

"Just so." He gives the book back. "Maybe you don't get the whole list done. That doesn't mean you shouldn't start, right?"

"I don't know," I murmur.

"Right?" he asks again, his voice leading.

"I guess so."

He hops off the bed, the enthusiasm he arrived with back again. "Good. Now that's settled, put on your swimsuit. I'll meet you downstairs."

He's gone before I can say, "Wait." I stare blankly at the closed door a minute then shrug to myself. I strip out of my lifeguard suit—apparently Cameron's observation skills are lacking—and pull out a bright bikini from my bottom drawer. Slipping on a sundress and some flip-flops, I grab the film and dash for the stairs. I'm three steps down when I turn back.

I have to find the camera, and for a second, I panic at the thought that it was in my car when it hit the tree. But then I see it, nestled into the bookshelf like a decoration. I grab it, throw it into my purse, and run down the stairs to where Cameron is waiting.

Chapter 10

We've been driving for twenty minutes now, and I'm recognizing less of my surroundings every minute. I've asked Cameron at least a half dozen times where we are going, but he's determined to surprise me. I play with the hem of my dress, curling the crocheted edge up between my fingers then pressing it flat against my legs. Curl and press, curl and press.

As soon as we left the house, I could tell we weren't headed to the community pool. Not that I thought Cameron was dorky enough to surprise me by taking me to hang out at my workplace, but he did have me wear a bathing suit. His dad belongs to the Muscatine Country Club—something he swears is only out of necessity because he has to schmooze clients on the golf course, but that we all know he secretly loves. But, ten minutes after leaving home, Cameron drove the truck past the entrance to the country club pool without even glancing at it. As far as I know, there is nothing resembling a pool this far out of town.

"You know," I say, turning in my seat to face him. I prop a knee sideways on the bench seat between us. "This could probably be considered kidnapping. I hope you've got a good lawyer."

"I think I can handle myself," he says with a laugh. Cameron's dad is one of the most well-known lawyers in Muscatine, and since he was in middle school, Cam's been planning to follow in his footsteps. "Besides," he continues, "I don't seem to remember forcing you into the truck."

"No, but I came under false pretenses and, um . . . extreme duress."

He stares at me, a barely concealed smirk playing at his lips. With one hand, he readjusts his grip on the steering wheel, and with the other he pulls a water bottle from under the seat. He holds it out to me. "Pretenses and duress. Right. How does that work, now?"

"Well"—I take a deep drink of the water, and I can feel the cold of it sliding down my throat to my stomach—"first, I thought we were going to a swimming pool, not to the middle of nowhere."

"Why would you think that?"

I gesture to my outfit. "Maybe because you said, 'Put on your swimsuit.'"

"But I never said anything about a pool. You know what they say about assuming things."

"Whatever. But, seriously, where are we going?"

He laughs and shakes his head. "You'll see. Now, what else?"

"What do you mean 'what else'?"

"I seem to remember you saying something about extreme duress. What's that all about?"

I slump back into my seat, a sigh passing through my lips. "Mom and Dad told me they are thinking of selling Storm's car, and I totally lost it. The things I said to Mom . . ." My stomach protests the memory.

"In pretty big trouble?"

"I thought I would be, but Dad just told me to go to my room, and then they were gone when we left, so I don't know what's going on. I thought for sure you were Mom coming to ground me for life when you knocked."

He flicks on the blinker, just before slamming the brakes and shifting the truck into a lower gear. The turn to the right is so sharp that I slip across the seat toward Cameron until the seat belt locks me into place.

"Sorry about that. The road kinda snuck up on me there."

I look around. We've only been off the highway for thirty seconds and already it's like we are in a different world. Trees push in at us from both sides, creating a hazy darkness. I remove my sunglasses. The truck bumps and lurches farther into the woods.

"The road?" I say. "I'm not sure this actually is a road."

"It used to be," he says, "when people used it more. Steven used to take me out here all the time before he went off to college."

"How is Steven?" I ask. I haven't seen Cameron's older brother since he was home for Christmas break, and then it was only in passing.

"Oh, crazy as ever. You know Steven. He's about to start med school, so my parents are thrilled."

"I bet."

"Ah, here we are!" Cameron pulls the truck to an abrupt stop and cuts the engine.

"Cam?"

"What?"

I squint out the windshield. "There's no *here* here."

He's already pushing open his door. "Can you just calm down and trust me? Get out." With that, he slips out of the truck and slams his door shut. I watch him cross in front of the truck, opening my door when he reaches my side. I hop out.

"I wish I would've known you were taking me to the middle of the freaking forest. I would've at least considered tennis shoes. Or were you planning on killing me and dumping my body before my shoe choice makes much difference?"

"When did you become such a drama queen?" He reaches his hand toward me, but then stops, his arm hovering in the air awkwardly. Confusion crosses his features for a moment, quickly replaced by the casual ease he usually wears. His fingers grip mine and he tugs my arm. "Besides," he says, "you shouldn't lie. We both know you still would've worn flip-flops."

I let him lead me through the trees, grateful for his grip on my hand when I slip on fallen leaves. Up ahead, I can make out the massive shapes of two giant boulders, the overgrown path we are on winding between them.

Cameron lets go of me just as we reach the boulders. "It's pretty tight here," he says then turns sideways and slips his slim frame between the rock faces. He's halfway through the gap when I follow him.

My dress snags at the rocks, trying to trap me in the tiny passage, and I have to work it loose every few shuffles of my feet. At least it's not one of my favorites; I'm pretty sure it's not going to survive this adventure.

I can feel the sun hitting my shoulder and the side of my neck, giving the first indication that I'm almost out of this increasingly claustrophobic space. I move forward more quickly.

"Wait," Cameron says, "let me . . ." His fingers brush down my arm, fumbling until he finds my hand again. "Okay, come on out, but stick close to the rock."

"Why?" I take another step, and then the boulders are behind me. My stomach jumps into my throat, and my head spins violently. I press my back to a rock, suddenly wanting nothing more than to be back between the crush of the boulders. "Where are we?" My voice is hysterical.

Cameron turns to face me, trapping me between his body and the rock. He squeezes my hand and bends his head down so we are face-to-face. I clamp my eyes shut.

"Anna," he says softly, "open your eyes." I shake my head. "Come on, I've got you. I won't let you fall."

My eyes pry open, one at a time. I can't see anything but Cameron's face, his brown eyes staring unwavering into mine. My breath catches in my throat, and my hands tremble. "This isn't funny," I say.

"I'm going to back up a bit," he says, but I grip his hand even tighter, refusing to let go. "It's okay, Anna. Just keep your back against the wall. As long as you can feel the rock, you're not close enough to fall, okay?"

I nod. At least, I think I nod, but I'm not sure my head moves at all. Blood rushes back into my fingertips after I force my hand to release his.

Cameron takes a step away from me, followed by another. He uses the toe of one foot to slip the shoe from the other, then repeats the process on the opposite side. His shirt comes off in one swift movement, and he drops it to the ground. He props the old Polaroid camera on one of his shoes, followed by his glasses.

"Number fifteen," he says.

"Number . . . fifteen? . . ." My voice sounds far away.

"Be brave with your life. It's not much, I know, but it's a start." And then he turns away from me and launches himself off the cliff.

I scream.

Chapter 11

I'm on the ground when Cameron makes it back up to me, my back pressed hard against the rock and my head between my knees. Air is escaping me, and I have to chase it down with each breath, forcing it through my nose to my lungs. Too fast. I know I'm breathing too fast, but it's all I can do at this point not to panic.

Cameron stands over me, cold water dripping from his swim trunks and hair, splashing by my feet. "Hey," he says, and I can feel him crouch down beside me. "It's fine, see? Not a scratch on me."

I don't look, but talk to the ground. "You seriously thought this would be a good idea?"

"Well, yeah."

"And you never considered that maybe you should—I don't know—warn me first?"

He drops to sit next to me, wraps a wet arm around my shoulders, and gently pulls me upright. I glare at him. He takes his arm back then bumps his shoulder against mine. "Honestly?" he says. "I knew if I told you what we were going to do, you would never come."

He's right. There's no way I would've voluntarily come here. "Yeah, because this is insane."

"It's fun."

"It's insane," I say again. "Throwing yourself off cliffs is not fun."

"How would you know?"

"Because—"

"Have you tried it?"

"I don't have to try it. I have a brain. It's not like you have to be a genius to know how dangerous and stupid and—"

"Be brave with your life, Anna. Be brave."

The argument dies on my lips. I can see the words in my mind, scrawled at a diagonal across the pages, taking up the full spread. Written bigger than any other task on the list. Is it because it's the most important, or because it's the last?

"I don't think I can," I whisper.

"Yes, you can," Cameron insists. "I'll jump with you."

"I'm not sure this is what she meant when she wrote that."

He stretches his legs in front of him, long and lanky. "Well, what did she mean then?"

"I don't know. To be brave. You know? Not just to do reckless things. To, I dunno, do things I wouldn't otherwise. To take risks."

"So, what part of that doesn't cover this?"

I glance straight ahead of me. The cliff drops off fifteen feet from where I sit, and below it, I can just see a sliver of river winding by. Before now, I never really thought about what she meant by those five words. "Be brave with my life." But it seemed somehow bigger than this. I tell Cameron so.

"I think you're right," he says. "But this is just a start. The first thing in a long line of your being brave. Maybe she didn't mean you should face your fear of heights by jumping off a cliff. But isn't that what bravery is?"

"I'm pretty sure nowhere in the definition of bravery does it say anything about cliff diving."

He laughs, and when he snorts, I laugh with him. "No, not that. But, you know, being afraid of something and doing it anyway."

I sigh. "You'll jump with me?"

"I promise."

"Fine," I say, standing on shaky legs, "but you better watch yourself, Andrews. You still have your turn to be brave."

. . . . . .

Cameron has jumped three more times already. Each time he dives from the cliff, I make my way that much closer to the edge of the rocks. Now, I'm looking down at the water below, thankful that I didn't eat before coming. My insides squirm as I watch Cameron pull himself out of the water and make his way back up the steep path toward me.

This is impossibly high. There is no way I can do this. Like, physically impossible—I'm pretty sure my legs won't let me jump. They are working independent of my brain now, overriding my commands in their efforts to keep me safe. This must be what true fight-or-flight mode feels like—the body taking over in a desperate grasp at self-preservation.

"You ready?" Cameron asks as he hits the top of the trail. He rubs a hand back and forth over his short hair, flinging water in all directions.

"No."

He stands next to me, close. Arm to arm, he wraps my hand in his. I shiver.

"You ready?" he asks again.

"Yes." The word is out of my mouth before I can take it back. I'll never be ready, ever, but I need to do this. I can do this.

"Should we count to four?" Cameron asks.

"Four?"

"Well, I figure three might not be enough time for you to get ready, but by the time we get to five, you'll probably wuss out."

A laugh rises in me, but I'm too nervous to let it out. I nod instead. "Four."

He pulls me even closer to him, if that's possible. "I'm not going to let go of you till we hit the water, so that means you really have to jump on four if you don't want to be dragged off this cliff."

"I'll jump," I say, sounding way more confident than I feel.

"Okay, then. One."

My legs tingle.

"Two."

My breath is coming too fast again.

"Three."

Black spots push at the edges of my vision.

"Four!"

My knees are bending, my muscles contracting, legs working beneath me. My feet leave the ground, and I'm in the sky. Falling, flying. Anchored only by my hand tight in Cameron's. Air rushes past me, pulling my hair from my back and into a wild swirl around my head. We fall forever. We fall for no time at all.

The cold is a shock, pulling us under in a flash. Cameron pushes my hand from his, and I'm alone, twisting in the water. Instinct takes over, and I'm swimming, swimming toward the sky. The sun grows brighter through my closed eyelids.

I break the surface, and laughter escapes me. True, light-hearted laughter. My body is buzzing with adrenaline, and suddenly I'm not sure my skin can hold me anymore. I tread water, spinning slowly to look up at the cliff above me.

Holy. Crap.

"You did it!" Cameron swims to me and throws his arms around my neck. We fall back under the water, my mouth filling with it. A tangle of arms and legs, we roll in the river, pushing off each other and crashing back into each other, until we finally find our way to shore. I cough out about a gallon of water.

"Sorry," Cameron says sheepishly as he climbs out of the river next to me.

Around a cough, I say, "No worries." I look at the cliff again. "I cannot believe I just did that."

"You were incredible!" He looks like he's going to hug me again, but stands back, grinning excitedly instead.

"I feel incredible! That was so . . ."

"Incredible?"

"Shut up. That was terrifying and amazing and . . . I can't believe I did that."

"We can do it again," he says.

I laugh then cough as the water irritates my throat. "Don't push it."

"Okay, no more jumping, but come on." He grabs my hand again. When did we become so comfortable with each other that we'll grab hands like this without a single thought? As kids, we held hands all the time, but then something shifted. Before high school, before the cheer squad, everything changed, and suddenly Cameron was a boy and I was a girl and holding hands meant something. I'm not sure when the shift happened, can't track down when it all changed, but one day we were two kids playing make-believe, and the next we were awkward and distant.

Now, he holds me tight as we make our way back up the cliff, my legs growing increasingly shakier each step of the way. At the top, he grabs the camera, never breaking contact with me, and holds it in front of us. "Smile," he says. He wraps his arm around my shoulder, keeping hold of my hand so my arm crosses over my chest. He's warm against my side. I lean my head against his chest.

The flash pops, and the camera spits out the undeveloped film. Cameron lets go of me and pulls it out, holding it in front of us as we wait for the image to appear.

Suddenly, I'm overwhelmed with the excitement of this day, and I can't stand still for another second. "Come on," I say and snatch the picture from his hand. I set it carefully on top of Cameron's shirt. "That'll take a couple minutes."

Hand in hand, we jump again.

Chapter 12

I clutch the picture between my fingers, staring at it. My hair is wild, wet and wavy around my face. My cheeks are flushed and my eyes bright. Cameron's skin is pale against my tan shoulders, his arm tight around me. I trace the lines of our fingers with my eyes, following the tangle of how they link together. The muscles on Cameron's arms and shoulders stand defined, and I wonder, when did the scrawny boy next door grow up into this man? He's still the same Cameron I've always known—long and lanky, all sharp angles and stretched limbs. But wrapped in all that is a man's body, and I'm surprised at how much that surprises me.

"You've been staring at that since we got in the truck," Cameron says. "Has it changed?"

"No," I say, but I don't look away from the picture. Because I can't take my eyes from Cameron's face: the smile softer somehow than normal, stretching his cheeks up toward faint creases around his eyes. He's not looking at the camera. No, his attention is directly on me, and looking at this picture, I blush, as if he were still staring at me like that.

"I'm pretty sure there's a Sharpie in the glove box," he says.

I pop it open and riffle through the contents until I find the marker. It's well loved, the writing on its case mostly worn away. I pull the cap off with my teeth.

The marker glides smoothly across the slick surface of the picture. My handwriting is sloppy, nothing like the decorative scrawl I'm so used to seeing on Storm's Polaroids, but the words I write over the image excite me:

Today, I jumped.

. . . . . .

Cameron turns the truck down our street, two houses from my own. The Monte Carlo is still in the driveway, thankfully. I'm still riding the high of this afternoon, and I can't go back yet.

"Hey," I say, turning toward him, "I know we're almost home, but could you maybe take me to Aunt Morgan's house instead? I just . . . I don't wanna be home yet."

"Um, sure. But . . ."

"But what?"

"You know you'll have to face them eventually."

"I know." I look at the picture again, see the excited flush in my cheeks. "Just not yet, okay?"

He drives to the end of the block then turns back toward town. It takes only five minutes to get to Aunt Morgan's from ours, and Cameron knows the way. We ride in silence. He pulls into the driveway behind my aunt's car and steps on the parking brake. "You going to mark that one off the list now?"

I shake my head. "I don't think so," I say.

"You were brave today, Anna."

"I know." A smile spreads across my face. "But it's like you said. It's just the beginning. I don't think I can mark it off the list until being brave is just how I am. Until it's my normal."

He's nodding, his smile matching my own. "Well," he says, "here's to a summer of being brave."

I push open the truck's door, but don't move to get out. "Hey," I say.

"Hey back."

"Thanks for today. I actually had a lot of fun."

"Me too," he says as he shifts the truck into reverse. "I'll see you later, Anna."

I watch him drive away then make my way up the sidewalk to the door. Knocking quickly, I open the door and let myself in. "Aunt Morgan?" I call into the dark house.

"Office!" she yells.

Her office is a mess. Boxes are scattered along one side of the room, and the massive desk she usually does all her paperwork on is covered in deep stacks of books. "Whoa," I say, "did your office explode? Marco."

"Polo." She groans and pulls herself off the floor behind the desk. "Sorry about the mess."

"What happened?" Aunt Morgan is hyperorganized. Her house looks like it should be featured in an issue of *Real Simple*. I've rarely seen a dirty dish in the sink, much less chaos like this.

"Oh, you know"—she waves her arms around the space—"I thought it was about time to paint this place."

"And that involved an earthquake first?"

She shifts a stack of hats off her office chair and drops into it. A couple years ago, Aunt Morgan decided that being an RN didn't demand enough time, so she started a small business selling crochet hats and scarves online.

"No. I had to empty the shelves so I could paint them, and I figured as long as I already had all this stuff out, I might as well go through it and see if there's anything I could get rid of."

"Let me guess," I said, "you got sucked into looking through all your books and haven't actually gotten anything done?"

"Well, no."

"When is your next shift?"

"In two days."

A stack of papers sits on top of a pile of books. I pick it up and flip through the sheets—orders to be shipped out. "Tell you what," I say. "I'm calling Rosa's for a pizza. I'll help you get your orders out, and then we can paint together. I have some things to tell you."

. . . . . .

Aunt Morgan was in nursing school the summer Mom and Dad spent at the hospital with Storm. She was living in a crappy apartment on the far side of town and had a horrible commute to class every day. So when Mom asked her to move into our house and watch me, she jumped at the chance.

Having Aunt Morgan there that summer was amazing. She had always been my favorite aunt, listening to my stories and playing all the silly games I made up. That summer, she let me sleep in her bed with her at night and surprised me at school with McDonald's for lunch—something Mom and Dad would never have done.

Since that year, Aunt Morgan has been my "person"—the one I go to when I'm having a hard time or when I have a tough decision to make. After my first boyfriend broke up with me, she held me while I cried then got me a pint of Häagen-Dazs and stayed up late watching *The Notebook* with me, even though she had a twelve-hour shift the next day. When Jovani and I had sex for the first time, I came to her, and she listened without judgment then took me to the clinic for birth control.

Now, we're sitting on the living room floor, leaning against the couch, finishing off the pizza. Aunt Morgan has a very strict no-food-in-the-living-room rule, unless I'm in need of girl talk, so when I paid for the pizza and immediately carried it in here, she knew whatever I had to talk about was serious. We each grabbed a slice, and I told her all about the list: finding it, telling Cameron, cliff diving, everything.

"So," she says, wiping her fingers on a wrinkled napkin, "what's the problem?"

"It's really not that big of a deal," I say, trying to play it cool.

"Banana, we better not be eating on my living room rug for 'not a big deal.'"

I sigh and pull my hair over my shoulder, winding it into a loose braid. "It's just . . . I can't do the list."

"Why not?"

I reach for the last breadstick. "Did you know Mom and Dad aren't getting me another car? And they want to sell the Monte Carlo."

"No . . . I didn't know that. But—"

"How am I supposed to take a road trip without a car? Half the things on that list I can't do here in town."

Aunt Morgan stands. "You want some more root beer?" I shake my head, and she crosses to the kitchen. Pouring herself a full glass, she returns and says, "Have you told them about Storm's list?"

"No."

"Why not?" She drops onto the couch behind me and starts undoing my messy braid. Aunt Morgan loves playing with my hair, with anyone's hair, really. Sometimes I wonder if she would have been happier if she'd become a cosmetologist instead of a nurse.

"I dunno." I sigh. "It's just, they are so sad, you know? I feel like I can't bring her up around them, like they'll break or something."

"They might surprise you."

"Maybe."

We sit together in silence, her fingers in my hair, a half-eaten pizza in the open box on the floor. An old truck passes, puffing smoke out its exhaust pipe. On the sweeping oak tree in the front yard, a pair of squirrels plays tag, circling the trunk at Mach speed.

"Hey, banana?"

"Hmm?"

"Have you thought that maybe . . ." She twists my hair into something complicated at the back of my head, lets it drop, and starts twisting again. All without saying another word.

"Maybe what?"

"Maybe you shouldn't do the list?"

I spin around to face her. My hair pulls at my scalp until she realizes what's going on and releases it. "What? Why?"

"I think it's a really good thing you want to do. Just . . . maybe you should be having your own adventures instead."

I shake my head in disbelief. "These *would* be my adventures."

"Oh, I know, but they wouldn't really be. This was Storm's thing, not yours."

"It used to be both our thing," I spit back. "Remember? We used to do this together. Every summer."

Aunt Morgan looks at me with that look of pity I'm so used to seeing, the one I hate. The one I've never seen on her face before. "Sweetie," she says, and I hate how patronizing she sounds, "you guys haven't done one of these lists in years."

"I got busy."

"I know, I know. But"—she hesitates, and I know she's weighing the cost with telling me the truth against the cost of just dropping the subject—"did you ever think that maybe that wasn't why?"

"What do you mean?"

"When you got to high school, you tried so hard to do your own thing."

"So?"

"Maybe your sister stopped giving you these lists so you could keep doing that—have your own life."

My vision blurs. "I don't want my own life like this! I want what we had. Why did she have to leave?" I'm crying in earnest now.

Aunt Morgan slides off the edge of the couch and wraps her arms around me. I snuggle into her soft body, fitting into her embrace perfectly, as if her arms were molded by all the other times she's held me like this. She strokes my hair and rubs my shoulders. Kisses the top of my head.

"I didn't mean to make you upset," she whispers. "I'm sorry."

I shrug.

"Banana? I want you to really, really think about this, okay? Maybe it's best to just leave this alone. You should have your own adventures."

"No," I say immediately. "I'm doing this. I'll figure out a way. This list will give me the best summer I can have, I promise."

"I hope so," she says, pulling me tighter.

Chapter 13

I make my way downstairs the next morning as soon as I hear movement in the kitchen. Mom and Dad still weren't home when Aunt Morgan dropped me off last night, and when they finally returned, they went straight to their room without a word to me. I can't remember a time when my parents were so upset with me that they wouldn't even talk.

The smell of coffee welcomes me to the kitchen. Mom's back is to me as she cuts fruit into a bowl. She's wearing her bathrobe, the deep purple one Storm and I bought her for Christmas last year. I watch her for a minute, taking in her familiar movements as she makes the same breakfast she's eaten every morning for as long as I can remember.

I clear my throat. Mom stiffens, but doesn't otherwise acknowledge me. "Mom?" I say.

"Yeah?" She doesn't turn around, just keeps on making her breakfast.

Taking a step closer, I say, "Can we talk? I'm really sorry about—"

She turns, bowl in hand, but doesn't quite face me. "It's fine, Anna. I have a lot of work to do, so . . ." Mom breezes out of the room, never once looking at me.

I fill a cup with coffee and sit at the table, but don't drink. This is bad. After the accident, when Mom was walking around the house like a zombie, we didn't talk for days. But this is different. Then, she was overcome with grief; now, she just doesn't want to talk to me. To be in the same room with me.

The floorboards squeak behind me, and I turn, expecting to see Mom. Instead, Dad stands just inside the doorway, already dressed for work in his khakis and button-down.

He eyes my full coffee cup then looks down the hall, the way Mom went. "Wanna go grab some breakfast, kid?"

. . . . . .

We go to Marilyn's, a tiny little diner down the road from Dad's office. We pick a corner booth in the back and order our usual—steak and eggs for dad and a waffle with strawberries for me. After the server leaves, Dad takes a slow drink of his orange juice.

"What happened yesterday?" he asks.

Even though I knew it was coming, his question somehow throws me. I stall for a minute, twisting my straw wrapper into a little worm then dripping water over it the way Storm taught me when we were kids.

Finally, I say, "Do you remember the lists Storm used to make every summer?" He nods, and I continue, "She did one for this summer."

Dad's eyebrows shoot up, and he leans across the table, closer to me.

"I found it in her room a couple nights ago. I can show you when we get home if you want."

He nods, staring at the table between us. "I'd like that," he says.

Our food comes, and we take a moment to thank our server, but neither of us eats. After a few moments of strained silence, I say, "I'm sorry for how I acted yesterday. For what I said."

"Thank you," he says with a tired smile. "Where did that outburst come from, Anna?"

I shrug and spear a strawberry with my fork, but don't raise it to my mouth. "It's just . . . I want to do her list," I say. "Me and Cameron. We want to do it together, the way we used to when we were kids."

"Okay?" Dad pokes at his food. The server comes by and eyes our plates. She looks like she's about to ask if everything's okay, and Dad gives her a tight smile and quick nod. She moves on her way.

I'm not sure how to tell him what I need to, so I decide to just dive in. "When you guys said you were selling her car and that you didn't want me to drive, I . . . I snapped. So much of the list"—I sigh—"There's things like go in a lighthouse and this dive-in theater in North Carolina she wanted to visit. And I can't do it if you and Mom want to keep me so close all the time—and if I don't have a car."

"Pumpkin," he says. He pushes his plate away. "Your mom is just—*we* are worried. That's all. Can you understand where we're coming from?"

I nod. "I do, really. But I'm not her, Dad."

"We know that."

"Do you?" My voice is louder than I intend, and the man across the aisle from us shoots me a sharp look. I calm myself and say, "Do you really? Because it feels like I can't be myself and do the things I want anymore."

Dad sighs and leans back into his bench, his arms crossed over his chest. "What do you want, Anna?"

What *do* I want? I'm so thrown by the question, by him asking me so directly, that I don't know how to answer for a moment. "I guess," I start, "I just want to be able to do the list."

"Okay . . . ," Dad says. He has his thoughtful face on, and it makes me perk up. I lean forward and wait.

After what feels like eternity, he says, "Your mom can't know."

"*What?*" I yell. The man across the aisle glares again.

"Calm down," Dad says. Quietly, he continues, "She's really freaked out right now, Anna. I see what you're saying, and I want to support you. But your mom is in a difficult place right now."

"I know she is. But do you really think we shouldn't—"

"I'll talk to her," Dad interjects. Finally, he takes a bite of egg. I follow suit with my waffle. It's cold now, but still delicious. "We will work something out, sweetie, I promise. I just need you to . . . let me handle it, all right?"

"Okay," I whisper. I don't know what he has in mind, but I do know my dad. He protected me from the monsters under the bed when I was a kid; he patched up scrapes and bruises when our adventures got out of hand. He's always been there, the rock of our family. If anyone can make this work for me, it's Dad.

Chapter 14

"Ugh," I moan when I open the door for Aunt Morgan. She looks as tired as I feel.

"Don't tell your mom," she whispers before taking a huge gulp of coffee, "but I'm pretty sure God's not even awake yet."

I laugh. "But they have the whole flight ahead of them. He's bound to wake up by the time they land."

The parentals come downstairs, looking disgustingly perky. Aunt Morgan winks at me and crosses to where Mom is standing with her carry-on bag. "Sorry I'm cutting it so close," she says. "You two about ready?"

"Yeah," Mom says. "Thanks so much for doing this, Morgan. We owe you."

Aunt Morgan waves her off. "Don't worry about it. Your house is way nicer than mine. We'll be fine."

A week after my breakfast with Dad, he and Mom sat me down in the living room for a talk. Things were still shaky between me and Mom, but I'd apologized again, and it was getting better day by day. They looked nervous that morning, like they had bad news to tell me, but I knew whatever it was, I could handle it. I'd already heard the worst news, and I was still alive.

"Honey," Mom said, "we have something to run by you."

I looked at Dad, and he gave me a nod and a tiny smile. "Okay?"

Dad's smile grew. "Pastor Willitz knows a man who runs Christian couples retreats, and he's doing one that's just for couples like us."

"Couples like you?"

Mom cleared her throat, looked at her lap. "Couples who have lost a child. It's a special retreat with speakers and exercises to help us cope and deal with our grief."

I couldn't believe it was really happening, that Dad had found a way to make things work for me with the list. I wanted to run across the room and hug him. But I'd promised—Mom couldn't know. Instead, I forced myself to stay calm as I asked for the details. "Where?"

"The group rents out a lodge at a lake in Montana," she said. She immediately followed with, "We don't have to go, honey, if it'll be too much. I know you've had a hard time, too, and—"

"It's okay," I said, trying not to sound like it was *too* okay. "I understand. How long will you be gone?"

"Three weeks," Dad answered, and I did some quick mental math. Three weeks was long enough to finish the list, if we worked fast.

As soon as we finished our conversation—both Dad and I reassuring Mom about a dozen more times that I would *really* be okay spending the time with Aunt Morgan—I ran next door to Cameron's, and we started to plan.

Now, I help the parentals load their suitcases into the back of Mom's SUV and climb into the backseat. It is time—I have to say good-bye to my parents, but then I can say hello to the biggest summer of my life.

. . . . . .

"Ugh, I can't." I stare at the plate of eggs Aunt Morgan slides in front of me after we get back from the airport. "I'm too nervous."

"You need to eat something," she says.

"Seriously, I think I'll puke if I eat that."

"Gee, thanks." She spears a piece of egg with her fork and pops it into her mouth.

"You know what I mean. I'm just not hungry."

"Whatever you say." She grabs my plate and sits across from me. Piling the scrambled eggs onto toast, she asks, "When are you leaving?"

I shrug. "I don't actually know. Cam had a few things to finish up this morning while we were at the airport, but he said he'd come over after. I have no idea when."

Just then, as if he heard us, there's a knock at the front door followed by Cameron's voice. "Hey, anyone up? Decent?"

"Kitchen," I call, and a moment later, he comes through the dining room door. He's wearing khaki shorts and a faded T-shirt with MODEL UN written across the chest. "Hey," I say lamely.

"Hey back. You about ready?"

I nod and stand up. Turning to Aunt Morgan, I say, "Thanks again for this. I'll call."

"Hey, Cameron," Aunt Morgan says, "why don't you go get the car ready? Anna will be out in a minute."

"Sure, no problem." He turns back toward the foyer. "Just the suitcase and backpack, Anna?"

"Yep." Once he's gone, I ask Aunt Morgan, "What's up?"

"You know I love you. . . ."

"And I love you." I'm not sure I like where this is headed.

"I want you to be really sure this is what you want."

"It is."

She nods. "Okay. I think you need to find your own place in the world, but if this trip is how you're going to do that, I won't stop you."

I round the table to where she's sitting and hug her from behind. "You're the best. I'll miss you."

She catches my hand as I start to leave. "Wait." She rushes to her bedroom.

When she comes back, she's carrying a leather satchel. It looks worn and used, but somehow brand-new at the same time. She hands it to me, and I look at her, questioning. She gestures for me to open it.

Inside, a camera stares at me. Nikon is stamped on the top of it, and its lens is huge. In a separate compartment, I can see another, slightly smaller lens. "What is this?" I ask.

"A camera."

"Okay, I got that, but—"

"Use it." She latches the camera bag shut and drapes the

strap over my shoulder. "Take pictures of everything."

"Thanks," I say, "but we actually have Storm's old Polaroid. And our phones."

She laughs. "That film is three dollars a shot. Save those for the special pictures."

I hug her again, pressing my face into her hair and inhaling deeply. "You're the best, Aunt Morgan."

"Don't you forget it. I love you, banana."

"I love you, too."

Cameron is leaning under the hood of the Monte Carlo, tinkering with the engine. His T-shirt is pulled up a couple inches above the top of his jeans, and the slice of pale skin brings back the rush I felt when jumping off that cliff with him. Of being brave. I remove the camera from the bag and fiddle with the controls. I have no idea what I'm doing, but I raise it to my eye and focus on Cameron.

The shutter is way louder than I thought it would be, and he turns his head toward me. He stands and faces me, a smile on his face. Shutting the hood, he asks, "You ready?"

I nod.

Chapter 15

"Where to?" Cameron coaxes the car to life and revs the engine a couple times then turns to face me.

"I—I don't know. The coast?"

He laughs so hard he snorts. "You have no plan at all, do you?"

My smile is so big I'm sure I look deranged. "Hit the road, finish the list. That's the full plan. As long as we make it to Wilmington and Carolina Beach, we can figure out the rest on the way."

"Okay." He shifts the car into reverse, and we roll down the driveway. "To the coast."

We head toward the interstate, and I settle into my seat, propping my feet up on the dash. Cameron cruises right past the entrance ramp.

"Where are we going?"

"You'll see," he says.

A minute later, he turns east on the tiny state highway I'm sure nobody ever uses.

"Any particular reason we are going this way?" I ask.

"A few, actually. One, this is a way better adventure than taking the exact same route everyone else in Iowa would take." I have to agree with him. I gesture for him to continue. "Two, the speed limit is lower, so while we won't get there quite as fast, we can"—he cranks the driver-side window down—"enjoy some fresh air. And three, you'd never agree to do this on the interstate."

"Do what?"

The car's slowing now, and Cameron flicks the blinker on. We pull to the side of the road. "This," he says and slides out of the car.

"Where are you going?" I call through the open window.

He circles around the front of the car and opens my door. "Scoot over," he says. "You're driving."

"Very funny. I don't know how to drive stick."

"I know. Now, scoot over."

I stare at him. "You're serious."

"Yup." He nudges me over the gear stick into the driver's seat. "You ready?" he asks.

"No."

"Good. How much do you know about this car?"

"That Storm loved it more than pretty much anything else in the world and that if I make the engine explode she will haunt me for the rest of my life?"

Cameron stares at me blankly, and I blanch at my own bad joke. I shake my head and grab the gearshift. "Sorry."

"Well, you already know how to drive, so I'll get you through the stuff that's different from an automatic. For one, this doesn't run nearly as smoothly as your car did, so don't freak out if it hiccups a bit."

"Got it. Hiccups, no big deal."

"That little pedal to the left of the brake is the clutch—"

"I know what the clutch is," I say, a bit snappy.

He holds up his hands in mock surrender. "All right, skipping ahead. Push the clutch in and shift the car to first gear."

"Which one is first?"

Cameron points at a tiny diagram at the top of the gearshift. It looks like a little H with a tail hanging off one side. Tiny numbers are written at the tip of each line, worn down with years of use, but still legible. "Top left," he says.

I work the stick into first. It slides into place with a satisfying *thunk*.

"Now, push the gas a bit. Don't worry about the clutch yet. Just push the gas." I do, and the engine growls at me. "Good. You hear that? It's okay. Don't worry about revving the engine too high, okay?"

"Um, okay?"

Laughing softly, he says, "Storm was always so scared of revving too high that she would kill the car over and over again because she didn't have enough power going through the engine when she'd let up the clutch."

"I remember that," I say. "It was Dad's fault. Remember when he tried to teach her to drive manual in the Audi? I went with them once, and it was the worst. Nothing but him saying, 'Feather the gas,' and her freaking out if the engine revved at all."

"I bet if he'd just let her rev the engine a bit, it wouldn't have taken her two months to learn to drive her car."

"Oh my gosh, I forgot how long she made you drive everywhere! I still can't believe she insisted on getting this car when she had no idea how to drive it."

"That was your sister. Once she saw this beauty, she had to have it. Nothing else would do."

"Yeah." I smile.

"All right, time to get moving," Cameron says. "This time, I want you to rev the engine a bit, then slowly release the clutch."

I do what he says. The car rumbles beneath me, and I barely move my left foot off the floor.

"Maybe not that slow," he says, "or we will be sitting here all day."

My foot speeds up. The car lurches forward, a bull released from the gate. It shudders twice and then stops. "Crap."

Laughing, Cameron says, "It's fine. Just crank her up and try again."

"What is it with dudes insisting cars are girls?"

"Don't look at me," he says. "Your sister's the one who named her Beatrice."

"Oh, right." I turn the key, but nothing happens. *Clutch*, Cameron mouths, and I press my foot to the floor. This time, Beatrice roars back to life. I try again. And again. On the fourth shot, the car lurches, but this time, instead of dying, it keeps rolling forward. I turn the wheel, easing us out onto the highway. We cruise.

After a few seconds, the engine is screaming at me. "You need to shift!" Cameron calls over the noise.

"How do I do that?"

"Push the clutch in." I do. "And move the gearshift into second. Then release the clutch."

The car jumps as I shift, but it keeps driving. I laugh, feeling light and bubbly. Cameron walks me through the gears until we are shooting down the highway, the wind in my hair and a smile on my face.

. . . . . .

Three hours later, I see a tiny café at the side of the road, so I slow the car and turn into the parking lot.

"I'm starved," I say as I guide us into a spot. The car shakes and shudders, and I mash the brake.

The engine dies.

"Well, that went well," I say.

"Just put the car into neutral next time before you stop. It's right in the middle of the gears, where the stick is loose," Cameron says, clarifying.

"Got it. Let's eat."

The café is tiny—just four tables and a short counter with a pie and a handful of cookies on it. A bell jingles as we breeze through the door.

"I'll be right with y'all," a short woman calls from near the kitchen. "Just go ahead and sit anywhere."

"I don't know if we can find a place," Cameron whispers. "Maybe we should ask Boo Radley over there."

The old man at the corner table turns and glares at us through hazy eyes. I nudge Cameron with my shoulder and shush him before leading us to the table closest to the door.

The woman comes over and drops two glasses of water in front of us. I take a quick sip and try to hide my grimace. It's warm. "What can I get for ya?" she asks, scratching a pencil deep into her frizzy gray hair.

"Um, can we see a menu?" Cameron asks.

"Ain't got one."

"Okay, then. Turkey sandwich?"

"We're out of turkey."

Cameron looks at me, his mouth trembling with suppressed laughter. I hide my own smile by looking down and taking another sip of the awful water.

"What do you have that's good?" Cameron tries.

"It's all good, hot stuff. Just pick something."

"Tell you what," Cameron says, giving her a shaky smile, his cheeks blazing. I turn a laugh into a cough. "Why don't you surprise me?"

"Whatever," the woman says, turning to me. "And you?"

"I'll just, um, have whatever you're bringing him."

She sticks the pencil into her bun and walks back to the kitchen without another word. I lean across the table. "If I eat dog today, I am blaming you."

"You picked the place."

"Yeah, yeah."

We sit sipping our water for a few minutes until the woman comes back holding two plates. She drops them onto the table unceremoniously and stalks back to the kitchen. It's some sort of sandwich—pulled pork, maybe?—with coleslaw and a generous heaping of barbeque sauce. Next to the sandwich is a pile of . . . something.

"What are these?" I ask, picking one up. It flops between my fingers.

"I think they are . . ." Cameron picks one up and takes a cautious bite. "Yep. Fried pickles."

I eye the breaded thing in my hand and notice a slight green hue showing through.

"They're pretty good," he says. "Try one."

He's right. In fact, the whole meal is delicious. We eat in record time then wait for the woman to come back to the table. Twenty minutes later, there's still no sight of her. Cameron walks to the counter and leans over it, peeking into the kitchen. "Hello?" he calls.

Nothing. He tries again.

"She probably ran home," Boo says from his table. "Jus' leave some money on the table."

Cameron looks at me while saying to the man, "We don't know how much we owe."

"Don't matter. Jus' leave whatever much you wanna."

Cam shrugs and pulls out his wallet, but I wave him off. "I got it," I say, dropping a twenty onto the table.

"You don't have to—"

"This is my trip. I'll pay."

He slides the wallet back into his shorts. "You can pay for lunch," he says, "but this is *our* trip, so that won't work every time."

"Fine," I say, and we make our way back to the car. I toss the keys to Cameron then climb into the passenger seat.

"You sure you don't want to keep driving? You were doing fine."

Shaking my head, I say, "I'm tired. Just wake me up when you want to switch, okay?"

He nods, and we pull back onto the highway. I'm out before the café leaves the rearview mirror.

Chapter 16

I wake up as the car slows to a stop. Rain is pounding the windshield, and the sky outside is dark.

"Where are we?" My neck is stiff, stuck at an unnatural angle while I was sleeping.

"Some little town a bit past Cincinnati," Cameron says.

"Cincinnati?" I blink the sleep from my eyes. "How long was I out?"

"A while." I stare at him, and he shrugs. "A long while."

A flickering hotel sign shines through the passenger window. ENDER HOUSE, it reads, but if I squint, I can see a *B* has burned out. Bender House.

"And what," I say, "we're staying at the Bates Motel tonight?"

"We have to stay somewhere," he says. "I made some calls as we were driving into Cincinnati. All hotels are full due to some big festival or something. This was the first place I could find us a room. We'd keep going, but I can barely see through the rain."

"All right," I say, reaching into the backseat to grab my bag. "Let's go, then."

The motel lobby has been kept up about as well as the sign. Tiles are missing on the floor, and mismatched floral couches flank either side of a nicked wood table, a tired-looking man reclined in one of them. A middle-aged Latina woman stands behind the counter.

"Hi," Cameron says. "I called about an hour ago about a room. Cameron Andrews?"

She types something on her computer then looks up at us. "I'll need some ID," she says in in heavy accent, "and a credit card."

Cameron steps in front of me, blocking my attempt to pay, and slides his driver's license across the counter. The woman picks it up and scrutinizes it.

"Sorry," she says, dropping in back to the Formica, "but you have to be twenty-one to rent a room."

"Seriously?" Cameron sounds desperate.

"Serious. So unless your girlfriend here is old enough, I'm sorry."

Cameron turns to me, his hands behind his neck, squeezing his forearms against his temples. "I guess we can try to keep going," he says slowly.

"I'll vouch for them," a gruff voice says from the couch. The man is sitting upright now, flipping his wallet open and pulling out his ID.

"I dunno . . . ," the woman says.

The man stands up and tosses the license onto the counter. "Come on," he says, "I'm old enough. I'll vouch for them."

Reluctantly, the woman types the man's information into the computer, and Cameron and I thank him profusely. He waves us off and drops back onto the worn couch.

"You're in room eight," the woman says, handing a huge key across the counter to Cameron. "Checkout by ten."

"Thank you," he says, and we walk outside, waving a friendly good-bye to the man.

Room 8 is at the end of the building and around the corner, one of only two doors on the side of the small motel. The door creaks when we open it, and a musty smell attacks us as soon as we step inside. I cough. When the light flickers on in protest, we examine the room.

There's only one bed, a tiny double, and no other furniture except a small stand with a TV on it. The TV is at least twenty years old, a giant box with a rabbit ear antenna sticking out at odd angles from behind it. We make our way into the room, shutting the door behind us.

The door hits the frame and swings back into the room. Slower this time, Cameron pushes the door. Nothing. He jiggles the knob, pulls up on it, and rams the wood with his shoulder.

"What's going on over there?" I ask.

"It won't latch." As if to prove his point, he lets go of the door. It drifts open.

"Are you sure?"

Cameron steps aside and lets me try, to no avail. No matter how we try to force it, the door will not latch. Finally, as I'm trying in vain one more time, Cameron shoves the TV table over to me.

"You can't be serious," I say.

"Look, I'm tired, and you don't know how to drive that car

nearly well enough to drive in the rain at night. Let's just go to sleep. We'll leave early."

I peek out the door. If possible, the rain is coming down even harder than a few minutes earlier. I can't see the road from where I stand. He's right. "Fine," I say.

Cameron goes into the bathroom, and I lower myself to the bed, digging in my bag for my phone. It takes forever to turn on, but when it does, I'm immediately flooded with notifications. Eight missed calls and nineteen text messages. I ignore them all and tap PLAY on the only voice mail.

"What the eff, Anna? I waited for-frickin'-ever for you at the pool. Finally, I go in and what do I find out? You quit yesterday? When were you planning to tell me?" She huffs a breath of frustration. "Where are you? Call me. Or don't. Whatever."

Sighing, I drop onto my back. I should've told Piper and Jovani what I was doing. And part of me wanted to. But the lists were never their thing. They belonged to Storm, and Cameron, and me. So I didn't say anything, just left town without a word to my two best friends and tried to ignore the guilt chewing at me. Holding my phone above my face, I tap out three quick messages. The first to Aunt Morgan:

ME: Hey, sorry so late. We found a room for the night. I'll call tomorrow. Love you!

The next to Piper:

ME: I'm sorry. It's a long story. I'll tell you soon, I promise.

And the last to Jovani:

ME: Are you as mad at me as Pip is?

Then I turn my phone off before any of them can answer.

We get ready for bed quickly, brushing teeth and changing into pajamas—me in shorts and a tank top, Cameron in loose sweatpants and a plain white T-shirt. I come out from the bathroom, braiding my hair over one shoulder, to find him standing awkwardly beside the bed.

"Um," he says, fidgeting, "you go ahead and take the bed. I'll sleep on the floor."

One look at the dingy carpet tells me it probably hasn't been vacuumed ever. I'm suddenly very thankful that I'm still wearing flip-flops.

"Don't be stupid," I say. "The carpet's disgusting." I pull the covers down and slide into bed, doing my best not to think about what's happened in this bed in the past. I pat the spot next to me. "Come on."

"You're sure?"

I nod, and he turns the light off. The bed groans as he climbs in next to me, mumbling a soft, "Good night."

I stare into the darkness. He rolls to one side then another. Coughs lightly. We've been lying here maybe five minutes when he rolls onto his back again.

"You awake?"

"Wide."

"Can't sleep?"

"Nope."

"Me either," he says. "Which is stupid, because I'm exhausted."

A thought hits me. "We could play Truth," I say.

His laugh echoes in the small room. "Man, I never thought I'd play that game again."

"Same here," I admit. Not after she left us.

"So, Anna, truth or truth?"

"I think I'll take truth for two hundred, Alex."

"What, exactly, is going on with you and Jovani?"

"Wow." I laugh. "Last time we played this game you asked me things like, 'What's your favorite ice cream flavor?'"

"Butter pecan," he says without hesitation.

"You know it." We lie in silence for a moment, just the sound of our breath filling the air. Then I say, "We're friends. Really, really close friends, but friends. That's all."

"Friends with benefits?"

I think back to that day in my room, Jovani's lips on mine, my hands on his belt, and my face floods with heat. I hope the darkness of the room hides my flush. "Okay, you got your answer. My turn."

My mind blanks. The game was so much easier when we were kids and our questions were simple and innocent. Now, lying next to Cameron, I don't know what I want to ask.

"Any time now," he says.

"Fine. When do you leave for school?"

"Seriously? That's what you want to know? The big truth?"

I laugh. "No. I just couldn't think of anything else."

Cameron nudges me with his elbow. "Mulligan," he says. "You can have another one."

My voice is soft, my throat tingly, when I ask, "Are you a virgin?"

"Whoa." He clears his throat. "That's, uh—"

"Sorry," I rush to say. "You don't have to answer that."

"It's okay." He pauses for a moment. "No, I'm not. You?"

"No."

"Jovani?"

"Yes."

He chuckles. "So, benefits, huh?"

Smacking his arm, I say, "No. Not really. We've dated. In the past, I mean. But not anymore. Who was it for you?"

His voice is soft. "You remember Candace?"

Her image pops into my mind, all dark hair and skin. She was a fixture at Cameron's house for a few months, and then we never saw her again. "She moved, right?"

"To Washington."

"Is that why you broke up?"

"Nah. Things weren't working out anyway."

"Why not?"

He's quiet for a long time, and I start to wonder if he's going to answer me at all. Then he says quietly, "She was jealous."

"Of?"

"Storm." He sighs. "She didn't get how it was between us."

I roll onto my side and prop my head on my hand. Heat radiates from him. It's something I've wanted to know for ages, and this might be my only chance to find out. "How were things between you two?"

"Come on, Anna, you know how it was." He sounds almost defensive.

"Was it ever . . . I mean, did you ever? . . ."

He sighs. Then says, "Once, almost."

I spring up in the bed and spin to face him in the dark, sitting cross-legged. "You did? When?" The bed groans, and the light flicks back on. Cameron's stretched across the gap between the bed and the wall, one hand on the floor to prop him up. His other hand reaches back toward me, so I grab it and pull him back onto the bed. He leans against the wall and pulls his knees to his chest.

"I said *almost*," he stresses.

"Yeah, yeah. When?"

"You sure you want to hear about this?"

I nod, pulling my bottom lip between my teeth.

Cameron pulls at the collar of his shirt. "The night before graduation. The night before"—his voice breaks off, and he coughs—"so, yeah," he finishes lamely.

"I had no idea," I whisper. "I didn't even know you guys were . . . together."

"We weren't, really," he says. "Storm just wanted to once before—it was a graduation pact." His face is blotchy red, and his eyes fill with tears. He coughs, again.

"A pact?"

"You know, like, 'If I'm still a virgin by graduation, we'll sleep together.'"

"You guys seriously had a sex pact? I had no idea people actually did that."

He laughs, but it sounds forced. "You know how she was," he says, and I laugh with him. *You know how Storm is.* How many times growing up did I hear that phrase? "You know how your sister is . . ." was Mom and Dad's default way of explaining her oddities. Cameron would say it with a shrug before following her on one of her crazy adventures. And we never argued with her, just followed along, because we did know. We *knew* how Storm was.

"Was it weird?" I ask him.

He nods. "Yeah. It was. And if I'd known . . ."

"You wouldn't have done it?"

His head is shaking now, slowly. "Well, we didn't really do it, anyway. I totally freaked out. I just wish one of my last memories of her wasn't such an awkward moment."

I turn and lie back down. Cameron follows suit. "Wow," I whisper. My eyes are suddenly heavy.

"Wow what?"

"Just wow."

Cameron turns the light off. I roll onto my side, his heat against my back, and drift to sleep, thinking that maybe Storm's not gone after all, but right here in bed between me and Cameron.

Chapter 17

We wake before the sun is up, and I am so ready to leave this place. We dress in the same clothes we wore yesterday then scoot the TV table back into place in front of the bed. The same man from yesterday is sleeping on the couch in the lobby when we enter, and we creep to the desk.

When Cameron hands the key to the woman, she whispers, "He was here all night. Wife kicked him out. You two are very lucky he didn't want that room."

I look back at the man. He looks younger in his sleep, his face less haggard. A smile pulls at my lips, and I feel irrationally hopeful that he and his wife will work things out.

Cameron thanks the woman, and we leave the Bender House behind.

Our drive is uneventful. We don't talk, except to give directions or ask if the other is hungry or needs to stop for a bathroom break. There's no music—the stereo is one of the things in this car that never got fixed—only a soundtrack of wind and tires on the road to keep us company. In the light of day, our conversation from last night creates an uncomfortable atmosphere around us. I don't know what to say to Cameron, and his silence tells me he doesn't have anything more to add.

So he drives, and I watch the road, neither of us knowing where we are going other than east, to the coast. We've been in the car all day, stopping only for fuel, hitting up drive-thrus for food. My back aches, and I know Cameron has to be exhausted, but when I ask if he wants me to take over, he waves me off with a grunt.

I'm reclined in my seat with my feet on the dash, fighting sleep, when I see the sign. I sit up straight. "Take the next exit," I say.

Without a word, he puts the blinker on and downshifts. A mile later, we merge onto another, larger highway.

We are forty miles from the Virginia coast, and traffic is insane. Cameron weaves us down the road, grumbling when a car cuts us off. "Where are we going?" he asks.

"There was a sign back there for Virgo Beach. I thought we could check out the boardwalk or something."

"Whatever," he says then he's silent again.

I watch him from the corner of my eye. His face is hard. The muscle in his jaw pops under the skin, and I watch as he tightens his hands around the steering wheel until his knuckles whiten. He's barely talked to me today, and I can't quite figure out how to ask him what's wrong.

"I just thought it'd be cool to see it for ourselves," I say. I don't know why I feel the need to explain myself, but a surge of anger is building in me, coming fast. "You know, since Storm thought it was so funny." My voice is sharp and spikey.

Cameron glances at me, his face tight, and gives a tiny nod. He still doesn't speak. I huff out an irritated breath and turn toward the window. I don't know what his problem is, but I need to not let it ruin this for me. I was so excited to see the sign for Virgo Beach and I try to hold on to that excitement now.

A few years back, when I was in sixth grade and Storm and Cameron were in seventh, Storm was obsessed with the show *Virgo Beach*. It was this superdramatic teen soap opera, supposedly real life, but we were certain nobody was really like the people on the show. Still, fake as it seemed, she loved it, never missed an episode, and made sure Cameron and I were there to watch with her.

On the show, they tried to make Virgo Beach look like this amazing coastal town, like a smaller version of Virginia Beach. But around the edges of the scenes things were really run-down and it showed how Virgo Beach wasn't a shiny vacation destination at all. That's what Storm loved the most about the show—how nothing was what they tried to make us think it was.

We make our way into the little town, and Cameron turns us toward the boardwalk. He's still not given any indication that he recognizes Virgo Beach. I was so certain he would be excited about it, too, that he would want to see it as badly as I did. But he just sits in the driver's seat, rigid, like he's annoyed at the world. Or maybe just me.

"There's a spot," I say, pointing to the side of the road between two SUVs. Cameron turns in without a word and steps immediately from the car. I stare at him in disbelief for a moment before climbing out myself.

"I have to call and check in with Aunt Morgan while we walk," I say, a hard edge still in my voice, and pull my phone out.

"No problem." He shoves his hands deep in his shorts pockets and heads in the direction of the boardwalk, leaving me to trail behind.

Nobody answers at the house, so I call Aunt Morgan's cell. It rings four times, and I'm preparing to leave a message when she answers, breathless. "Hey, banana! Where are you?"

"Where are *you*?" I can barely hear her over the music in the background.

"Downtown at Rush. It's Cassie's birthday, so we're out celebrating." I check the time on my phone. They sure started the party early. The music quiets; she must've stepped outside.

"Sorry I just sent a text last night. I didn't think you would want me to call that late."

She sighs loudly into the phone. "Anna, it's only the first day, and you've already broken our one rule."

"I know, but—"

"No buts." She giggles, and I can tell she's had a couple drinks. "Call me. Every night. We promised your dad. Okay?"

"I promise. And I'll try to be earlier from now on."

She's talking to someone else now. I can hear the soft murmur of her voice, but can't make out the words. "Thank you," she says to me. "I gotta get back in there, but you be safe, all right? And have fun."

"I will. Thanks, Aunt Morgan. I love you."

"You too." She hangs up.

I should call Piper, too, but if I'm being honest, I'm a bit scared. Her reply to my text last night was less than happy. Maybe I'll give her some time to calm down before I call. Instead, I dial Jovani. He doesn't answer, and I don't leave a message. He didn't respond to the text I sent last night or the three I added this morning.

Cameron is a good thirty yards ahead of me, walking fast. I jog to catch up, bump his arm with my shoulder. "Hey."

"Hey?"

"What's up?"

He looks down at me, a barely concealed smirk on his face. "Nothing. Boardwalk, beach, sweaty tourists, overpriced chili dogs. What's not to love?"

"Oh, don't be like that."

He smiles for real now. "Sorry. I'm just tired."

"You could've let me drive! Why didn't you just relax and get some sleep?"

"Because if I let you drive in that traffic, I'm pretty sure the transmission would be lying back on the highway dead and beaten."

"Shut up!" I nudge him again. "I'm not that bad."

"If you say so." He laughs and throws an arm around my

shoulder, pulling me close to his side. It feels a little forced, but at least he's trying. I tuck into his armpit like a little kid, and he squeezes. "Let's just get me some food, and I'll be better," he says, releasing me.

"Food is always a good idea," I agree. I loop my arm around his. "Where to, sailor?"

Directly in front of us is a rundown hot-dog stand with only three people standing in line. He nods toward it. "That looks good to me."

I'm not as sure as he is. "I dunno. It looks a little . . ."

"Ghetto?"

"Exactly. And, like, nobody is eating there. Now, what does that tell you?"

"That it's the best food on the boardwalk," he says.

"I don't follow."

Waving an arm in an arc, he says, "Look around. All the shiny, clean places with huge lines? What do you notice about the people in those lines?"

"Um, that they are about to get delicious, E. coli–free food?"

"No. They are all fancied up in sleek dresses and too-cool-for-school shorts. They have makeup on and sparkles on their flip-flops."

"Your point?"

"They look like they just stepped off the beach and threw something over their swimsuits, but they are trying too hard. Now"—we step closer to the dingy hot-dog stand, and he points at the people in line there—"look at them."

Crowded around the stand are two girls and a guy. They look about our age, maybe a little older. College students, probably. The boy's khaki shorts are frayed at the bottom and his flip-flops are so dirty the tan strap is almost black. The girl on the left wears a simple sundress, green and slightly wrinkled. Her black hair is in a messy ponytail that falls down her back. The other girl is in cutoff denim shorts and a gray tank top. Wet spots bleed onto her shirt from the bikini top below. She's laughing loudly, her whole face lit.

"And?" I say.

"Locals," Cameron whispers. "They are here because it's where they belong, and they know where the best food is. Ergo, we'll eat here."

Laughing, I say, "Did you seriously just say *ergo*?"

"You know you love it."

"You're a nerd."

The group in front of us steps to the side as we approach, and the man behind the counter calls out to us, "Hey, what can I grab y'all?" He's young and ridiculously handsome. Maybe this wasn't such a bad idea.

"What's good?" Cameron asks.

"You really think I'm going to say any of my grub's bad, man? It's all good."

"Fair enough. I'll take a long dog with onions and cheese." Cameron turns to me. "And whatever Anna wants."

"Um," I say, searching the board behind the man's head. "I dunno. Surprise me."

"You sure you wanna do that?"

I nod. "Give me your favorite," I tell him.

"Whatever you say, little lady." He winks.

Cameron laughs softly, quickly covering his mouth and coughing. He looks down at me with one eyebrow cocked. He doesn't have to say it for me to know what he's thinking. Did he seriously just call me "little lady"?

"Hey," the girl around the side of the cart, the one with the wet tank top, says, "you'll want to add a cone of fries to that. I promise." As if to prove her point, she pops one of her own fries into her mouth and chews it emphatically.

"I guess we need some fries, too," Cameron tells Cart Guy. Turning to the girl, he says, "Thanks."

"M'hmm," she mumbles then turns to stare at me. "You're really pretty," she says bluntly.

I pull my hair around my shoulder and force myself not to braid it. "Um, thanks," I say.

They are all staring at us now, and I feel like I should be behind a display case in a museum. Thankfully, before things get any more awkward, Cart Man hands a fry cone across the counter to us. I pop one in my mouth.

"Holy crap!" I exclaim. "These things are amazing!"

"Told ya," Tank-Top Girl says. "Miguel makes the best food. What's your names?"

"I'm Anna." I lean against Cam's arm and nod toward him. "And this is Cam."

"How long have you two been together?"

Cameron chokes on a fry and launches into a coughing fit.

"Oh, we aren't," I say.

"Well, you totally should be. You look great together."

"Thanks, I think." I pause, then ask, "What's your name?"

The girl's face brightens, and she says, "I'm Sabine, and this is Nina and Courtland."

"Court," the guy says. "Just Court."

"Well, Just Court," I say, "it's good to meet you. You, too, Nina."

Nina waves at me, holding a sloppy hot dog to her mouth with her other hand. Finally, Miguel passes our food to us. I get a red checked cardboard boat piled high with beans, coleslaw, and some sort of red sauce.

"Southern Dog," Court says. "I hope you have an iron gut, girl."

"There's a hot dog under there?" I say at the same time Cameron says, "No worries there. Anna can eat an overweight construction worker under the table."

"Gee, thanks," I say.

"That's a good thing," Cameron insists. "Guys like a girl who can eat."

"Especially those overweight construction workers," Nina says. Her voice has a slight accent that I can't quite place. "You two want to come eat with us?"

I throw a quick look at Cameron; he shrugs, so I nod and we follow Nina, Court, and Sabine across the boardwalk to a miraculously empty table.

We say nothing while we eat—the dogs are messy and take all our concentration. My Southern Dog is the most disgustingly amazing thing I've ever eaten. The beans are tart, the coleslaw sweet. And the red sauce is some sort of hot sauce—not Tabasco, but something similar. It adds just enough heat to make my nose drip.

When I finish, I wipe my face and lean back in my chair. Sabine says, "What brings you to Virgo Beach?"

"You're doing it again," Nina says.

"Am not."

"Please. You should be a politician. You're totally doing it."

"Doing what?" Cameron asks, his mouth full of fries.

"Sabine has taken it upon herself to be Virgo Beach's official welcoming committee," Court says. "After you tell her what brings you here, she'll ask how long you'll stay. Then if you need a map or for someone to show you around."

Cameron laughs. "Well, sorry to disappoint, but we'll probably only be here for tonight." He looks at me, eyebrows raised, as if asking for confirmation. I shrug, give a slight nod. This isn't the right place to continue the list.

"Any plans for tonight?" Nina asks.

Cameron and I shake our heads.

Suddenly, Nina is shouting so loud I almost fall out of

my seat. "Eh, Miguel!" He turns, facing us, but says nothing. "Where's the party tonight?"

He yells back, just as loud. "Bonfire at my house."

Nina looks down at her phone and says, "Look, we gotta go, but meet us back here at nine if you want to come with, okay?"

"Oh, you totally want to come," Sabine says. "Miguel throws the best parties."

"Okay, thanks," I say. "We'll think about it."

With waves and murmured good-byes, the trio leaves, and it's just me and Cameron again, staring at the boardwalk.

. . . . . .

"You're seriously not coming?" I'm standing in the tiny bathroom of our tiny hotel room, trying to work my hair into submission. I've braided and unbraided it about three times, to no avail. Finally, I pull it into a messy topknot. It's as good as it's getting tonight.

When I step into the room, Cameron is lying on the bed, flipping through channels on the appropriately tiny TV. "Did you hear me?"

"Of course I heard you," he says. "You were standing fifteen inches from me."

"And?"

"And I answered the first four times you asked, so I figured I didn't really need to answer this time."

"Humor me," I say.

"Fine. Yes, Anna, I'm really, really not coming."

I drop onto the bed next to him, crossing my legs at my ankles. Taking the remote from his hand, I turn off the TV and whine. "Come on, Cameron, it could be fun."

"I'm tired."

"You're eighteen, in Virgo Beach with no parentals to be seen, invited to a party—by a couple hotties, I might add—and you are going to sit in the smallest hotel room known to mankind and do what? Watch *Duck Dynasty*?"

"I was actually thinking of giving *Project Runway* a shot."

"You're kidding."

"Yes, I am. Now, give me that." Cameron dives for the remote, and I hold it as far off the edge of the bed as I can. My hand hits the wall. Cameron's hand wraps around the remote, just above my fingers, and he pulls. I refuse to let go.

Tugging back with my remote hand, I snake my other hand up his side and into his armpit, tickling him. He jerks back, fast. So fast that his elbow cracks me in the jaw. I pull my own hand back to my face, forgetting about the remote until the buttons smash into my cheek. I cry out and the remote clatters to the ground.

"Oh man, are you okay?" Cameron sits up and leans over me.

My eyes fill with water, blurring my vision. "Ow," I moan.

"I am so, so sorry."

I wave him off. "I know. It's nothing. Don't worry about it." To prove my point, I sit up and face him, smiling.

Cameron's face runs white. "Oh man."

"It's nothing," I say again.

"It's something," he says. "The whole side of your face is red."

Shrugging, I say, "It'll be gone in a few minutes."

Cameron picks at his fingernails, looking up at me every few seconds, guilt etched on his face. My jaw throbs. I just hope it doesn't leave a bruise. He clears his throat as I smooth the front of my tank top.

"Fine," he eventually says.

"Fine what?"

"I'll go with you. Get your shoes on."

I squeal like a little girl and throw my arms around his shoulders. "Thank you, thank you! I really didn't want to be a loner tonight."

"Whatever," he says. "If this is lame, though, I fully reserve the right to bail on you. Swollen jaw or no."

"Duly noted."

Chapter 18

Nina and Court are sitting on the table when we arrive, five minutes after nine.

"Sorry we're a bit late," I call to them.

"No worries," Nina says, hopping to her feet. "Five minutes doesn't constitute as late in anyone's book around here."

"Cool. Where's Sabine?"

Court stands. "She's already up at the house."

"Trying to get into my brother's pants," Nina adds.

"Is . . . Miguel?"

She nods. "Sabine doesn't like him. She tells me all the time." Nina rolls her eyes. "But get a couple drinks in her, and she seems to forget all about that."

"You guys ready?" Court asks.

Cameron nods, reluctantly, and I say, "Show us the way."

The walk is not a long one, just straight down to the beach and then a few hundred yards south. I can see the light of the bonfire as soon as we step onto the sand. Noise follows directly on its heels. Loud music, bass pounding through the night. Laughs and screams mixing together to form a typical party soundtrack. The ocean crashes to our left, its steady rhythm keeping pace with our steps, and I find myself drifting toward it—it calling me to its embrace.

Flip-flops in hand, I make my way across the beach until I hit cool, compacted sand. Three steps later, water tickles the edge of my feet, caressing my skin with its cool touch. By the time we reach the party, I'm walking midcalf deep, soaking in as much of the power of the ocean as I can, relishing the mist on my face and the salt air curling around me.

We stop a few yards short of the fire, and Nina and Court break off to talk to some friends. It's only now that I realize Cameron is in the water with me, his jeans rolled up over his shins, one leg higher than the other. His flip-flops are shoved into his back pockets. In the flickering light of the fire, I can see where the water has glued his hair to his legs.

"You ready?" I ask him.

"We could just stay out here," he answers.

It's tempting. I can't imagine anything in that house being better than the feel of the ocean rolling over my feet. But Sabine's spotted us and is emphatically waving us over.

"Let's go up," I say. "Sabine might dislocate a shoulder if we don't."

When we get to her, she's yelling, "You made it!" She throws her arms around me, hugging me tight. She smells strongly of citrus and alcohol. When she lets go, she immediately pulls Cameron into an equally tight hug. "You guys want a drink? Come on, I'll show you where everything is."

Sabine traipses up the beach toward the house and, with a shrug, Cameron follows. I fall into step after one more glance at the ocean.

"How many do you think she's had?" he asks.

"I dunno," I say. "That greeting didn't actually seem like much of a departure from this afternoon."

"I can hear you," Sabine singsongs. "I'm not drunk at all." She belches.

While it seems like every person in Virgo Beach is at the bonfire, the house is practically barren. A couple people flow through the living room and a girl pounds on the door of what I assume is the bathroom, but the kitchen is empty. The sink is full of ice with cans and bottles of beer poking through, a random hard cider peeking out from one side. Bottles of hard liquor crowd the counter, red plastic cups stacked in between.

Sabine says, "How drunk do y'all wanna get? We've got the lightweights in the sink and the heavy hitters on the counter."

"Water?" Cam asks.

"No can do, handsome." She grabs a Miller Lite from the sink and tosses it to him. "This is as close as we can get to that."

"Uh, thanks." He wipes the can on his pants and cracks it open. I notice he doesn't drink.

She turns to me. "What about you?"

"I don't care. Something good."

Her face lights up and she sets to work at the counter, pouring liquids into a cup at lightning speed. Twice, she holds the concoction to her nose and takes a deep sniff before adding more booze. With a final splash of something clear, she spins, sloshing some of my drink onto the floor.

"Madam," she says, "your drink."

It's a vicious color, one I imagine is usually reserved for toxic waste. The smell is intense, burning my nose. Sabine is staring, so I put it to my lips and take a tiny sip.

"Oh my gosh! That's insane." The drink tastes exactly like Sour Patch Kids.

"Right? It's my favorite."

"I could drink this all week long," I say and pull another swig. I don't know how she did it, but the alcohol has no bite. It's just sweet and sour and green and delicious. I drink more.

Half a cup later, the room is spinning. "Whoa," I say, "this stuff is strong."

Cameron grabs my arm and tugs me gently toward the door, leaving his full beer can on the counter. "Let's get outside so you can have some fresh air."

The fire is even bigger than it was before, and I watch as a huge guy in jeans and a plaid shirt throws another pallet into the blaze. The crowd cheers, and Sabine skips up to him.

"Clem, you gotta meet my new friends," she slurs, pointing in our general direction. "This is Anna and Christopher."

"Cameron," I correct. Cameron says nothing.

"Hey, man," Clem says, clapping Cameron on the shoulder. "How's it going?"

"Fine."

"Chris isn't a big talker," Sabine slurs. "Hey, have you seen Miguel?"

Clem guffaws deep and low then takes a swig of his drink. Foam clings to his mustache. "Lover boy went down to the water. Something about skinny dipping. Run, princess. This may be your only chance to see him in the buff."

"Shut up," she laughs, but takes off toward the ocean.

My mind is buzzing, stuck on those two words: skinny dipping. Can it really be this easy? I squint against the brightness of the fire and look down to the edge of the beach. Five or six shadows run and spin near the water, and soft laughter drifts to my ears.

A hand waves in front of my face. "Earth to Anna," Clem says. I ignore him, turning to Cameron. "Number six," I say.

He stares at me.

"The list." How could he have forgotten? This is the whole purpose of our trip. "The list, Cameron! Number six: Go skinny dipping."

He looks to the ocean then back to me, slowly. "Now?"

"Why not?" I'm already walking toward the water. "Don't you see—it's fate."

He scrambles to keep up with me. "Fate, Anna? You're drunk. Let's just do this another time, okay?"

I kick my shoes off as soon as I hit the compacted sand. It feels cooler now than it did on the way to the party. Cameron grabs my hand and pulls me to a stop. "Anna, come on."

I tear out of his grip and spin to face him. "No, you come on. This is why we're here, Cam. To complete the list." I pull my tank top over my head in one fluid movement and drop it to the ground at my feet. Cameron stares at the sand to my left as I step out of my shorts. Standing in only my bra and panties, the cool ocean breeze plucks up goose bumps on my skin.

"Last chance," I tell him. "You in or out?"

He says nothing.

I drop my panties to the sand and reach behind me to unhook my bra. As soon as I'm free, I'm running to the ocean.

The water's cold, a lot colder than I thought it would be in July. I gasp, my muscles seizing, and I freeze in place, the water licking my upper thighs. My arms are crossed tightly across my chest, and I clasp my hands around my upper arms. Squeezing, I will myself to warm up. A wave hits me, advancing the cold up to my belly button.

"It helps if you just dive in. Do it all at once," a deep voice says shockingly close to my ear. My arms automatically tighten over my breasts, as if he can see anything in this dark.

"Miguel?"

"Hey, Anna," he says. "Glad you came." Heat radiates from his body—he's standing close to me, and suddenly all I can think about is how ridiculously naked I am, only water separating us. I shift back, trying not to draw attention to the move—pretty sure I'm about as subtle as a giraffe in a coffee shop.

He splashes me, laughing. "I'm serious, just duck under. It'll be warmer after."

When I don't reply, he says, "I'll do it with you. Count of three, okay?"

"Four," I say.

"Huh?"

"Count of four."

"Okay, whatever you say." He counts, slowly, and on four, I let my legs turn to jelly.

The water covers my head, cold and intense and wonderful. I stay beneath the surface, letting the waves move me softly over the ocean floor, until my lungs burn. Then I stay a bit longer, finally rushing to the surface when my body starts screaming for breath. The air hits my skin, rushes into my lungs, dances through my hair. It's cold now, and the water is like a warm hug, holding me tight, keeping me safe. Miguel is still there, so close, but now I'm relaxed, caring about nothing beyond the sensation of the ocean flowing around my body. It's speaking to me, singing lullabies, tempting me to become part of it. I could stay here forever.

Clouds shift, and the moon shines down on us, silvery, glinting across the ripples in the water. We bob with the waves, and more people splash in to join us. I can't make out faces, don't care who they are. I slip onto my back on top of the ocean. Water invades my ears, shutting out the world, and I'm all alone, just me and the ocean. And thoughts of Storm. Number 6.

Chapter 19

Cameron's not on the beach when I swim to shore. I slip into my clothes, forcing them over my sticky, wet skin. With a wave to the rest of the group, who are still splashing in the waves, I head back to the bonfire.

I do a full loop around the blaze, and Cameron is nowhere to be seen. Clem is reclined in a beach chair, Sabine perched on his lap. She smiles at me and waggles her fingertips. The fire dries my skin, making it feel tight, the salt itching my pores. I ask Sabine, "Have you seen Cameron?"

"Who?"

"Chris," Clem says with a smirk.

"Oh yeah! He came back up about twenty minutes ago and asked me to tell you, um . . ."

"That he went back to the room," Clem finishes for her.

I'm nodding, but not sure why. "Oh, okay. I should probably go, too. Thanks for inviting us."

"You want us to walk you back?" Sabine asks. One look at her face tells me that the last thing she wants is to leave Clem's lap right now, so I shake my head.

"I'll be fine." I give her a quick hug.

"My last name is Martin," she says. "Find me on Facebook?"

"Will do. Thanks again."

The walk back to the hotel is quiet, the boardwalk having gone to bed while I was at the party. The rhythmic rush of the ocean is my only company as I make my way through the streets. I creep into the room, tiptoeing through the dark. Cameron is asleep on the bed, snoring softly, so I climb in next to him, wide awake.

The ocean is still on my skin, the rush of the night still in my heart.

. . . . . .

"Let's go," Cameron says, too loudly, the next morning. I pry my eyes open, squint into the light of the room.

"What time is it?" I croak.

"Seven thirty."

I roll over and pull the blankets up to cover my head. "You did not seriously just wake me up at seven thirty in the morning."

"We were on the road way before this yesterday," he says. I hear the sound of a zipper followed by the shuffle of items being shoved into his bag.

"Yesterday, we were in the creepiest motel in the continental US. Seriously, what's the hurry?"

He sighs. "I just don't want to be here, okay? Let's move on."

"I'm going back to sleep."

The bed bounces violently and the blanket is jerked away from me. Cameron is inches from my face, anger painted all over his face.

"What the hell, Cam!" My anger matches his.

"Have a good night?"

"Yes, thank you. Now, leave me alone."

"Get up."

"No."

His face softens a tiny bit. "Please, can we just get on the road? You can sleep in the car."

I pull the pillow from under my head and press it over my face. "What are the chances you'll let my sleep if I say no?"

"Not great," he says.

"Fine." I sit up, throw the pillow at him. "But we are stopping for coffee."

The boardwalk is dead this early in the morning, yet we manage to find a little espresso stand tucked into the side of a building. It's ridiculously overpriced, but I'm willing to barter my firstborn for a good latte at this time of day.

The barista hands us our drinks, and Cameron turns toward the car, but I stop him and head the other way.

"Where are we going?" He's still angry.

"I need to grab a picture." I pull the Polaroid from where I tucked it into my purse and head to the beach. Cameron follows. Once we're on the sand, with no buildings between us and the water, I stop and raise the camera to my eyes.

"Sure you don't want to strip down for that, make sure it's really accurate?"

"Shut up," I snap. "Just take my picture."

He grabs the camera from my hand, and we burrow our drinks in the sand. I walk down the beach, just to the high-tide line, then turn to face him. Throwing my arms out from my sides, I tilt my face to the sky and remember the freedom of floating last night, nothing separating me from the rush of the ocean.

"Okay, crazy girl," Cameron calls, "we're done." He's holding the picture in one hand, waving it back and forth slowly. He smiles as I approach him, and it shocks me to find how much I've missed seeing that smile since yesterday. I reach for the picture.

Cameron pulls his hand back, keeping the photo just out of my grip. "Nope," he says. "Not until we are in the car."

We kick the sand on our slow walk back, knocking one another like bumper cars as we make our way through the hills and valleys of the beach.

"Where are we headed next?" Cameron asks as we cross the boardwalk.

I shrug. "I have no idea. South, I guess."

At the car, Cam opens my door for me then says, "Outer Banks?"

"Okay? . . ."

He runs around the front of the car and slides into the driver's seat, cranking the engine. "I did some research last night when you were . . . you know. Outer Banks—"

"When did you have time for research? You barely left before me."

He waves me off with a flip of his wrist. "Don't worry about it. They have lighthouses and parasailing, and it's on the way to Carolina Beach."

"Meaning, it's pretty much perfect?"

"Exactly."

I recline my seat, prop my bare feet on the dashboard. "Outer Banks it is. Onward, Jeeves."

. . . . . .

"Why do you think she wanted to do it?" Cameron's voice cuts through the silence of our drive just as we leave Virgo Beach.

"Do what?"

"Skinny dipping. I can't figure that one out."

I shrug. "Who knows. Why did she put any of these things on the list?"

He flicks on the blinker and switches lanes, passing a motorhome pulling a car and a boat. The Monte Carlo feels like an ant next to an elephant. "The lighthouse thing makes total sense."

"It does?"

"Yeah. Don't you remember that summer your grandma took us to the library, and Storm would get the same book, like, every week?"

"Kinda, I guess." I don't remember at all, but I can't bring myself to admit out loud that I've forgotten. It's like forgetting a piece of Storm—a piece of myself—and I won't do that. Can't.

"The girl in that book lived in a lighthouse. Well, not *in* a lighthouse, but her dad was the lighthouse keeper or something, so they lived right next to it. And she got to go up into the lighthouse all the time, and I think it was magic. But maybe I made that part up."

"How did I not know that?"

He shrugs. "Don't know. But Storm talked about it all the time. For years. She would go on and on about how she wanted to find an old, decommissioned lighthouse and rehab it to live in. I guess that's a thing you can do. She saw a show or something."

I have no words. She was my sister, my idol. The person I knew better than anyone else. And I had no idea how much she loved lighthouses, that she wanted to live in one. We used to tell each other everything, make our crazy plans together, and I feel empty inside knowing that I was left out of this one—or had maybe been too busy to listen.

"You okay?" Cameron's voice is soft, lacking the lightness it had just moments ago.

"Fine," I say.

"Liar."

"I just don't get why she didn't tell me. If she loved lighthouses so freaking much, how did I not know about it?"

"I don't know, Anna. It's not like she went around telling everyone that."

"You just said she talked about it all the time!" I'm yelling now, but I don't care.

Cameron goes silent, focusing all his attention on the road. The drive is beautiful, all lush trees and cow-dotted fields, the ocean peeking through occasionally, as if to remind us it's still there. Up ahead, I can see the flashing lights of a construction crew. I watch the car in front of us, reading the stickers plastered over every inch of its back bumper. VIRGINIA IS FOR ALL LOVERS. WHAT DID SHAMU EVER DO TO YOU? OBX.

"What's OBX?" I ask Cameron, happy to change the subject, to force myself not to dwell on lighthouses and Storm.

"Where we're going."

"The Outer Banks?"

"Yup." That's all, no further explanation, just one word and he goes back to staring out the windshield.

Turning to face him, I tuck my foot under the other thigh and say, "I'm sorry I yelled at you."

He waves a hand dismissively and looks at my lap, to the picture I'm clutching there. "How'd it turn out?"

The Polaroid is slightly blurred, the early morning light making the image more yellow-gold than it should be. It's beautiful. I stand there, my gauzy sundress drifting around my thighs. Head back, hair falling in manic waves around my shoulders. The sun dots the upper right-hand corner of the image, spilling rays across the frame, obscuring me.

"Perfect," I say.

"What are you going to write on it?"

"I dunno." I grab the Sharpie from the glove box then hold

it hovering over the picture. "What do you think?"

"I think skinny dipping with a bunch of people you don't know at all is insane."

"What, would you rather I'd gone skinny dipping with you?"

Cameron makes a soft choking noise, and I watch him from the corner of my eye. His knuckles whiten and he readjusts his grip on the steering wheel. Red splotches rush into his cheeks.

"I got it!" I say, adjusting the Sharpie. I lower it to the image, right over my chest. *It wasn't the same without him.*

Cameron cranes his neck toward me, and I yank the picture out of his view. "Uh-uh," I tease. "No peeking."

"You're seriously going to go on this trip with me, dragging me along to all your little shenanigans, and you won't even let me see what you wrote?"

"Pretty much." I tuck the picture into the book, at #6: Go skinny dipping.

"I know where you keep the book," he says. "I can just look one night while you're sleeping. Or when you're on one of your thousand daily bathroom breaks."

"You could, but you won't." As I say it, I know it's true. He won't look if I ask him not to, because that's just how Cameron is. How he's always been. I slide the book back under my seat and say, "And I don't go to the bathroom a thousand times a day."

He laughs, loud, and when he snorts, the tension drifts from my shoulders. It's good to have him back.

Chapter 20

I lean back in the chair and fold my hands over my stomach. "I think I'm going to explode."

Cameron's hand freezes in midair, a spoonful of yogurt halted on its path to his mouth. "Too much?"

I look around our hotel room, taking in the crazy amount of food still left uneaten. "Yeah. Just a bit."

Yesterday's drive to Nags Head took all day. It's just over a hundred miles from Virgo Beach, but there was construction on about ninety of those miles. Crews had the road torn up every few miles, and we spent much of the day waiting for flaggers and pilot cars. Cameron and I talked the whole time, reliving stories of our childhood. We laughed and cried, remembering Storm, and it was exactly what we needed.

Drivers all around us grew more and more frustrated. Horns beeped regularly, and the guy in the truck in front of us threw a rude gesture out the window. The flaggers looked like they'd rather be anywhere else. But me? I could've stay in the car, in our memories, forever.

By the time we got here, we were exhausted, so we decided to wait till this morning to do any exploring. I called Aunt Morgan on the way here, and she snagged us this room. Then I called Piper, holding my breath until she answered.

"You have two minutes to tell me what's going on," she said, her voice deadly cold, "and it better be good or I'm hanging up."

I stumbled over my words at first, but before long, it all poured out of me. Piper listened way longer than the two minutes she gave me. When I finished, all she had to say was, "Wow." I could count on one hand the number of times Piper had been speechless, but she definitely was then.

Things weren't perfect between us, but it was a start.

This morning, Cameron woke up early and ran downstairs to bring up more food than we could possibly eat for breakfast. Now, I'm not sure whether I need a nap or to puke. I'm stuffed.

Cameron drops the spoon back into the yogurt cup, his bite abandoned. "Maybe we should take a walk or something. You'll want to digest a bit before we get there."

"Get where?"

"I booked us for a parasail tour at nine."

The room spins, and my breakfast fights at my throat in earnest now. "You *what*?"

"Number Fourteen. Go parasailing. They have great tours here."

"I know what number fourteen is." I bend forward, dropping my head between my knees. The compression doesn't help my full stomach, but at least I can breathe again. I take deep, slow breaths—in through the nose, out through the mouth.

"What's up?" Cameron's voice sounds far away. A hand is on my shoulder now, warm and comforting.

"You have got to stop springing all these heights on me."

"No, this will be different," he insists. I raise my head just enough for my eyes to meet his, to make sure he's being serious. His expression is soft, concerned. "I promise. You start on the ground, so by the time we're up high, you'll be having too much fun to care."

"We?"

"Yeah, we. You didn't think I would let you go parasailing alone, did you? We are going tandem."

I manage to sit up. The room isn't spinning anymore, and I'm pretty sure breakfast is firmly stuck in my stomach—for the time being at least. "Lead with that next time, okay?"

He laughs. "I'll try," he says. "Now, go get dressed."

. . . . . .

"Aren't you two just the cutest little couple I've seen all week?" The woman at the parasail shop circles toward us from behind the counter. She's an explosion of pink—magenta tank top with white and pink rhinestones, white Bermuda shorts, fuchsia platform sandals. Her lips are so bright they nearly blind me, matching the hot pink streak in her platinum A-line. She looks to be about forty-five, and as she comes toward us, I brace myself for a hug. She looks like a hugger. She doesn't disappoint.

"Oh, we're not a couple," I say into her Aqua Net–scented hair, but Cameron, beside me, simply says, "Thanks."

She holds me back at arm's length. "Well, you're just the tiniest little thing. I'll have to dig in the back rack to find a harness that fits you."

Is she serious? In her platforms, she's a good four inches shorter than I stand in my flip-flops. I glance at Cameron, who's watching me with an amused smirk on his face. "Um, I'm Anna," I say.

"Oh, honey pie, I know. Got your name written down. Your beau here told me all about you. Don't you worry your pretty little face, dear. We'll take good care of you." She grabs my hand in one of hers, Cameron's in her other. Her eyes mist over, and I'm afraid her smile might actually break her face in two. "Listen, I gotta go make sure everything is ready for y'all and find you some harnesses. I'll be back in two shakes of a lamb's tail, but if you need anything before then, you just holler for me, ya hear? My name's Bobbi Rae."

"Thanks, Bobbi Rae," Cameron says, his voice betraying laughter. She beams even brighter, if possible, then drops our hands and scuttles to the back office.

I raise an eyebrow and stare at Cameron. "Look at you, charming Miss Bobbi Rae. She might just take you home with her tonight." I do my best to mimic Bobbi Rae's thick accent, but end up sounding like I belong in a bad country music video.

"I dunno. I think you were more her style, you pretty little thing." He nudges me with his arm. I roll my eyes.

I stroll around the room, which is pretty barren—just a desk with a computer and some brochures on it, and a single stool perched in front of it. A water cooler stands in one corner, little paper cones piled on the tiny table beside it. The walls are covered with pictures.

I lean in to one of the corkboards. It holds dozens of pictures, all of people in the sky, life jackets and harnesses wrapped around them, a rope tethering them back to Earth. All those people who have been where we will be in mere minutes.

I feel Cameron beside me, sense the heat of his body over my shoulder. "You ready?" he asks in a whisper, his mouth right at my ear.

"They all look like they're having fun."

"That's because they *are* all having fun." He leans a little closer, until his chest barely brushes my back. I lean, without thinking, into him. Just enough to let him know I feel him, but no more. His breath tickles the side of my neck. He opens his mouth to say something, and I turn my face toward his.

"Y'all two ready?" Bobbi Rae's perky drawl drops in from behind the office. I jump. Away from Cameron, from whatever was just happening. My toe smashes into the wall, and I curse under my breath.

"You okay?" Cameron barely contains his laughter.

"Shut up," I say, trying to glare at him, but I can't force

myself to look him in the eyes. To Bobbi Rae, I say, "We're as ready as we'll ever be."

"All right. I always suggest fliers use the restroom first. You'll be out there a while."

"Oh, I'm okay, thanks."

"She's lying," Cameron says. "Use the bathroom, Anna. You'll regret not."

"Whatever, nerd."

Bobbi Rae gestures to a door I hadn't noticed before. Just like the wall on either side of it, the door is completely covered by photos of parasailers. I push, and it creaks open.

A few minutes later, Bobbi Rae herds me and Cameron through the back office and out onto a walkway. "Just follow this straight down to the marina, and Leroy will be waiting at the boat. You can't miss it."

She's right. There is no way we could possibly miss Leroy. He's equally as brightly colored as Bobbi Rae—wearing an electric-blue tank top with **PARASAIL AWAY!** emblazoned on it in hot pink. His orange swim trunks clash violently with the rest of his outfit. He stands in front of a huge white boat with a chrome light bar arching over it. A bundle of rainbow material sits at his feet.

"Leroy, I presume?" Cameron says as we approach him.

"That's me. Y'all must be Cameron and Anna. Bobbi Rae has been yapping about you two since the minute you called. It's 'bout all she'll talk about this morning." His accent is just as strong as Bobbi Rae's, but where her voice is nasally and high, his is rough and raspy.

"What did you say when you called?" I whisper to Cameron.

"Oh, nothing important." He rubs a hand across the back of his neck then holds his other out to Leroy. They shake. "Thanks for doing this, man."

"No problem. Y'all ready to get fitted?"

Leroy directs us to strip down to our swimsuits. Suddenly, I'm wondering if a bikini is at all appropriate for parasailing. Will the harness pull at things? I feel woefully underdressed. Goose bumps prickle my skin, despite the warmth of the morning sunshine.

Leroy's bent over the boat's open back bench, rummaging around in it. After a minute, he stands back up, two neoprene life vests in hand. "These should fit," he says, handing them to us.

We zip and clip into our life vests. Mine fits like a second skin, and I twist side to side, making sure it doesn't hike up. Perfect. As soon as I'm done with my checks, Leroy stands in front of me, a complicated-looking harness in hand. He helps me step into the leg holes then sets to work wrapping straps around my torso. He tugs so tight, I fall forward, bracing myself on his shoulders.

"Careful, sweetheart," he says.

"Sorry."

"Don't sweat it. Everyone does it. Just gotta make sure you're in here good and tight."

Once Leroy is satisfied I'm not going to fall out of my harness, he does the same to Cameron and ushers us into the boat. He offers a hand when I step in and, not wanting to hurt his feelings, I accept. His palm is rough and calloused and so hot it almost burns to touch. "There you go, dear," he says.

We troll out of the marina, drifting our way past dozens of boats docked in neat rows. We glide by a buoy marking the end of the no wake zone, and Leroy pushes the throttle flat. The boat rockets off, zooming parallel to the shore, dancing over the waves.

The wind rushes through my hair. I close my eyes and feel the salty air caress my skin. Cameron sits next to me; I can feel him there, an ever-steady presence next to my frantic being. I relax my legs until my knee rests against his.

The boat slows, and I open my eyes. We are in open water, bobbing gently. A tiny hamlet is cozied into the coast to our left, and the vast, wide ocean lies to our right, stretching out forever.

"Y'all ready for the ride of your lives?" Leroy asks. I nod, unable to find my voice.

He leads Cameron and me to the back of the boat, where he asks us to stand side by side. He clips our harnesses together, tethering us to each other. It seems oddly appropriate, the two of us stuck together now by more than memories of my sister.

Leroy checks the parachute, deems it safe for use, and hooks it up to us. No going back now. I glance at Cameron. He's staring down at me, smiling.

"What?"

"Nothing," he says, but he doesn't look away.

Leroy sits back in the captain's chair. "Last chance," he calls back. "Y'all ready?"

"Ready, Leroy," Cameron says. "Let's do this."

Leroy pushes on the throttle and the engine grumbles. The wind picks up with the boat's movement, rushing past us. We start slowly, barely moving at all, then pick up speed steadily. I focus on the back of Leroy's shirt, the rainbow parachute with a phone number beneath it. My heart thumps in my ears, equal parts excited and terrified.

The parachute billows behind us, catching the air, and my feet slip backward. My stomach drops, and I choke on a scream. I'm still on the boat, standing on the platform, but my feet continue to slide, slowly edging toward the drop off. Automatically, I reach for Cameron's hand.

The back of my knuckles brush against his. I'm frantic, panicked. He wraps his hand around mine, holding me tight, and readjusts to intertwine our fingers. I squeeze, risking a glance at him. He's watching me. His eyes are bright, alive with excitement. A wide smile explodes on his face. Our feet leave the boat.

I forget to breathe, just squeeze his hand tighter. For a

moment, we hover, just off the back deck of Leroy's boat, and soon we drift upward. Slowly at first, then faster and faster still. We rise, soaring into the sky, the boat below us growing smaller as we float toward the clouds. My heart is beating double time, tap dancing across my rib cage, and still I'm not breathing.

The rope finally grows taught, and I gasp air into my burning lungs. When I exhale, I laugh. "This is incredible!"

Cameron pulls my hand to his chest. "Feel," he says. "My heart is racing."

"Mine too."

"I know." His smile is dazzling in the clear air.

"How high do you think we are?"

"About a thousand feet."

"Seriously?" I look down at the boat, and I'm barely able to make out Leroy in his fluorescent outfit.

Cameron nods. "It's the highest they go," he says. "I asked."

My heart speeds up again. But it's a different feeling now. There's no fear—just exhilaration. I relax into my harness until I'm sitting in the sky. Just me and the boy next door, up here in a world of our own.

"Thanks for this," I whisper.

I'm not sure he hears me, but after a minute, he brushes my knuckles across his lips and says, "You're welcome."

We float above the ocean for nearly an hour, the towns and islands of the Outer Banks drifting by below us. The water is so blue from this angle that it looks like a cartoon. Blurry white lines mark where the waves roll to shore.

A gull flies beside us, the sunlight glinting off its feathers, creating a subtle rainbow in the sea of white. It keeps pace with us, cooing gargling coos, just loud enough for me hear it singing.

"I think you found a friend," Cameron says, and I nod, not taking my eyes off the bird. My hand is still in his, warm and safe.

"I think I shall call him George," I say.

"I don't know," Cameron answers. "Looks more like a Spock to me."

"You're a geek." I pull his hand closer to me, until I can wrap my arm around his. I lean my head to his shoulder.

My stomach drops out from under me, like I'm on a hyper-speed elevator. Cameron and I dip forward then rock back into our seated positions. The boat is slipping slowly through the water, and Leroy stands at the back, cranking the rope back in, lowering us. It seems like we've been up here forever and no time at all, and I don't want it to be over.

The descent is slower that the ascent, and I take the last few moments we have to soak in the excitement of being up here, where the birds live. Cameron sighs softly beside me. And then we're touching down. At some point, Leroy throttled down so the boat is idling in the water. He unclips the parachute, and I pitch forward.

"I got ya," he says, reaching a hand out, steadying me. Cameron wobbles beside me, and Leroy reaches toward him. "Careful, buddy. Your legs'll be a bit shaky."

As if to prove the point, Cameron stumbles and reaches out to catch himself. But there's nothing there, so he pinwheels his free arm around, trying to regain his balance. It all happens in slow motion. One second he's there beside me, trying to stay upright on the back of the boat, and the next he's falling. The harness, where I'm clipped to him, tugs at me first, followed closely by his hand, still gripping mine. I reach for Leroy's hand, but can't find it, so I grab the parachute instead.

Cam and I hit the water together, all legs and arms and parachute fabric, dancing a close tango under the salty waves. I manage to find the carabiner that clips us together and release it, so we're connected now only by the vast expanse of the chute. When we break the water's surface, everything is rainbow, just me and Cameron in our own world under the parachute. His face is blue, with a purple streak crossing his forehead.

The pull is magnetic as I bob there, staring at him, seeing him—really seeing him—possibly for the first time. We drift together, the space between us seeming suddenly huge after the last hour glued to each other's sides.

The color shifts, light changing, the parachute being pulled off our heads. Bright sunlight hits my eyes, and I close them against it, wishing to stay hidden by our rainbow world. Leroy's voice is loud. "Careful there, cowboy! Y'all all right?"

Suddenly, I'm laughing. Giddy, hysterical laughter, all the excitement and exhilaration and ridiculousness of this morning catching up to me. "We're good, Leroy," I manage between giggles.

He lowers the ladder, and we make our way back into the boat, where Leroy guides us into seats. The ride back to the marina is quick and silent.

"Thanks so much, Leroy," I tell him. "That was amazing."

"Don't thank me, darlin'. Thank this fella of yours." He winks at Cameron.

As we head back up the walkway toward the office, I ask Cameron again, "What did you tell them when you called?"

"Nothing. I just set up an appointment."

"You know you're a terrible liar, right?"

"I know no such thing."

"Well, you are. Now, what did you tell them?"

He grins and bumps into me. I almost fall off the path. "That's for me to know and for you to try to find out," he says.

"What are we? Twelve?"

Bobbi Rae comes rushing out of the office, her face all smiles. She bounces over to us and pulls me into a bone-crushing hug. Her tank top is wet when she lets go, but she doesn't seem to notice. "How was it, sugar?"

"It was amazing," I gush. "I never wanted to come back down."

"Oh good. Why don't you go get dressed? Leroy will be back up with your pictures in just a minute."

"Pictures?"

"Oh yeah," she says as we walk back into the building. She arcs her arm around the room, at the picture-covered walls. "We take them for all our riders, dear."

"Thank you, Bobbi Rae," Cameron says. He digs through his pile of clothes and pulls the Polaroid out, holding it to her. "Would you mind taking one of us with this?"

"Anything you want, baby boy." She takes the camera, turns it around in her hands. "Whoa, I ain't seen one of these in years. Where'd you get it?"

My voice grows quiet when I say, "It was my sister's."

Bobbi Rae nods knowingly, and I toss Cameron a curious glance. He stares straight ahead.

"Where do you want to be?" Bobbi Rae asks. "Outside?"

"No," Cameron says, "let's take it in here. Against the wall so all the other pictures can be our backdrop." We walk to the far wall, careful not to let our wet life vests touch the pictures, and stand there awkwardly.

Dropping the camera back to waist level, Bobbi Rae says, "All right, you two. Take off the vests and look like you like each other." She winks, huge and comical.

We shed our life vests and drop them into a bin Bobbi Rae points out behind the counter. Then we cross back to the wall and stand, bare skin and wild hair and excited faces. I wrap my arms around Cameron's waist, and he rests a hand lightly on my hip.

The camera is ejecting the film just as Leroy walks in and plants a loud kiss on Bobbi Rae's cheek. "Good ride," he says. Then he pats her on the butt and walks into the back room.

Cameron and I slip into our clothes. I layer a sundress over my wet bikini, and he disappears into the bathroom, returning with his swim trunks in hand and jeans slung low on his hips. I notice how his gray T-shirt hugs his frame and wonder when I started noticing things like that.

Five minutes later, Leroy's pictures in hand, we leave him and Bobbi Rae. I practically skip back to the car. Spinning a circle in the parking lot, I say, "That was the most incredible thing I've ever done!"

"How's the picture?"

I take the Polaroid from his outstretched hand. "What happened to not seeing them till we're in the car?"

"Whatever." He laughs then leans into me, reaching his long arm up over my head, easily plucking the picture from my grip. He disappears into the car and emerges with the Sharpie from the glove box then braces the photo on the roof of the Monte Carlo. I watch as he writes a caption over our bodies.

Together, we flew.

"It's perfect," I whisper. I nudge him aside then dig the

journal out from under the seat and slide the picture between the pages.

My muscles are still taut with anticipation, craving the excitement of just moments ago. I stand up and rub my hands across the front of my dress. Bouncing on the balls of my feet, I say, "I am so jazzed! I feel like I can do anything!"

"You sure about that?"

I nod.

"Good," he says with a grin, reaching a hand toward me.

Chapter 21

Cameron grasps my hand and tugs me along the sidewalk, ignoring my questions of where we're going. We walk for two blocks before he stops suddenly in front of an unassuming blue door.

"Where—"

"Shhhh. Just . . . come on."

A soft bell tinkles as we enter the building, which is dark, smelling strongly of incense. The walls are painted the same color blue as the door, and they are covered with black-and-white sketches. It takes me only a moment to realize they are sketches for tattoos.

"Cameron," I start to say, but another voice speaks over mine, high-pitched and chipper. "Welcome!" a girl says.

She's short, maybe five foot two, with purple hair cut into and a fierce pixie cut. Her eyes are crystal blue, and a tiny red gem sparkles on one side of her nose.

"Um, hi," I say.

"Do you guys have an appointment?"

Cameron leaves me at the door and crosses to meet her. "No," he says, "but here's the thing . . ." His voice fades until I can't hear what he says.

The two of them talk for a few minutes then the girl waves me over. "First tattoo? Don't worry. Jim is super good. The best."

Cameron is watching me, and I'm watching the girl, shocked. She stares back at me in anticipation, so I nod and say, "It's silly, though. I don't even know what I want. That's stupid, right?"

She shakes her head, glances at Cameron for half a second then back at me. "Not stupid at all. But make sure you pick something you want, okay? You gotta live with it for a long time." I stare, dumbfounded, so she says, "We have some books you can look through."

"That'd be good."

"Awesome." She comes out from behind the counter and leads us to a couch in the lobby. Three huge binders are sitting on a coffee table. "Take as much time as you need. Jim doesn't have any appointments until tonight, so he'll wait for you. This book has large color work, this one has small color work, and that far one has the black-and-whites, simple stuff."

I immediately reach for the third book and pull it into my lap. I flip through the pages, Cameron watching over my shoulder as I breeze past flying birds and blowing dandelions and stylistic arrows. Some of them are great, stuff I can imagine getting done, but nothing really speaks to me. I get to the end and immediately turn back to the beginning.

"Nothing?" Cameron asks.

I shrug. "I don't know. I liked some of them. I'm just not sure . . ."

He's turning the pages now, taking more time than I did, really scrutinizing each image. He stops at one page, flips to the next, then turns back again. "What do you think about these ones?"

The page is filled with words, flowing script on soft skin. *Let it be; no regrets; though she be but little, she is fierce.* I read tattoo after tattoo, studying the way the letters flow into each other and twirl on the skin. My eyes are tracing the decorative letters of a tattoo that reads *sisters* when viewed one way and *friends* the other, when it hits me.

"Keys," I say, holding my hand out to Cameron. He fishes them from his pocket, and the second I grip them, I run from the room, full out until I reach the car. Panting, I unlock the door and pull the journal from under the seat. In an effort to calm my heart and steady my breathing, I force myself to walk back to the shop, the book hugged tightly to my chest.

Cameron looks up as soon as the bell jingles my return. He studies my face closely and his eyes fall to the book.

"I've got it," I tell the girl behind the counter.

"Coolio." She pulls a clipboard from a box behind her. Passing it to me, she says, "I just need you to fill this out and have your brother sign it, since you're underage."

I nod, dumbly, and sit next to Cameron. "Brother?" I whisper.

"Yeah, sis. I explained how our parents are gone, but I'm your legal guardian, and I am giving permission for you to do this." He fishes his driver's license from his wallet and slides it under the clasp on the board. "They'll need that." I make sure my last name matches his, hoping this works.

Paperwork in, the girl leads us through a beaded curtain to another room. This one is bright. White and clinical. Four chairs line the room in a neat row, spaced evenly at wide intervals. They look like dentist chairs. Each one is in front of a small vanity and a massive mirror. A large man occupies one chair, laid fully out, facedown, with a petite Japanese woman etching a dragon over the expanse of his broad shoulders. The other three chairs are empty.

"Hey, Jimbo," the girl calls through an open door, "they're ready."

The man who joins us now is thin and dignified looking. He wears black slacks with a black, short-sleeved button-down tucked into them. His hair is short and neatly combed, and he wears thin, wire-framed glasses. The rest of his appearance stands in stark contrast with the vintage sailor tattoos covering his forearms and snaking around his neck.

"I'm Jim," he says in a quiet voice, holding a hand out to me. His handshake is smooth, gentle.

"Anna."

"What are we doing today, Anna?"

I lay the book on the closest chair and flip through the pages until I hit #15: Be brave with my life. I point. "This. *Be brave.*"

He nods. "May I?" I hand him the book, and he studies the words flowing over the page, the unique calligraphy spelling out my tattoo, at the same time messy and beautiful. He hands it to the purple-haired girl. "Can you make me a copy of this, please, Allie?"

She nods and dances from the room, book in hand. While she's gone, Jim and Cameron introduce themselves, Cameron playing the brother card. I'm pretty sure Jim doesn't believe a word of it, but he doesn't call us out on the lie. He turns to me. "Where are we putting it?"

I don't hesitate. Immediately, I point to the right side of my rib cage, just below where the strap of my bikini wraps around my torso. "Here."

He winces. "That's a sensitive area. It'll hurt worse than normal."

"I can take it," I say. It can't be any worse than the pain I've been carrying with me since Storm's been gone.

"If you're sure."

I nod, and Allie comes back through the beads. She hands the journal to Cameron and the copy paper to Jim. To me, she gives two blue and red gel caps. I stare at the pills resting in my palm. "It's just Tylenol," she says. "You don't have to take it, but if you do it now, it'll help a bit with the pain. There's bottled water in the cooler if you want."

The pills stare at me from her palm. "Can't," I say. "I'm allergic. Do you have any Advil?"

She shakes her head, and Jim says, "Sorry. Advil might make you bleed more. No bueno."

Shrugging, I ignore the pills and cross to the cooler to pull out a bottle of water. I take a deep drink as I cross the room. Jim is bent over the vanity by one of the chairs, sketching onto a thin sheet of paper with a blue marker. I sit.

"Why the ribs?" Cameron asks.

"Dunno." I shrug. "Just seemed like the right place."

"Ready?" Jim says. I nod, hoping I look more confident than I feel. He holds up the paper he was working on, the stencil he'll use, and there it is, the words I'll have on my skin for the rest of my life.

Be brave.

After I pull my dress down to my hips, Jim reclines the chair and has me lie on my left side, my right arm draped over my head. He pulls on a pair of gloves and cleans my skin with something cold.

"All black?" he asks. I nod.

A buzz sounds by my head. In the mirror, I see Jim adjusting the tattoo gun until the buzzing is even, humming. A tiny pot of black ink sits in front of him.

"Here we go," he says.

My body tenses the second he touches my side, anticipating the pain. It's intense, white-hot, like a demonic kitten scratching me over and over with laser claws. Jim works slow and methodical, taking his time to make sure each line and letter looks just right. I squeeze my hands into fists and clench my jaw.

Suddenly, my endorphins kick in, and I know what people mean when they talk about a "tattoo high." The pain is still there, burning away at my rib cage, but I no longer care. There's something cathartic about it, almost soothing. My face relaxes, and before long, I find myself drifting off, existing only in my own world.

The click of the camera shutter, followed by the mechanical buzz of a Polaroid being spat out into the world, draws me back, and I open my eyes to find Cameron standing in front of me, watching the progress. He sets the picture on the vanity, well away from Jim's setup, and lays the camera beside it. "How are you doing?"

"I'm fine," I say. "It hurt bad at first, but it's no big deal now."

"Good."

"Even better," Jim says then pauses for a shockingly long time before saying, slowly, "we . . . are . . . done."

He turns off the tattoo gun, and in the sudden silence, I can hear the man on the other chair snoring softly. I don't blame him. Jim wipes my side one last time with a soft paper towel then follows up with some sort of lotion. "You ready to see it?"

He raises the chair up, and I slide off, standing on wobbly legs. With a deep breath, I turn toward the mirror and raise my arm.

It's perfect. Better than I imagined. The tattoo, the words, her writing—it looks like it belongs there, hugging the side of my body. I could have been born with it, it fits so well. Tears rush to my eyes, and my nose burns.

"It's amazing," I say. "Thank you."

"Of course," Jim says in his soft voice. "Let's get you covered up." He slathers the tattoo with some kind of gel and tapes a rectangle of plastic wrap over his work. As I'm repositioning my dress, Jim goes over the care instructions with me. He hands Cameron a small tub of gel. "Make sure she uses this."

Jim turns back to me. "Thank you for letting me work on you, Anna. It's been a pleasure." He gives me a loose hug, kisses me on the cheek, and disappears through the back door.

Allie is leaning back in her chair reading *Rolling Stone* as I approach the counter. I pull my wallet from my purse, but she waves me off. "Your brother already took care of that."

"Oh, okay. Thanks for everything," I say lamely. We step back out onto the sidewalk.

"What did I say about paying for things?"

"I don't know what you're talking about," Cameron says.

"Liar." I link my arm with his. "Thank you for today. It was awesome."

"Oh, it's not over yet." He grins a Cheshire cat grin.

"What else could you possibly have planned?"

"You'll see. But first, lunch."

Chapter 22

We find a café nestled in a corner near a row of tourist shops. The tables are covered with red-and-white checked oilcloth, and the walls display rows of plates featuring kittens playing with yarn and kids frolicking hand in hand through fields. The front counter holds a glass display case, packed with more pies than I've ever seen in one area.

As soon as we step through the door, a woman calls out to us, "Go ahead and sit wherever you'd like. I'll be with you in a second." She's gorgeous, with creamy skin and vibrant red hair pulled up in victory rolls. She wears an old-fashioned diner dress—short-sleeved with a Peter Pan collar—a starched white apron contrasting the dress's bright aqua. Her upper arm is a tangle of black and gray lines, a tattoo swirling from her elbow to somewhere hidden by the dress. She has thick, black eyebrows and about six sparkly earrings in each ear. It's like looking at a bizarre time warp.

Cameron picks a table close to the window and we sit, the journal, camera, and recent Polaroid placed in the table's center. I look like I'm sleeping in the photo, stretched on the chair, Jim positioned behind me, leaning over and working the letters into my skin. I touch my side. It feels hot through my dress—tender, but not painful.

"This one doesn't need a caption," I say, plucking up the picture to take a closer look. Cameron snapped the photo just before Jim declared my tattoo finished, so the only caption I need is already there: "Be brave," etched permanently on my side. I slip the picture into the journal.

"Here y'all go," the woman says, dropping a couple menus on the table along with two glasses of water. "Sorry about that. I was having a major sweet tea catastrophe back there."

"No worries," Cameron tells her. "Can I actually get some of that sweet tea?"

"Oh, me too, please," I echo.

The waitress's laugh is deep and throaty. "All right. Y'all want the stuff I just dropped on the floor?" She winks at Cameron and whisks back to the kitchen.

She's back almost immediately, two tall glasses in hand, a slice of lemon perched on each rim. As she sets down the tea, she eyes me curiously. "Hey, didn't I see you running into Jim's earlier?"

I nod.

"I thought that was you. It's hard to forget that hair. It's gorgeous. Mine is supposed to be blonde, you know, but I could never get it to look like yours. I tried and tried to get that effortless beachy look, but it never stuck. So I gave up."

I'm trying to imagine the girl in front of me with my pale, golden hair. It doesn't match the vibrant look she has now. "I love your hair," I say. "How long does it take to style?"

She cups one hand over a victory roll. "It took me forever the first time. For. Ever. But now that I've beaten it into submission, it goes pretty quickly. So, what'd you get?"

"Uh? . . ."

"Your tattoo? Jim did all of mine. He's the best in town, not that he has much competition. But he's such a nice guy, right? What'd you have done?"

I gesture lamely to my side. "It's, uh, right here, my sister's—"

"Here," Cameron interjects, saving me from my own lameness. He fishes the picture out of the journal and hands it to her.

"Oh, that's great!" she exclaims. "That lettering is amazing. Where'd you find it?"

"My sister wrote it."

Handing the picture back to Cam, she says, "Well, she's really good. You should tell her to sell designs to studios. She could probably make some cash."

"Um . . . thanks. I'll do that." My face burns. I stare intently at the table.

"I guess I better give y'all a couple minutes to look at the menu. Just holler when you're ready. Name's Sam."

"Thanks, Sam," Cameron says, and she walks away, practically bouncing into the kitchen. "Anna, you okay?"

"Fine." I shrug, forcing nonchalance.

"She reminds me of her."

I follow his gaze to where Sam disappeared.

"Storm had that same intense retro thing going on, ya know?" he says.

"Yeah."

"Remember that one summer my mom thought she would take up portrait painting?"

A laugh bubbles up my throat. "I'll never be able to forget. She made us sit still for hours."

"She always gave us cookies at the end, though, so it was worth it."

"Those cookies were the only reason I agreed to do it." I crack my menu open and skim past the offerings.

"That was the year Storm starting dragging me to those vintage clothing stores," Cameron continues. "My mom told her she looked like some old model from the black-and-white photo days, and Storm just ate that up. Wanted to dress like the model and everything."

"Bettie Page," I say. I remember the day like it was yesterday. Mrs. Andrews had us over for portraits, maybe the third time she'd painted me. She'd just finished mine, and I was digging deep into the cookies. As she arranged the couch for the next painting, I asked, "How come you never paint me and Storm together?"

She turned to me, a streak of golden paint under one eye, and said, "Because, Miss Anna, you are all gold and yellow and bronze, a palette of one color, and your sister"—she paused, beaming—"Stormy is a study in contrasts."

She was right, I realized as I looked at us both in the mirror, standing side by side. My blonde hair faded into tan skin, pale brown eyes matching the glow of my cheeks. Beside me, Storm was all milky skin, black hair, and vibrant blue eyes. Everything a defined line, standing in stark contrast.

"Come on, Bettie Page," Mrs. Andrews said, leading Storm across the room to the couch. I'd never seen my sister smile so big.

Now, Sam dances back into the room. "Y'all ready? Sorry if I couldn't hear you calling. It gets kinda loud back there."

"That's fine," I say, glancing at my menu to the first thing that stands out. "I'll have the fish and chips and a side of slaw, please."

"Excellent." She grabs my menu. "What about you, handsome?"

Cameron passes his own menu to her. "I'll try that blue cheese bacon burger with the home fries."

"Good choice." She winks. "My favorite. Y'all want some hush puppies to nibble on while you wait?"

"That'd be great, thank you." Once she's gone, I ask Cameron, "Well, what are we doing after this?"

"Nice try."

"Come on, you know you wanna tell me."

Shaking his head, he leans back in his chair, arms crossed over his chest. "Not a chance."

My phone buzzes. I want to ignore it, but just in case it's Aunt Morgan, I fish it out of my purse.

PIPER: what the hell? not answering my calls now?

Swiping my screen, I see that I missed seven calls this

morning. I didn't even think to check for messages after parasailing. I tap out a quick response.

ME: Sorry! My phone was silenced.

PIPER: so call me. NOW.

I sigh. Talking on the phone is about the last thing I want to do. I love Piper, but she can be exhausting. She tends to thrive on drama. But she is my best friend, and I left her behind without even telling her. If our roles were reversed, I don't know that I would have acted any differently than she did. At least she's calling; maybe she's decided to forgive me for ditching her. I wave my phone and tell Cameron, "I gotta call Pip. I'll be right back," and step outside.

She answers immediately. "About time!"

"Sorry. Cameron woke me up at the butt-crack of dawn to take me—"

"I don't want to hear about your trip right now."

I'm taken aback. I guess she hasn't forgiven me after all. I try to shake her words off, ignore the harsh bite to her voice. Leaning against the café's brick wall, I wait for her to continue.

"Guess what?" She's back to her chipper self, the need to spill gossip more intense than her anger. "Taylor had this party last night, right? Just a small thing, movies and whatnot, but, like, everyone was there."

I slip down the wall and sit cross-legged on the sidewalk, watching tourists as they pick their way through shops lining the street.

"Anyway, I'm like not loving the movie Luke picked, so I decide to wander around and see who else is there, and I go out into the backyard, and guess what I see?"

"I have no idea," I deadpan.

"Jovani and Shelly! They were out on the swing where anyone could see them, just making out. Like, full-on make-out, like it was no big deal. I could've killed him."

"Why?"

"Why?" She's yelling now, working up to full-blown rant mode. "Because you're my best friend, that's why! I can't believe he'd do this to you. I mean, I know you totally abandoned us, but still."

"I didn't abandon you," I say evenly. "I'll be back soon."

"How soon?"

"Soon-ish . . . but, Pip? If Jo wants to make out with Shelly, that's fine. We like Shelly, remember?"

She scoffs into the phone. "Yeah, right. You know you two are perfect together. Admit it, this drives you crazy."

I suppress a sigh. "Really. It's fine. He's free to kiss whoever he wants. I think Shelly's great for him."

A voice sounds in the background, and Piper says, "Hey, I gotta go. Chase is here." She hangs up before I can say anything.

Back in the café, the plate of hush puppies is empty, and Cameron is staring at his burger. A basket of fried fish and french fries sits in front of my chair, a ceramic bowl heaped with coleslaw next to it. "You didn't have to wait for me, you know."

"I didn't. You totally missed out on those hush puppies." He picks up his burger and takes a giant bite, a look of ecstasy on his face. After he swallows, he asks, "How's Piper?"

"Ugh. I don't wanna talk about it. Let's just eat."

. . . . . .

An hour later, Cameron parks the car and turns to dig through the stuff in the backseat.

"Here," he says, rotating back and dropping Aunt Morgan's camera bag in my lap.

"Where are we?"

"Just wait." Cameron purposely parked at the far end of the lot, facing a giant tree so I can't guess where we are. I know we haven't left the Outer Banks, but that's the only hint I've been given.

"You ready?" Cameron asks. I nod.

He leads me to a paved trail where three kids are running around, jumping over the single-chain fence lining the path. An older woman—their grandmother, maybe—sits on a bench, taking pictures. We walk past them, over a short hill, and I see it.

The lighthouse stands proud on the shore, the keeper's house just in front of it, tall reeds flanking both sides. A black spiral reaches around the tower to the top. Beyond it, the ocean is gray and white-capped, the sky a pale blue with wispy clouds stretching across it.

"Wow," is all I can say.

"Cape Hatteras. You ready to go in?"

"Are you serious?" I bounce on the balls of my feet, making the camera bag swing wildly. It hits my tattoo, and I grimace. "Ow."

"Let me take that." Cameron slips the bag from my shoulder and loops it across his chest. We step up to the front of the lighthouse where a man in a tan park services shirt stands waiting.

"We the only ones?" Cameron asks.

The man nods toward the path and says, "I think so. The kids seemed a bit freaked out by the idea of going in."

Cameron hands the man some money and receives two tickets in return. I almost argue, but my purse is back in the car, and I know Cameron would wave away my money anyway. He's already made it perfectly clear that he's ignoring my request to pay for this trip myself. We wait another minute or two for any stragglers, and when no one shows up, the man opens the door.

"I'm Rick by the way," he says. "I guess I'm your personal tour guide this afternoon. Usually, this tour is self-guided, but I have to check out the lighthouse anyway, to make sure nobody left their stuff behind. Y'all ready to climb? We've got two hundred fifty-seven steps ahead of us."

With that he starts climbing the seemingly endless staircase, and Cameron gestures for me to ascend next. He takes up the rear. We climb and climb and climb, Rick occasionally pointing out bits of the lighthouse walls, telling anecdotes about its construction, but mostly only our breath, heavy, fills the air. Forever we rise, turning and turning and turning, until we can see the lamp at the top. It's massive, a bulb surrounded by a mirrored casing. Windows circle the walls. We finally spill up onto the platform. I gasp. From up here, the ocean looks eternal. I cross to the eastern window and stare out over the water. A few boats dot the horizon, and I can just make out the shapes of people on the beaches below. "This is amazing."

"Y'all want to know how the light works?"

"Yeah," Cameron says immediately, and Rick launches into his explanation. It's interesting, I'm sure—Cameron is hanging on to Rick's every word—but I can't make myself listen. Everything up here is surreal. I buzz with excitement. I can't believe I'm here, at the top of a lighthouse, living Storm's dream.

This morning seems so far away already, like parasailing happened a lifetime ago. Without a word, I take Aunt Morgan's giant camera from Cameron and raise it to my eye, taking more pictures than I'll ever actually need. Next to me, Cameron snaps even more with his phone.

Cameron steps up next to me, just close enough for our arms to brush. "It's pretty neat, isn't it?" I nod.

Rick clears his throat behind us. "I've gotta head back

down," he says, "but if you two promise not to stay too long, you can hang out for a minute before I lock up for the evening."

"Thank you, Rick," Cameron says.

"And don't touch the glass." He turns to leave, but Cameron calls for him to wait.

He holds the Polaroid camera out to Rick. "Would you get a picture for us?"

Nodding, Rick takes the camera, eying it curiously. We stand together beside the giant bulb. I smile, and Rick clicks the shutter. Then he hands the camera back to Cameron and descends the stairs.

Cameron holds the picture at his side, facing toward his pants. We watch the ocean roll beneath us as we wait for the image to develop. After longer than necessary, he turns the picture upward. In it, Cameron is giving me bunny ears, his tongue sticking out.

"Nice," I say.

"Just keeping it real."

He's standing closer now, so close. If I were to lean back, his chest would break my fall. He sets the camera and picture on the ledge, next to an expanse of knobs and buttons. When he draws his arm back, he takes my hand in his, twirling me around to face him.

Has he always been this tall, or is it just because we are so close now? I tilt my head up to see his face. "Today was awesome," I whisper.

In response, he leans down. His nose brushes against the side of mine, tickling. Our lips meet. The kiss is tentative, hesitant—so soft it's almost not a kiss at all. Once, twice, three times, his lips feather across mine. And then I melt into him.

He wraps his arms around my waist, holding me tight, and I snake one hand to the back of his head; the other I brace flat against his chest, sandwiched in the warmth between us. My mouth opens, and his tongue slips between my lips.

My heart leaps around my chest, a bird fighting to get free of its cage. I pull Cameron's lower lip into my mouth, teasing it with my teeth, and he groans softly, the sound vibrating into my palm.

When we break apart, my hands are shaking. "Whoa," I whisper.

"Yeah."

"We should, um . . . we should get going."

"Yeah," he says again. He bends down and places one last soft kiss on my lips before, hand in hand, we descend the lighthouse stairs.

Chapter 23

#5: ~~Meet my soulmate.~~ Fall in love.

The words stare at me from my lap. I'm curled up in a chair next to the window, the curtain propped open just enough for me to see the notebook pages in the light from the streetlamps. Cameron is on the bed snoring softly, one arm thrown over the empty space on my side of the bed. The clock next to him reads 5:22 a.m.

I can't sleep.

After we left the lighthouse yesterday, we spent the rest of the afternoon and evening on the beach. We played in the ocean, made sandcastles. Made out in the waves, our bodies slick against one another, salt water bobbing around our shoulders. For dinner we went to a seafood restaurant near the beach, sat at a window overlooking the sound, and ate by candlelight. The day was perfect—the evening, if possible, better. Back at the hotel, we fell into bed and tangled in the sheets, our lips hungry for each other. We kissed deep into the night, the rush of excitement keeping us awake until, finally, we drifted off in each other's arms.

Then I woke up, and anxiety set in. What was I thinking? This was Cameron. The boy next door—Storm's best friend.

My lips are still tender with the memory of his kisses, but my stomach is knotted, tight, with what we've done. How could we, even for a moment, get so lost in each other that we forgot her?

The sheets rustle. Cameron rolls over, his eyes barely open. They lock on me, briefly, then squint at the clock. "What are you doing up?" he asks, his voice thick with sleep.

"Couldn't sleep."

He pulls the covers open. "Come here." His smile is soft and sleepy, and his eyes unfocused.

I look at the journal again. *Meet my soulmate.* Why are those words crossed out, replaced with *Fall in love*? They are so similar, but a million miles apart, too. I've never really believed in the idea of soulmates, of just one person for each of us, but Storm must have. Why else would she have written that?

"Anna?"

I'm standing before I even know what I'm doing, crossing the small room and crawling into his arms. His embrace is warm. Safe. His lips press to the top of my head, and I lay my cheek against his chest, listen to his heartbeat, steady and slow. I lace my leg between his and draw circles on his shoulder with my finger.

"What's going on?" he asks. I feel the question, rumbling through his chest below me, more than hear it.

"Nothing."

"Anna?"

"Just thinking about Storm," I say.

His breathing stops only for a second, but it's long enough for me to notice. My finger freezes midcircle.

He clears his throat. "Is it because Storm and I . . . because we? . . ."

My heart stops, stalls in my chest, and then jump-starts into high gear. How could I have forgotten? Storm and Cameron were in bed how we are now, tangled together, skin to skin, sweaty . . . he said almost, that it didn't actually happen, but still.

I bolt upright, extracting myself from his arms. I run to the bathroom. Locking the door, I sit on the toilet lid, my elbows on my knees and my hands in my hair. My stomach roils. I focus on my breath.

A soft rap sounds at the door. "Are you okay?"

"Yeah," I manage to say, my voice shaky. "Just not feeling so great."

"Can I get you something?"

"No. I'll be out in a minute."

I wait for five before I splash cold water on my face, force myself to pull it together. It's just Cameron. So we kissed. It's not like neither of us has kissed someone before. This doesn't have to be a big deal. Last night was an accident, a fluke, a combination of adrenaline and high emotions coming together into something that never should've happened. It's in the past, and now we can move on to finish the list. I can do this.

But when I walk out of the bathroom and see him sitting on the bed in his pajamas, with one side of his hair sticking up, a look of concern etched on his face, there's a tug, a lurch, deep in my gut, and excitement rises in me. I can't help it.

"Better?"

"Yeah. Sorry." I sit next to him, lean into his side as he wraps an arm around me. My breathing becomes a bit quicker, shallower. This shouldn't be happening, I know, but it is. I'm falling for Cameron Andrews. And despite the thousand reasons I shouldn't, despite freaking out just moments before, I let myself.

. . . . . .

"You wanna drive?" Cameron asks after we leave the hotel lobby. He dangles the car keys in front of me, one eyebrow raised comically high. I snatch them from his grasp and run to the car, leaving him behind.

I'm already in the driver's seat, the car rumbling around me as Cameron stows our bags in the trunk. He climbs into the seat next to me then leans across the midconsole and gives me a quick kiss. "Where to now?"

I shrug. "South? We're bound to get to Carolina Beach eventually, right?"

"Sounds good to me."

I kill the engine three times trying to back out of our spot, then once more while leaving the parking lot, but eventually we make it onto the road. The drive through town is brutal—this place has more stop signs than any tiny beach hamlet should—but I manage to get us all the way to the highway without any more problems. I smile smugly at Cameron.

It lasts for about an hour, this easy driving, until I slow down for a truck. The car shudders, reminding me to downshift. Clutch to the floor, I pull the car from fourth to third.

The grinding sound is horrible.

I try again, and I hear the same grind. I push the gearshift back to fourth, but the result is no better.

"Clutch," Cameron says groggily.

"I'm pushing the clutch!" Panic is rising in me. I pump the clutch, trying any gear I can. Finally, with a hiccup, the car pops into second. It jumps forward, the engine revving. Automatically, I shove the clutch to the floor again. Braking, I pull to the side of the road.

The car jumps in the gravel, and I stomp on the pedal even harder. I'm about to shove it through the floorboard and, just as I'm sure the engine is going to die, Cameron pops the stick shift out of gear and into neutral. We stop, the engine rumbling softly.

"What just happened?" Cameron asks.

Setting the parking brake, I lean back and press my palms to my eyes. "I have no idea. Everything was fine, but then it just started to freak out."

"What did you do?"

"I didn't do anything!" I yell.

Cameron eases my hands from my face. "Calm down. I'm not saying you did anything wrong. I just need to know what happened so I can try to figure out what's going on with the car."

"I was just driving along, and then this truck was going really slow, so I tried to downshift, and . . ."

Cameron is nodding slowly. "Press the clutch," he says.

I do. Once it's to the floor, Cameron works through the gears, trying out every one and producing that same metallic grind in each. "Clutch is out."

"What does that mean? We're just stuck here?"

"No. But it does mean I need to drive now, okay?"

We switch seats without speaking, and Cameron kills the engine and puts the car into first gear. He signals and waits for traffic to lighten up. Finally, he says, "Ready?" I nod, and he starts the engine.

The car rolls slowly at first then jumps forward onto the road. When Cameron shifts to second, the gears grind again, so he waits a moment and tries again. The stick pops into gear. The car shakes a little, but we keep moving. The transitions to third and fourth gears go smoothly, and we're back on the road.

"You are a genius."

"I try." He reaches across the console and wraps my hand in his. I turn mine over, and our fingers intertwine, our hands resting on my upper thigh. "I think I saw a sign back there for New Bern. We can make a pit stop and see if we can get the car fixed."

"You can't keep driving it like this? Seems to be working."

"It's too hard on the transmission. It'll get us to town, but we shouldn't try to push it too far until we can get a new clutch."

Cameron revs the engine high whenever he needs to downshift, moving the stick slowly until it pops into gear when he upshifts. It takes us two hours to get to New Bern, and once there, we stop at the first mechanic's shop we pass.

It's a small shop with just enough room for two garage bays and a lobby housing three chairs. One bay has an old pickup lifted in it, and the other is, happily, empty. Cameron pulls the car in front of the empty bay, careful to pop it into neutral before shutting off the engine.

Almost immediately, a weather-beaten man in greasy coveralls is standing next to the car. "What can I do ya for?" he asks once we are out of the car.

"Clutch went out between here and the Outer Banks," Cameron explains. "Any chance you can squeeze us in for a fix?"

"What year?"

"1970."

The man whistles. "That's a great car you got there, kid. We don't see many of these old Carlos around here. We're kinda swamped, though. Y'all got a couple days?"

Cameron looks at the empty bay then at me, and I nod. What other choice do we have? We could look for another shop, but the car was acting pretty shaky by the time we rolled into town, and I'm not sure how much farther we should push it.

We follow the man into the lobby and watch as he navigates through several screens on the computer. "All right," he says after a couple minutes. "We can get a new clutch here pretty easy, but it's going to be Monday morning before we can get the work done. Maybe Sunday if we're lucky."

I look at the OPEN sign hanging on the front door, standard Monday–Friday hours listed on it, with Saturdays by appointment only. "Are you open on Sunday? I don't want you to have to come in just for us."

"Oh yeah. We don't take new cars, but we got a guy who's one of those Seventh-day Adventists. Does the church stuff on Saturday, so he comes in on Sundays to finish up extra work."

"Sounds good," Cameron says. "How much is this going to cost us?"

"The part'll run you about one-fifty, and I'm guessing labor will be about four hundred unless we find something in there that causes problems."

In the back of my mind, I can see the money draining from my savings account. The credit card Mom and Dad gave me a year ago is in my purse if things get desperate, but they'll see anything I charge, so it's not an option I want to pursue.

Cameron passes our keys to the man and the three of us walk out to the car to get our bags as he points out a place down the street, where we can catch a bus that'll take us into the center of town. We walk toward the bench he indicated, and I pull out my phone.

"Hey, banana!"

"Hey, Aunt Morgan," I say, my voice not nearly as chipper as hers. "We're in New Bern."

"Wow. Don't sound too excited about that."

"The clutch went out," I say, "so we're stuck here for a couple days."

"Ouch. That sounds expensive."

"Yeah. Hey . . . can you maybe look for a room for us? Something not too expensive? We're waiting for a bus but we have no idea where we're actually going, and I really don't want to deal with it right now." After Bender House, it's easier to have Aunt Morgan rent for us anyway.

"Sure thing. How long do you think you'll be there?"

"The mechanic said they won't finish till Monday, so through the weekend, I guess."

"All right. I'll figure something out. Talk to you soon."

"Thanks, Aunt Morgan." I hang up and drop my phone into my purse. Cameron is rubbing my arm, soft strokes on my bare skin. I snuggle closer to him. "I'm glad you're here."

"You better be," he says with a laugh, "or you would've been completely stranded back there."

"Shut up. Not just because of that." I crane my neck, reaching my lips for his, and kiss him, soft and slow.

My phone ringing breaks us apart, and I scramble to get it, heat flooding my cheeks.

"Hey, what'd you find?" My voice is breathless.

"Okay, so rooms around New Bern are hard to find. But I got you one at the Bradham B&B."

"Bed and Breakfast? How expensive is that going to be?"

"Don't worry about it. My treat."

"You don't have to do that."

"I know. I want to. You guys have some fun there, okay?"

"Thanks. I love you."

"Love you, too, banana-face."

Just as I hang up, the bus comes into view. Cameron gathers our bags, and we step to the edge of the sidewalk. The bus squeals to a stop and the doors open with a hiss of air.

"Where's the Bradham B&B?" I ask the driver as we board. I dig through my purse for some cash to pay our fare.

"We go right past there," he says. "I'll stop for you."

"Thanks so much."

We find a seat, halfway to the back, between a middle-aged woman in a skirt and blazer and a bunch of high schoolers crowded around a video playing on an iPad. We stow our bags under the seats and sit.

The bus winds through the streets, past huge, old houses with magnolia trees shading expansive lawns. We cross a river, and then we're flanked by brick storefronts, their glass windows painted. People stroll the sidewalks, and virtually no cars drive past.

We stop twice, letting people on and off. Soon the driver turns a corner and stops in front of a giant Victorian house painted sky blue. "Here you two go, the Bradham B&B."

The house is beautiful. It has a wide front porch with Adirondack chairs lining it, small tables separating each. The front door is intricately carved wood with an etched glass window set near the top. Inside, the lobby boasts a high ceiling and sculpted molding, with a giant oriental rug covering the hardwood floor. We cross the room to the marble-topped counter and ding the bell.

"Hi!" a voice calls from the back, followed by a petite woman. "Oh, you must be Anna and Cameron!"

"That's us."

She removes a key from the wall and waves us toward the stairs. "Well, come on. You're lucky. We have a wedding party staying here, so we have only one room left. I'm Nancy," she says as an afterthought before starting up the stairs. She leads us past the second floor and on to the third, where we stop on a small landing with one door on each side. She unlocks the door on the left and we enter the room, which is huge, with a massive four-poster standing in the center. There's a round table on either side of the bed and a wardrobe against one wall.

"You have your own bathroom through there," Nancy tells us, "and we serve breakfast from six to nine. If you need anything, I'll be right downstairs."

We thank her, and she leaves. "How much do you think your aunt is paying for this?" Cameron asks as soon as he's sure Nancy is out of earshot.

"Too much, probably," I say, "but I intend to enjoy it." I dive onto the bed and wrap myself in the huge comforter. Nestled into the warmth, our late night and early morning catches up to me, and I suddenly feel exhausted.

"I'll be right back," Cameron says and slinks out the door before I can say anything. He's gone less than a minute, and when he returns, his breath is heavy.

"You okay?" I ask, yawning.

He nods and holds up a piece of paper, and I wave him closer. It's a wedding invitation.

"Where'd you get that?"

"It was on the counter when we checked in. You didn't see it?"

I shake my head. "And what, you just decided to swipe it?"

"I'll give it back. I just wanted the details."

"Why?"

"Because we are crashing a wedding tomorrow night."

Chapter 24

"Cameron."

Nothing.

I shake him. "Cameron."

"Mmmm?"

"Are you awake?"

"No."

"I'm hungry."

"It's dark."

"Starving."

"What time is it?"

"Doesn't matter. I'm hungry."

With a groan, he rolls over and grabs his phone from the bedside table. "Ugh. It's three fifteen in the morning. Go to sleep."

"Can't. I'm hungry."

"It's not my fault you went to bed without eating anything."

"Yes, it is."

"Oh, really? How do you figure?"

I snuggle into his side and press my mouth to his neck. His pulse beats under my lips. "Because you were so warm and comfy and I didn't want to move and I fell asleep. Your fault."

"You're not going to let me go back to sleep until you eat, are you?"

"Not likely."

"Fine. Let's go."

We sneak from the room and tiptoe down the stairs. The house is dark, only a small lamp emitting light into the lobby. The dining room is just to the side, and we make our way through it to the kitchen.

The kitchen is huge, with stainless-steel appliances. It's shockingly modern in a house filled with antiques. Cameron pulls open the fridge, and light spills out onto the floor.

"Are we supposed to be in here?"

"Probably not," he says, piling food into his arms. "But if you don't eat, I'll never sleep, and I'm tired." He sets to work assembling a sandwich at lightning speed. He hands it to me, then puts the ingredients back into the fridge.

"Oh my gosh, this is the best sandwich I've ever eaten," I say around a mouthful of food. "Seriously, I want to have this sandwich's babies."

"As long as you do it fast." Cameron grabs my hand and leads me back into the dining room.

Just then, a light flicks on in the next room, and a voice calls out, "Hello? Is someone down here?"

It's Nancy, who is maybe the nicest woman ever. She probably wouldn't care that we took some food if we explain how hungry I am, but still, I panic. Dropping to the floor, I pull Cameron with me, and the two of us crawl under the massive dining table. I sit back on my knees and take another bite of the sandwich. Seriously, best ever.

The overhead light flickers to life, and I watch a pair of sock-covered feet round the table and head into the kitchen. "Hello?"

Cameron doesn't really fit under the table. He looks like a marionette shoved into its box, all long limbs and sharp angles, bent into this tiny space. His head presses against the underside of the table, and he is glaring at me. I stifle a laugh.

I slip my sandwich onto one of the chairs and drop to my hands and knees, lean forward, and press my mouth to his. He kisses me back, and we stay like that, blissfully uncomfortable, until well after the light is turned off and Nancy is back in bed.

Up in our room, nestled into bed, I finish my sandwich. After my last swallow, I say, "Thanks for the food."

"You owe me."

"I know." I wrap an arm over his chest and nestle my head into the hollow of his shoulder to drift off again, safe in his arms.

. . . . . .

We sleep in, missing breakfast completely. By the time we've showered and gotten dressed, it's almost lunchtime. The wedding is at four, so we have a few hours to kill before crashing the party.

The B&B is a whirlwind of bridesmaids getting ready, running through the halls half-dressed, their hair in rollers.

The bride is set up in the sitting room next to the lobby, a team of stylists circling her, tugging at her hair and touching up her makeup. Her dress hangs in the corner, immaculate and sparkly.

"Did that invite happen to mention a dress code?" I whisper to Cameron. I sound like I'm trying to talk around marbles, but I'm not sure how else to form my words. Accents are even harder when you try to whisper, I'm quickly learning.

"Your British accent is rubbish," he says in an accent that is, admittedly, way better than mine, if still not exactly *British*.

"Bollocks."

"Do you even know what that means?"

"Whatever. What are we supposed to wear?"

He sneaks the invite from behind the camera bag, reading it as he crosses to the counter. He puts it back where he swiped it from then returns to me. "It says black tie optional."

"Meaning we should probably wear something nicer than anything we brought. We don't have money for this."

"Oh, ye of little faith." He winks, waving at the bride and her entourage as we exit through the front door.

He leads me through the streets, past storefronts and boutiques, his phone glued to his hand as he follows the directions on-screen. Dresses hang in windows, and I spot at least three that would be wedding appropriate, but Cameron doesn't slow down. Finally, he stops in front of a nondescript building and points to it with a flourish. "We're here."

"Um, okay?" A small wooden sign hangs off the wall, decorative script reading LOUISA JANE. We enter.

The store is small, crammed wall-to-wall with clothing racks. I can't make out any sort of organization to the chaos. Shiny dresses are smashed next to T-shirts and jeans, which are next to a long pair of footed pajamas. "We're never going to find anything here."

An old woman squeezes her considerable belly between two racks and stands in front of us. "Hello, dears," she wheezes. "What are we looking for today?"

"We have a wedding to go to this evening at Tryon Palace. Black tie optional," Cameron explains. "We don't have much cash."

She tuts, eyeing us from top to bottom. "Spin," she orders, and we do, bouncing off each other as we turn in the tight space. When we're facing her again, she stares intently, a slow smile breaking over her face. "I have just the thing. Wait here."

She disappears into the racks, the only indication that she's still in the room is the sound of metal hangers clanking against one another. She mumbles to herself. A door slams. I look up at Cameron, questioning, and he shrugs.

The woman comes back, and we follow the line of shaking clothes racks as she makes her way toward us. She has two garment bags draped over her arm. "Black one is for you," she says, pointing her chin at Cameron. "And the white is yours," she tells me.

We take the bags. "Do you have a fitting room?" I ask.

She looks at me like I just kicked her puppy. "No need. It fits, I promise."

"Thanks," Cameron says, pulling out his wallet. "What do we owe you?"

She waves him away. "Just bring them back tomorrow."

"Seriously?"

"Yeah. It's a secondhand store. Nobody cares if the dresses are a little used."

We thank the woman again, promising to return the clothes first thing in the morning, and start back toward the B&B.

. . . . . .

The dress is stunning. I stand in front of the bathroom mirror, turning to admire it from all angles. The shiny fabric is deep purple, almost black. It's strapless, a black leather band holding the bodice snug just above my bust. It hugs my body, falling to my knees. The woman even put shoes in the bag, black wedges with delicate silver beading.

I tease my hair, trying to add some volume to my waves, then gather it over one shoulder, working it into a loose bun. I slick on some lip gloss and call it good.

Cameron's standing at the wardrobe when I come back into the room, his back to me. His clothes fit equally well. He's wearing a slim gray suit and black shoes. He turns.

"Wow," he says. "You look . . . wow."

"You're not so bad yourself, chap." Under the gray suit coat, he's wearing a white shirt, the top button undone.

"You ready?"

The bridal party is already gone, and the house is quiet in their absence. "Cheerio."

"You really need to go to England sometime to see how they really talk." Cameron's accent is subtle and flawless, having been refined throughout the day.

"Pishposh, old boy."

Outside, Cameron stops me from going down the steps and guides me to one of the chairs. "I called a cab," he says. "There's no way we are walking there in these shoes."

The cab pulls up a minute later, and we slide into the backseat. "Take us to the palace, Jeeves," I say to the driver.

"Ignore her," Cameron says and laughs.

Tryon Palace looms over us within ten minutes. The building is huge, standing proud on its neatly manicured lawns. The driver drops us off at the looped driveway. Cameron pays him, and we walk around the building, following a path of flowers and balloons. At the back, an arched trellis is set up, wild flowers woven into it. Rows of white chairs line either side of a grassy aisle. Guests mingle, hugging and kissing cheeks. We make our way to the back row and slip into two seats.

A man stands at the front of the aisle now, under the edge of the trellis, and the guests make their way to their seats. A black woman sits next to me, clutching her purse in her lap. "How do you know Sarah and Jasper?"

"Oh, I don't, really," I say, my accent faltering for a moment, "but my boyfriend here went to school with, uh, Jasper."

"That's nice. Where are you from, dear?"

"Iowa." She looks surprised, and I remember the fake British thing I've been doing. "I grew up in a small town just outside Manchester, but I came here to live with Grammy and Papi a few years back."

Music starts playing now, saving me from digging myself further into the hole I'm in. We watch the processional— flower girls and the ring bearer followed by four groomsmen escorting four bridesmaids. Then the bride steps up, her father on one side, her mother on the other, each of them holding one of her hands.

Suddenly, I'm crying. Like, shaking, trying-not-to-sob-out-loud crying. As I watch the beautiful bride make her way to her groom, it hits me that Storm will never get to do this. This wedding is the kind she would have loved—simple and beautiful and outdoors, fancy but understated. This could have been her, five years from now. Less even. Instead, she's gone, and she'll never get her perfect wedding.

Cameron grabs my hand and squeezes it tight. I squeeze back, holding on for all the comfort he gives, for the knowledge that he's here, missing Storm as much as I do.

But it doesn't last. Instead of the comfort I expect to feel, my skin crawls, burning where our hands meet. I pull my purse into my lap and extract my hand from his on the pretense of digging out a Kleenex. When my face is dry again, I link my hands in my lap instead of offering one back to Cameron.

The reception immediately follows the wedding, so as soon as those gathered all stand and cheer for the couple, we are ushered into one of the buildings behind the palace. It's decorated with strands of white sparkly lights, more wild flowers gathered in crystal vases around the room. A dance floor takes up one end, a group of round tables at the other.

We follow the crowd to the tables. Each is filled with name cards. Of course. There's a door off to the side of the room, and I make my way to it, slipping through quietly. Cameron follows. A man is in the room, putting the final touches on an enormous, ornate cake. He stares at me, the question clear on his face, so I hold up my phone. "I have to make a call. How do I get outside?"

Without a word, he points behind him to a door that is propped open with a box. I rush through it. Outside, I lean against the wall and tap my phone screen.

ME: Hey, it may be late before I can call tonight.

AUNT MORGAN: So call now.

ME: Can I not?

AUNT MORGAN: ??

ME: I'm fine. Just really tired. Still here in New Bern. Nothing new to report.

AUNT MORGAN: Okay, but call in the morning. I have the day off.

ME: Will do.

Cameron stands next to me, waiting patiently until I put the phone back in my purse. When I do, he says, "You okay?"

"I'm brilliant."

He reaches for my hand, but I pull it back, crossing my arms.

"Anna, what's going on?"

"Nothing."

"You lie."

"Bollocks. Let's just . . . wait."

Hurt crosses his face, but he shrugs and makes his way to a bench under the wide branches of a magnolia tree. We sit, not talking. I take my phone back out and scroll through my social media feeds, angling away from Cameron. With a sigh, he leans back, his own phone in hand, and we stay like that, together but separate, until music starts to thump its way over the lawn.

"Dinner must be over," he says.

"Great. Let's dance."

I allow the music to take me away. As soon as we're back in the building, I hit the dance floor, soaking up the beat, my body moving with it. It's a mass of bodies out here, all bouncing together, arms waving and dresses spinning. The DJ keeps us moving, playing four fast songs before slowing things down.

"And now, how about we have Mr. and Mrs. Hepworth out here for their first dance?"

The crowd erupts in cheers, and the bride and groom make their way to the center of the dance floor. The groom holds his bride tight as the opening notes of an old rock ballad play. We all watch as they turn circles around the floor, and then, one by one, other couples join them. I can see Cameron standing at the edge of the floor, watching me.

The man next to me is in his sixties. When he offers me his arm, I take it, and we spin around the floor. The songs blend together, slow, swaying songs melting directly into fast songs, bodies jumping. We do the Chicken Dance, the Hokey Pokey, and the Macarena. Sappy country songs and upbeat jazz.

Halfway through "(I've Had) The Time of My Life," I'm dancing with a boy about my age—the bride's nephew, I learned three songs ago—when Cameron approaches.

"Hey, Anna," he says, then turns to my partner, "mind if I cut in?"

The nephew, whose name I've forgotten, looks confused, like he didn't realize that this ever happens outside of movies. Probably it doesn't. But he steps aside, and Cameron sweeps me into his arms. I keep one hand on his chest, forcing some distance between us.

"What's going on, Anna?"

"I don't know what you're talking about."

"That's ridiculous, and you know it. It's like a wall went up between us during the ceremony, and I want to know why."

"I just think that we—what we're doing—"

"Can you cut the accent? I can't have this conversation with you when you're talking like that."

Anger prickles the back of my neck. "Fine," I say, my voice harsh and all-Iowa. "I think we made a mistake. Is that what you want to hear?"

"A mistake?"

"Yeah. You and me. It's a mistake. You kissed me, and I got caught up in it, and I shouldn't have let it keep going. It was a big, fat mistake."

"You know that's not true." The song changes, some fast-paced pop number, but we stay together, swaying back and forth.

"Cameron, don't you remember what this whole summer is supposed to be about?"

His face softens. "Of course I remember."

"So, being in a relationship with you is not part of that. I am doing this list, and you don't fit in it."

Cameron's hand presses against my lower back, and I let him pull me the slightest bit closer to him. "I could fit in, if you let me."

"No, you couldn't. What about number five?"

"Fall in love. What about it?"

The page flashes in my mind, the crossed-out words harsh and vibrant. "She wrote 'meet my soulmate,' Cameron. Not fall in love with a boy I've known my whole life."

"Didn't she cross that soulmate part out?"

My head is shaking, but I say, "Yeah, but it's still the same. I need to find someone. Meet a stranger and fall in love. Not . . . this." Even as I argue, the muscles in my arm relax, my elbow bending until we are pressed against each other, chest to chest, my hand flat between us.

He dips his head low, his lips just brushing my earlobe. Chills erupt across my skin, and I lean into him, already giving in. I can think of a hundred arguments, but my body craves him too deeply.

"Anna," he whispers, and the sound of him speaking my name sends shivers down my spine. "We all start as strangers."

I don't know who makes the first move, but our lips meet, hesitant, then hungry. And we're standing there, in the middle of the dance floor, couples spinning around us, kissing.

I could kiss him forever.

Chapter 25

The sun peeks through the window this morning, falling warm across my face, coaxing me awake. Cameron is lying next to me, one hand behind his head. He looks younger in his sleep. I press a gentle kiss to his lips.

He shifts, reaches an arm around me. The kiss deepens. He pulls me on top of him and tangles a hand in my hair. "Good morning," he murmurs into my mouth.

"Back atchya." I kiss him again. "What are we doing today?"

After a long kiss, he rubs a hand down my back, resting it just above the curve of my butt. "This."

"This is definitely nice," I say in between quick kisses, "but if you don't feed me, I'm liable to get nasty."

"Don't I know it."

"I'm just saying, I can't be held responsible for the things I say when I'm hungry."

He shifts, and I can feel his excitement. I run my fingers over his scalp, embracing his head with my forearms, and press myself into him. Forehead to forehead, I stare into his eyes then kiss him again, hard and eager. I'm ready to say that food can wait, to stay in bed all day, but my stomach grumbles a loud protest to that idea. Rolling off Cameron, I groan and stretch.

"Okay, okay. Point taken. Let's feed you."

The clock tells us we have fifteen minutes left to grab breakfast downstairs, so we plod to the dining room in our pajamas. It's empty except for pitchers of milk, juice, and water on the table.

Cameron pulls a chair out for me, and when I sit, he bows deeply to kiss my hand. "My lady."

"You're an idiot."

"I do my best. Be right back." He rounds the table and peeks his head through the kitchen door. "Hello?"

Nancy's voice rings out. "Oh, Cameron, dear. I'm so happy you two could eat with us today." She comes out into the dining room, and Cameron sits next to me. "Good morning, Anna," she says.

"Morning."

"We have waffles with strawberries this morning. Does that work for you two?"

"Sounds wonderful," I say, remembering my breakfast with Dad, not too long ago.

"How about some eggs? Would you like me to fry up a couple?"

"We're fine," I say at the same time as Cameron says, "That'd be great. Thank you."

Nancy laughs and looks to me for clarification. "Eggs would be nice," I say.

"Would you like some help?" Cameron asks.

"No, no, dear. You just stay there and enjoy. This is my job." With a wink, she disappears into the kitchen.

We don't talk, just sit at the massive table, shoulder to shoulder. Cameron puts his hand on my thigh, palm up. I run my fingernails over his palm, up and down his fingers, circling his wrist. I memorize the lines and contours of his hand, where it's hard and calloused, and where it's soft and silky between his fingers.

Nancy is back faster than seems possible for the amount of food she's carrying balanced precariously on her arms. Cameron hops up and helps her off-load the plates onto the table, despite her protests.

"Thank you so much, Nancy," I say. "This looks amazing."

And it is. The waffles are light and spongy, almost more angel food cake than waffle, and the strawberries are fresh, not frozen in syrup like I'm used to. We eat fast, and before long I feel like I'm about to burst.

"I need a nap."

Cameron laughs. "It's, like, nine thirty. How can you possibly be tired?"

"Food makes me sleepy."

"Too bad. We're going exploring."

Grabbing the front of his shirt, I yank him toward me. Our lips crash. "I can think of a few places I'd like to explore."

"I can't take you anywhere, can I?"

"Nope." I kiss him again.

. · · · ·.

An hour later, we're dressed and walking through downtown. We dropped off last night's clothes, putting the garment bags in a Tupperware box the old woman left in front of her locked shop, a Post-it note on top reading RETURNS.

We walk into an old-fashioned soda fountain, with Pepsi bottles lining the shelves and old metal signs hanging on the walls. It's crowded with people seated at all the tables, a few around a display case at the end of the store. Two empty stools stand side by side at the counter, and we beeline to them. The wall behind the bar is a collage of old black-and-white and sepia photos interspersed with the history of Pepsi. The man behind the counter is sporting an impressive walrus mustache. He smiles wide, his eyes disappearing in wrinkles, and holds up a finger for us. "Just one second."

As we settle onto our stools, Cameron grabs a plastic display card and reads: "The Birthplace of Pepsi, located in historic New Bern, North Carolina, is the actual site where Pepsi-Cola was first invented by Caleb Bradham in his pharmacy in 1898." He scans the rest of the card silently as Walrus Man makes his way toward us. I order two Pepsis and watch him pour them from the fountain.

"It's better here. Don't you think it's better here?" Cameron says, straw still in his mouth.

I take a small sip. It's sweet, the carbonation tickling my nose. "It's good," I say, "but I don't really taste the difference."

"It's better, I promise. More Pepsi-like."

"More Pepsi-like. Got it." With the straw between my teeth, I smile at him.

"Storm would get it," Cameron says. "She was a real Pepsi connoisseur."

"That she was." We kept a list of places in town that carried Pepsi in glass bottles, because apparently it's better that way. I could never tell much of a difference. Cameron is right; she would love this.

We drain our glasses and vacate our stools, waving off the Walrus's offer of refills. Cameron turns as soon as we hit the sidewalk, grabbing my hand and hauling me toward the water. We skip-walk to the marina.

"Where. Are. We. Going?" I say between breaths.

"Boat mocking."

I stop in my tracks, my arm jolting when it reaches the end of Cameron's reach. "What the heck is boat mocking?"

He pulls my arm, lightly. "You'll see. Just come on."

We amble now, a gentle stroll along the docks of the marina. Many of the slips are empty, their owners enjoying the weekend, but enough boats are still docked that the marina looks full. With the sun glinting off the water and all the masts standing tall in a row, it feels like we're walking through a painting, an artist's rendition of what the coast should look like.

"There," Cameron says, pointing. "That one." We walk up to the back of a huge blue boat. White and gold lettering is painted on the back, reading *In Deep Ship*.

"Okay? . . ."

He looks at me like I've sprouted a second head. "Okay? That's it? Come on, it's funny! Who names a boat something like that?"

"Whoever owns this one obviously."

"Funny girl."

"Whatever. What should a boat be named, oh, wise one?"

"I don't know. Something like"—he spins around, scanning boats, and rushes to one across a dock—"this! This is a respectable boat name."

"*Carpe Diem*? If you say so, Captain."

"What's wrong with *Carpe Diem*?"

"Nothing. It's just that you'll probably find three in every marina on the East Coast."

"It's not that common."

"I bet it is. *Carpe Diem* is like the Anna of boat names."

Cameron's smile is knowing when he says, "You always hated your name, didn't you?"

"Yes—no." I run a hand through my hair, fingers catching on the tangles, and I weave it into a braid over my shoulder. A quick search tells me I don't have a hair band, so I tie the end in a messy knot. "It's not that I hate my name. Anna's a fine name."

"Well, what's the problem, then?"

"Nothing. I like Anna."

"Liar. You used to try to change it all the time when we were kids. You made us all call you River for a month once."

I shrug, remembering. I'd loved the name River when I was little. "It's just—my parents. It's like they used up all their creativity with Storm, you know? How did they name one kid such a unique name, and then less than a year later all they come up with is Anna?"

My hand is in his now, and we slowly leave the *Carpe Diem* behind. "Do you remember what your parents were like before you and Storm were born?"

"You're kidding, right?"

He laughs. "Of course you don't *remember*, but from stories, I mean."

"Yeah. They seem like they were . . . different. More fun, less uptight."

"They were hippies."

"No—"

"They were! Total, honest-to-goodness hippies. Flower children. But then your mom got pregnant, and your dad got serious about his job."

"How do you know all this?"

"I listen. Your mom used to talk about it all the time, how your dad went from wanting to travel wherever the wind blew them to studying all night to pass his classes and get promoted. She said it happened practically overnight when she got pregnant with Storm."

When Cameron talks, I don't picture Dad, the middle-aged man with the receding hairline and small paunch—the Dad I know now—nor do I see the man with the long sideburns and flowing hair from the wedding picture hanging on the wall in our upstairs hallway. Instead, Cameron's words conjure an image of a third man, somehow better than either version of Dad I know. More handsome, too, like the hero in the romantic comedies Piper is always making me watch.

I can't tell Cameron any of that, though—can't admit how little I know about my own parents when he knows so much. Instead, I say, "I don't really see what this has to do with our names."

"Everything!" He throws his arms out, creating a huge circle in the air and nearly yanking my arm out of its socket in the process as he yells it. A man on a boat nearby—*The Last Chance*, I notice—stops his wipe-down of the instrument cluster and stares at us.

"Seriously?" I rub my sore shoulder with my free hand.

"Yeah. See, Storm—the name, not the baby—was a grasp at the hippie life they were leaving behind. It was the last vestige of who they were before they became parents. And by the time you came along—"

"A whopping eleven months later . . ."

"They were over it. They'd left that part of them behind. So they named you Anna."

"Let me get this straight. You're saying all it took for my parents to go from being creative, free-thinking hippies to giving me the most common name of all time was seeing the pee-stick turn blue?"

"Exactly. But I'm pretty sure Anna isn't the most common name of all time—I think Mary might be."

"Whatever."

We've stopped walking. My hand is hot in his. A gull flits behind Cameron's head, landing on the mast of a huge white boat named *Persephone*.

"That's a good name," I say, tilting my chin toward the boat.

He glances at it, barely, then looks back at me. "I like Anna better."

"You're a terrible flirt."

He steps closer. I can feel his breath on my face. "I can call you River if you'd prefer."

"Shut up."

"That, I can do."

He kisses me, hot and soft and firm all at once. Letting go of his hand, I loop my arms around his neck, my fingers in his hair. I memorize the feel of his body against mine, each curve and ridge and plane of his chest. His arms snake around my lower back and pull me to him even tighter, lifting me onto my tiptoes.

It's always been a fetish of mine, this desire to kiss some-one tall enough to get the tiptoes involved. But when you're five foot ten, even the taller guys are not really tall enough for that. But Cameron is, and suddenly the limbs that have always seemed just a bit too long are perfect for me.

This kiss goes on forever, our lips dancing, tongues exploring. My head is cloudy, shutting out the marina and all the boats, the man on *The Last Chance*, who might still be watching us for all I know.

When Cameron backs up, breaking contact for a second, I follow him, leaning back in. I'm not ready to be done yet; already my lips ache for more. He obliges, kissing me for a moment longer, and then pulls away, pressing his forehead to mine. The tips of our noses barely touch.

His breath comes in rapid bursts. I tilt my face up to his again, but he shakes his head slightly. "Hold on," he whispers.

Suddenly, his whole body is trembling. It's the barely noticeable shiver of someone who doesn't know yet that they're chilled. But it has to be ninety degrees out here on the dock, so I know he's not cold. He draws in a slow breath, his chest shaking with the effort.

"Are you okay?" I pull my head back from his so I can focus on his face. His cheeks are flushed, his lips slightly swollen. He keeps his eyes closed and nods.

"I . . ."

Just the one word, and he's silent again. The tremor has calmed, so now only his hands shake where they rest on my lower back. He opens his eyes, and they're bright as they stare into mine.

"Cameron?"

"I love you."

I blink. My face goes completely slack. I must look like the world's biggest idiot. I can't find my voice—not that I have any idea what I would say if I could speak. The sounds of the marina—gulls screeching in the distance, water lapping against the hulls of boats—all fade away, replaced by only the sound of my heart beating in my eardrums, erratic and too fast. I start to back out of Cameron's arms, but he holds me tight.

"It's okay," he says, breaking through the pounding in my ears. "You don't have to say it back or anything. I don't expect . . ." He clears his throat. "You just need to know. I had to tell you."

"How long?" My voice is barely a whisper.

"I don't think it's possible to put a time line to love. Once it's there, it's like there's never been anything else. Time bends, and suddenly I knew that I've always loved you." He rushes to talk over my interjection. "And I have. In one way or another, since I moved in next door, since that first summer together, I've loved you. Both of you. But this right now? It built up slowly over the past week, but it also came out of nowhere just a few minutes ago. I can't explain it, Anna. I just know that I love you, and if I didn't tell you right now, I'd be kicking myself for missing the opportunity."

Tears prickle at the corners of my eyes, and my whole body seems heavier. He's staring at me so candidly, everything written on his face.

"Thank you," I whisper. It's the stupidest thing I can say—a horrible way to follow up an "I love you"—but it seems to be exactly what he needs to hear. A smile lights up his face, the toothy, crooked smile I've always loved, and his eyes nearly disappear into it. And I do love that smile. I may not be ready to find out if I love all of him, but this is a start. I inch his head to mine and kiss him, right on the smile that melts my heart.

Chapter 26

The alarm clock blares next to my head, jolting me out of my dream. I swat at it until it stops then snuggle back into Cameron's embrace. He's warm against my back, and his arms flex just slightly, wrapping me tight. His lips rest on my neck.

"Anna," he whispers, his breath tickling the baby hairs behind my ear.

"Ugh."

"Anna, we have to get up."

"No, we don't." I tug the covers up around my neck, holding the comforter to my cheek. "Too warm. Need sleep."

"We're going to miss it."

"'sokay."

Cameron groans. "Anna," he says again, soft and low. "This was your idea." He kisses me, just behind the ear, then trails his lips slowly along my jaw, leaving a blazing path of heat everywhere they touch. I refuse to give in.

"It's time to get up." He brushes my hair off my shoulder and presses his lips there. Something jumps and rolls, deep in my gut. When he turns me, I don't resist, instead rolling to my back, eyes still closed. Cameron slips over me, holding his weight on his forearms, pressing down on me just enough to make me want more. I squirm under him.

"Wake up." He kisses each of my eyelids, one of my temples.

Presses his lips to my chin then the hollow of my throat. My back arches.

"Come on, Anna." His lips brush against mine, just barely. Soft enough to tickle, and then they're gone. His breath caresses the side of my face. I turn toward it, hoping to find his lips there.

Instead, I find that he's rising off the bed. Without thinking, my arms shoot out and grab him, pulling him back down. Our lips crash.

He comes out of the kiss laughing. "I knew I could get you up. Now, let's go." He jumps off the bed and slides into his flip-flops.

"No fair," I grumble, but I follow him, putting on my shoes.

Cameron pulls the comforter from the bed and leads me out of the room. The house is dark, but I can hear faint clattering coming from downstairs—Nancy preparing breakfast, probably. There's a trapdoor in the ceiling above us; Cameron pulls the cord and it opens, a white ladder sliding to the floor. We climb.

The widow's walk is small, just enough room for one Adirondack chair and a small table, which I can barely make out in the darkness. We pull up the ladder behind us, not wanting whoever is staying in the room across the hall to trip over it when they awake. Cameron sits, and I nestle onto his lap, draping the comforter around us.

Stars are still visible, but the sky is lightening just at the horizon, a royal blue bleeding into the blackness. From the roof, we can see over the other houses all the way to the water. There's just enough light now to make out silhouettes of boats in the marina. If I try hard enough, I can pretend to see the place we stood yesterday when Cameron told me he loves me.

I lean my head against his shoulder. "I don't think I've ever been up to see a sunrise."

"No?" He hugs me tightly. "I thought you girls always had to be up at ridiculous hours for cheer practice."

"Yeah, I guess we do, but I never pay attention. All I can think about is getting to school and getting practice over with."

"Don't you like it?"

"Yeah, I do like it," I say a little too excitedly. "It's just that practice is really early, and I hate getting out of bed."

"Yeah. Got that."

"And . . ." I turn in his lap, just enough so I can see his face. Since I joined the squad three years ago, I've been all cheer, all the time. We practice, we perform, and when we aren't doing that, we hang out together. I'm with the squad always, and the girls on the team are my best friends. So I've never said aloud what I'm thinking—I've barely let myself think it.

"And?" Cameron prompts.

"And it sometimes seems a little pointless, you know?" I force the words out as fast as they can leave my mouth, knowing that if I don't say them now, I never will. Once they're out there, though, I slow down to explain. "I mean, you did the debate team and all that because you want to be a lawyer, and Storm took every science class she could get into so she'd be ready for college. You were both in the Key Club and did volunteer stuff, and what do I do with my time? I jump around and clap my hands and go to parties."

"But you like it, right?"

I nod. "I do. I really, really do. But it's pretty pointless."

He shrugs. "If you like it, then it's not pointless."

"That's crap."

"No, I mean it. I did Key Club because Storm asked me to and there's no saying no to Storm. And the debate stuff? I'm a huge nerd—don't bother denying it, because we both know the truth. I didn't do debate because it gave me some greater meaning, though. I did it because I like to win."

"You don't say."

"You've noticed, huh?"

"Of course I've noticed. The whole world has noticed." I sigh. "But that's just the thing. You know what you want to do, and you do it. I don't want to be a lifetime cheerleader. I do it because I don't do anything else."

Cameron's quiet for a moment before saying, "Well, do you have any idea what you want to do after school?"

I shrug, not answering. I'd always thought I'd just follow Storm to the University of North Carolina. That's how I'd lived my whole life, following in her footsteps, always eleven months later, and I figured college would be no different. She was so passionate about the ocean, and since I didn't have my own passion, I told myself I was passionate about it, too. But now she's gone, and I can't follow her anymore. I have to make my own path, and I'm not sure I'm ready for that.

The sunrise starts in earnest now, a blaze of orange peeking above the water and reflecting on the waves. We grow quiet, and I settle back into Cameron's chest for the show.

The sky shifts through myriad colors, blue to orange to the softest of pinks, and finally to yellow just before the sun breaks out from its nighttime prison. I blink against its sudden brightness.

"Worth getting up so early?" Cameron asks.

I nod. "It's gorgeous. Where's the camera?"

"Oh crap." He starts to stand, and I slip off his lap to the roof. "Double crap! I'm sorry."

I'm in a fit of giggles as he helps me to my feet. "Did you really just say 'double crap'?"

"Shut up! I swore in front of your mom once, and I seriously thought she was going to cut out my tongue. I don't think I've said a curse word since."

"I think I remember that."

"You should. You're the one I cussed at." He smiles sheepishly. "Stay there. I'll go get the camera." He drops through the trapdoor, and I curl my feet under my butt in the chair and watch the light show.

He's back faster than seems possible, Polaroid in hand.

Before I know what's happening, he's snapped a picture of me, the camera spitting the film out with a mechanical whir.

"Thanks for the warning." I run a hand over my head, trying to smooth down my bedhead.

"You're beautiful," he says. "You have nothing to worry about."

"Charmer."

"You know it." He hands me the camera, and I stand, taking one step to the railing. The marina is lighting up now, the sun glinting off hulls and mast tips. It's coming alive down there, boats backing out of their slips, still more coming in from nighttime shifts. I hold the camera to my eye, putting the place I think we were standing yesterday in the center of the frame, and take a picture of the sunrise over the marina. It may not be the right place—it's probably not—but every time I look at this picture, I know I'll remember it as the place Cameron Andrews told me he loves me.

"Well," Cameron says, stepping behind me and wrapping his arms around my waist, "I don't know about you, but I'm starving. Someone insisted we get up before the sun."

"Shut up," I say, but I twist my neck around and kiss him.

. . . . . .

"Good morning, you two," Nancy chirps as we make our way into the dining room. Unlike yesterday, this morning the room is packed. The bridal party left yesterday, and now the B&B is filled with mostly middle-aged couples. They stare at us when we walk in—eight pairs of eyes, six with glasses, appraising our pajamas and unruly hair. Maybe we should've showered before coming down.

"Um, hi," I manage as I scan the room for a seat. There are two empty chairs, an elderly couple separating them. I give Cameron's hand a light squeeze then let it go and head to one of them. Cameron steps toward the other.

"Oh," Nancy cries, her fork halfway to her mouth, "wait, Cameron. You two can sit together. Harv, Jeanette, do you mind shifting down so Anna and Cameron can sit next to each other?"

The man to my left smiles at me, his light blue eyes watery and cataract-clouded. "Of course," he croaks and picks up his plate, circling around the back of his wife and sitting in the chair on the other side of her. She passes his coffee cup to him with a shaky hand.

"Thank you, Harv," Cameron says, patting Jeanette on the shoulder as he passes her to the recently vacated seat. Cheeks blazing, I take the chair next to him.

"I'll let Tom know you two are here," Nancy says, rising from her seat. "He'll have food out to you in just a minute."

"Thanks."

Staring at the table, willing the blush to leave my cheeks, I reach for Cameron's hand. My fingers intertwine with his, resting in his lap. With his other hand, he traces soft lines on my forearm, and I struggle not to laugh.

"So, Anna and Cameron, is it? Why don't you two tell us about yourselves," the woman sitting across from me says. She looks to be in her midfifties, with tightly curled black hair and cat-eye glasses. Her voice is sweeter than honey.

"Um, there's not really much to tell," I say.

"Nonsense, dear. Everyone has a story."

"That's the best part about Bed & Breakfasts, sweetie," another woman chimes in. "We love traveling and getting to know other guests."

"Don't know that we've met any quite as young as you two, though," a man I assume to be her husband—a hulking man with a tiny, red face and very little hair—says. "Are you college students?"

Cameron is oddly silent for once, so I say, "High school, actually. Well, I am for one more year. Cameron just graduated."

"Graduated?" the man bellows. "Congratulations, my boy. Where are you going to college?"

Cameron's ears are redder than red, but a tiny smile makes its way onto his face. "Yale," he says, pride leaking into his voice.

"Yale?" Jeanette perks up for the first time since we entered the room. Her voice sounds like it might shatter into a thousand pieces at any minute. "My Harv went to Yale."

"You did?" Cameron asks, turning to Harv.

"A long, long time ago." He laughs. "What are you planning to study?"

Harv and Cameron settle into a comfortable conversation about classes and campus activities and the rich Yale traditions, Harv telling a few particularly colorful stories of his time there. At one point, Jeanette punches him playfully and tells him to hush.

"How long have you two been married?" I ask them.

Jeanette's face is a mass of wrinkles, the skin folded over in so many ways it looks like a failed origami experiment. But the love in her eyes and the adoration she has for her husband shine through all of that, and she's beautiful. "It'll be sixty-two years next month," she says.

"That's incredible," I say, and the table joins in a round of congratulations.

Harv kisses the side of Jeanette's head, his lips loud and smacking, and she swats him off with a laugh. "This is our anniversary trip," he says. "I have a surgery in a couple weeks, so we want to get it in before that. We try to take a small trip every year."

"Nothing serious, I hope?" The honey-voiced woman across from me asks.

"Oh, no, no. It's nothing serious." Harv's voice is lighthearted, but concern etches his features, and Jeanette's eyes fill with tears. "So," Harv says, clearing his throat and clapping Cameron on the shoulder, "what about you two? How long have you been together?"

We look at each other, and I remember what Cameron told me just yesterday. Once it's there, it's like there's never been anything else. Has it really been only four days since our first kiss? It feels like this is all there's ever been—me and Cameron, together, as natural as breathing.

"Uh . . ." Cameron laughs and then says, "a bit less than a week?"

The woman across the table stares at us blankly. Her voice isn't nearly as sweet when she says, "And you're already on vacation together?" Her words drip with disapproval.

"It's not really like that," Cameron says.

"Well, what is it like then, young man?"

I want to kick her under the table. Anger crawls beneath my skin, making me twitch and squirm in my chair. The way she looks at me, her judgment and scorn, makes me want to lash out. Cameron squeezes my hand, no doubt trying to remind me where we are, to force me to keep calm, but I can't help myself.

My voice is deathly calm as I say, "It's like this: my sister, my best friend in the whole world, died. On graduation night. Here one minute, and gone the next, crushed to death in my car." The table is silent, stares of horror coming from all the guests. Cameron is squeezing my hand so hard my fingers hurt, but I can't stop. "Storm—that's my sister, the dead one—she wanted to take this trip, but she can't. And Cameron was her best friend since we were kids. So we came together. We did this trip because Storm can't, because she's dead. Is that explanation enough for you?"

Just as I finish, Nancy breezes back into the room, a tall, balding man behind her, carrying plates of food. She falters at the stillness in the room. "Is everything okay?" she asks.

Harv, who I'm learning is master of the poker face, breaks the silence for us. "Great, Nancy. Thank you for this wonderful breakfast." Sound picks up at his words, forks and knives hitting plates as everyone remembers to eat.

"Oh, don't thank me, handsome. Tom did this one."

"My compliments to the chef." Harv tips an invisible hat to Tom and winks at me. I mouth a thank-you.

The woman across from me continues to stare in shock as her husband finishes his meal, and then they leave in a rush. As soon as they are out of the room, chatter builds back up, my outburst thankfully forgotten.

Once we finish eating, Cameron stacks my plate on his and then asks Harv if he can take his.

"Don't worry about it, Cameron," Nancy says. "It's our—"

"I know! It's your job. But I feel weird not helping, so just let me, okay?"

"If you insist," Tom says. "You can put them in the sink, thanks."

Cameron takes a stack of too many plates to the kitchen, disappearing behind the door. As soon as he's gone, Tom asks me, "What are you two going to do today?"

"I don't know, actually. I don't think we have any plans."

"Have you checked out the trolley?"

I shake my head. "What trolley?"

"Hold on, dear." Nancy rushes from the room, heels clacking on the hardwood floors, and comes back with a brochure in hand. "The trolley is a historic tour. It'll take you through town and teach you a bit about the history of the buildings and stuff."

Tom butts in, "It sounds schmaltzy, but it's actually pretty neat."

"Thanks," I say as Cameron comes back into the room. "I think we'll do it."

"Do what?" Cameron stands behind me, and I hand the brochure to him.

"Tom and Nancy say it's a pretty cool ride."

"Awesome. Thanks." He squeezes my shoulder. "If we get ready now, we can catch the first tour."

We say our good-byes to Harv and Jeanette and make our way back upstairs. As soon as we enter the room, Cameron pulls me to a stop. "What happened down there?"

"I don't know. I just . . ."

"Totally lost it?"

"Yeah." Anger creeps up my neck at the memory of the honey-voiced woman staring at me. "It was strange. It was like, if I didn't say anything, I was going to explode."

"I think you did."

"I know." I shrug. "But it's done, and I can't change it."

Cameron draws me into his arms and hugs me. "If you want to talk about it, you know I'm here."

"I know," I whisper.

"It might make it easier if we do. Talk about it, I mean."

"I know," I say again. "But not now, okay? Now, I need to shower."

"Sounds good," he says, smiling. "Go get clean, stinky."

Chapter 27

The trolley picks us up three blocks from the B&B. It's shiny blue and open to the air, modeled like the old railcars in San Francisco. We climb aboard and hand our money to the smiling driver then pick a seat near the middle. Cameron motions me to the window seat, climbing in after me and laying an arm over my shoulder.

A small group of tourists joins us, filling up about three-quarters of the trolley, before the driver starts down the road, jingling the bell as we creep forward.

We learn the brief history of New Bern, spanning more than three hundred years since its founding. We pass the birthplace of Pepsi again, and I glimpse Walrus Man through the window. Over the intercom, the driver, Donny, explains much the same thing we read on the display card while we drank our sodas at the fountain yesterday.

As we cruise through historic downtown, Donny tells us of the ghosts that supposedly haunt the old buildings. Apparently, the trolley company also runs a historic ghost tour at night.

"We should do that," I say.

"The ghost thing?"

"Yeah. I think it'd be cool."

"Maybe we will, if we have time," Cameron murmurs against the side of my neck.

"If we have time?" I twist to face him. "What else do we have to do while we're stuck here?"

"Oh, I dunno." His hand slides up my thigh, and he leans into me. "Maybe this."

He kisses me, intense, right there on the crowded trolley. My mouth opens to him, automatically, his lips fitting there like they belong. My tongue flits across his, eliciting a soft moan deep in his throat.

Someone in the seat behind us laughs, but I don't care. I don't care about anything but Cameron's lips on mine. I press my hand into his chest, and he shudders under my touch. His hand slips under my shirt, running along the skin there, barely brushing the edge of my tattoo, which is still tender.

I'm hot, too hot. I can't be close enough to him. I want every inch of him to touch every inch of me. I arch my back into him, press against him as tight as I can. He leans back, panting.

"We gotta stop."

"No, we don't." I reach my lips to his again.

The people behind us break into laughter again.

"Yes, we do." He moves back into the seat, folding his hands over his lap. The trolley brakes squeal as we stop at a red light.

Pressing myself against his side, I pull Cameron's earlobe into my mouth and give it a soft nibble. His breath catches, and he moans again, so, so softly.

"No, we don't," I whisper. Then I climb over his lap and grab his hand, pulling him to the front of the trolley. "Hey, Donny, it's been a great ride, but I'm not feeling so great. Motion sickness." I gesture to my stomach, trying to sell it.

"Ah, I'm sorry to hear that. I might be able to find some Dramamine for you."

"That's okay, really. It's been an interesting tour, but I think I just need to lie down." I'm practically bouncing, eager to get off the trolley.

"Well, thank you for coming," Donny says. "You feel better, okay?"

"I will, thanks." I force myself to walk down the steps slowly, dragging Cameron behind me.

The light turns green, and the trolley rumbles off, turning down the cross street. As soon as it's out of view, I launch myself into Cameron's arms, my mouth crashing against his.

"Come on," I say when the kiss ends. I lead him into a little shop on the corner.

We weave through the aisles, passing by batteries and boxed crackers and coloring books, all lined up next to each other. The store has no organization I can figure out, other than drinks in the coolers around the perimeter. I finally find what I'm looking for in the fourth aisle we try, right next to a display of Cup Noodles.

I grab the box from the hook, and Cameron freezes, his hand suddenly tightening around mine. "Anna . . ."

I press my lips to his, mouth open. His stiffness melts almost immediately, and I know he feels it, too, this desire tugging at us, stronger than I want to fight.

"Come on," I say against his mouth.

"You sure?"

"Absolutely."

The man behind the counter seems bored as he checks us out, not looking directly in our eyes once during the transaction. But when he hands the bag and the change back to Cameron, he adds a soft, "Have fun, man." He maybe would be smarmier if he threw in a wink. Maybe.

The walk back to the B&B is long, the trolley having taken us more than a mile from where it picked us up. Anticipation drives us along, our pace quicker than normal. A red light catches us a couple blocks from the room, and we're immediately wrapped in each other's arms, lips together. This suddenly feels like the longest journey ever.

When the light turns, we practically run across the street and down the sidewalk to the B&B. Nancy is, thankfully, nowhere to be found, the lobby empty when we enter, and we make a beeline to the stairs.

We are in our room in record time. As soon as the door shuts behind us, we are connected again, bodies hot with excitement. Cameron holds me firmly, his arm against my side pressing uncomfortably on my tattoo, but I'm beyond caring about that. I want to be even closer.

Cameron backs us up until his legs hit the bed, and then we're falling, our lips barely separating as we land on the bed. I lie on top of him, chest to chest, my hair creating a cage around us, and I kiss him again, slower now, but no less eager. I press into him, slide my body against his, and he groans, loud this time. My body lights up in response to the deep rumble in his chest. His hands snake up my shirt, hot against the skin of my back. He spreads his fingers, palms flat, as much contact between us as possible. I lift my head, gasping to pull a breath in, and his mouth is on my throat in an instant, pressing kisses down the line of my neck. He reaches my collar bones, and his tongue plays in the soft hollow between them.

I need to feel more of him. The layers of fabric separating us mock me, taunt me with the barrier they provide. I sit up, straddling his lap, and pull my shirt over my head. Cameron has seen me in a bikini a thousand times before, but now, as I sit over him in just shorts and a bra, he stares at me, all awe and lust and beauty.

I rotate my hips against him, and his buck into me in return. Bending forward, I kiss him then hop off the bed and drop my shorts to the floor.

He peels his clothes off, never taking his eyes from mine, and we stand there, only feet apart, taking each other in. Even this close seems too far from him. I search the room, find the plastic bag where Cameron dropped it as we entered the room.

I pull out the box and remove one of the foil wrappers. We strip out of the rest of our clothes.

Skin to skin, we collide, every inch of my body on fire with the feel of him. He lays me on the bed then hovers over me, careful with his weight. He kisses me so tenderly it almost hurts, and then lowers onto me.

We're clumsy at first, trying to find a rhythm, one that is perfect for only us. But even as we come together awkwardly, not yet in tune with one another, something just feels right, for the first time in a long time.

When we're done, I curl up in Cameron's arms and press my face into the curve of his neck. I lie there until he falls asleep, his breath growing slow and steady, and I let his rhythm lull me to sleep, too.

Chapter 28

Sixteen hours. That's how long it's been since I last thought of Storm, since I last wondered what she would be doing if she were still here. Sixteen hours since we sat on that trolley, hearing about the ghost tours she would have loved. Sixteen hours spent curled up next to Cameron, shutting out the world, the memories, everything but each other. I can't believe I let myself forget.

I didn't, though—forget Storm. I could never, really. But as I sit here, in the passenger seat of her car, watching Cameron from the corner of my eye, I'm in awe that last night could have happened at all. That we could find so much joy in the sorrow we've been sharing.

"You ready?" Cameron asks, breaking the morning's silence. We're in the car, newly fixed and ready to go, still in the mechanic's parking lot.

"Ready." We pull onto the road, and I dig my phone out of my purse. "I'm going to call Aunt Morgan real quick, all right?"

Cameron nods, switching lanes while I dial. She answers almost immediately, her voice way too chipper for how early it is. "Banana!"

"Hi," I say into the phone, stifling a yawn.

"You're calling early."

"Yeah, thought I would check in. We just picked up the car—"

"How much did that cost you?"

"I don't want to talk about it." Cameron tried to share the cost of the repair, but I refused. My bank account is feeling the effects of that decision now. Still, between the two of us, we have enough to finish our trip, so we're fine. "Anyway," I say, "we're going to head down the coast today to Wilmington and Carolina Beach, and I don't want to forget to call when we get there."

"Do you need me to find you a room?"

"That's okay. I think we can manage. I'll call if we need help." We plan to check off #13: Sleep in the UNCW dorms, but if we can't find a way in, we will figure something out.

"Sounds good. Did you guys have fun this weekend?" I blush at the memories of yesterday and look sideways at Cameron. He raises an eyebrow in question. "Yeah, it was great," I tell Aunt Morgan.

"I'm glad. You sound happy."

"You know what? I am." A smile creeps up at the corners of my mouth.

Aunt Morgan laughs softly. "Good. You deserve to be. Oh— and, banana?"

"Yeah?"

"You guys were safe, right?"

I groan and roll my eyes, not that she can see the expression. "Of course we were," I whisper.

"Just making sure." Her voice is full of laughter. "Hey, I gotta go. My shift starts in an hour and I still have to shower."

"Okay. I'll talk to you later. Love you."

"Love you, too. And I'm really happy for you, Anna."

"Thanks." I hang up the phone and drop my head against the passenger seat, rolling it to look at Cameron. "She totally knows."

"Knows what?" He keeps his eyes on the road, navigating our way to the outskirts of New Bern.

"You know . . . knows."

Red flares in his ears, and his shoulders hunch slightly. "Oh," is all he manages to say.

"Don't worry about it, though. Aunt Morgan is totally cool. She won't tell the parentals, so you're safe."

We stop at a red light behind an old, blue truck with a rusty bumper. Cameron grabs my hand and places it into his lap, tracing the lines of my palm with a finger. He looks at me mischievously. "What do you think they'd do if they found out? That I deflowered their little girl, I mean? I probably wouldn't be invited over for Monday night dinners anymore, huh?"

The car slowly rolls forward as the truck ahead of us struggles its way through the intersection. "Well, you didn't actually deflower me, remember? I'm pretty sure Mom and Dad know I'm not their pure princess anymore. They just like to pretend I still am. But all bets are off if they find out about you and Storm. She was still their little girl."

My voice chokes in my throat, a noise somewhere between

surprise and sadness. Cameron's hand freezes above mine, and then he grips the steering wheel hard. Clears his throat.

"Sorry," I say, barely able to force my voice out. "That was . . ."

"It's fine." But his voice tells me it's very much not fine.

She's been here, with us, all morning. Reminding us of our loss, weighing heavily on our shoulders. Are we allowed to be this happy without her? It seems wrong, like we did something we shouldn't have. But I can't help it; even as I feel the guilt, my insides bubble with excitement and attraction and a ridiculous need to be close to Cameron. Last night wasn't enough for me. I want him, always.

"It wasn't fine," I say. "I wasn't thinking."

Suddenly, Cameron turns in his seat, checking behind us, then jerks the car to the side of the road and stomps the parking brake.

"Whoa. Is everything okay?"

He turns to face me, pain etched across his features. "Anna . . . ," he whispers.

My heart stops, my shoulders tense, creeping up toward my ears. This is it—I can see it in his eyes. Last night was a mistake. I was a mistake. I brace myself for the letdown, but it doesn't come. Instead, he stares at me, his face a jumble of emotions, unsure of which will win. I feel sick, disbelief and amazement crushing me. He still says nothing, until I can't stand it anymore. I would rather just get it over with and move on. Just pull it off fast, Mom always told me when I had to remove a Band-Aid as a kid, and it won't hurt as much. So I say, "Listen, last night wasn't a big deal, okay, so you don't have to—"

"What?" His shock stops my words before I can finish my sentence. "Last night was a *huge* deal."

"It doesn't have to be. We can just pretend . . ."

He leans across the car and touches his mouth to mine, hard and hot. This kiss is unlike any of the others. This one isn't sweet and tender, exploring new territory, nor is it the rushed, lust-filled kisses we shared yesterday. This kiss is a declaration, firm and unmistakable: he wants to be here, with me, no questions. We break apart, and I gasp for air.

"Will you just shut up and listen?" he says.

I nod.

"Anna . . ." He pauses, his eyes searching my features, trying to read my thoughts as he finds the right words. "If I had known, I wouldn't have done it."

"Wouldn't have—"

He holds up a hand. "Just wait, okay? I have to say it. If I had known that you and I—that any of this were pos-sible—I wouldn't have done it. Storm was my best friend. Sometimes I thought she was my other half, that we were soulmates. But I didn't love her."

"Yes, you did."

He nods, a smile softening his face. "Of course I did. But not in that way. Not like—not like I love you. I did it because she made me promise. It was a stupid pact, and sometimes I can't believe I actually went through with it, but you know—"

I finish for him, talking over his words. "Yeah, I know how Storm was."

He laughs, a little forced, but close to the Cameron laugh I love, the one I can't help but laugh along with. Suddenly, his face turns serious again. "I don't want her to hang over us."

"She'll always be here," I whisper.

"She will. And I am so incredibly happy about that. That's the only thing that keeps me going without her, knowing that she's here with us, in our memories. I see her when you smile, Anna, and it breaks my heart and makes me love you even more, all at the same time." With the side of his hand, he wipes a tear from under my eye.

"I never thought we looked alike at all," I say.

"You don't." He laughs again. "Until you smile. Then you two—you're the most beautiful girls I've ever seen. But, this"—he draws my hand to his mouth, kissing it lightly, then presses my palm flat to his chest, his heart beating fast and strong—"I want this to be just us. I want to be able to be with you and love you and kiss you whenever I want. I don't want to feel guilty about what happened with Storm. Okay?"

My breath shudders as I try to calm myself and find my voice. "I feel like it's wrong to be so happy when she's gone," I admit.

"But it's not. It's okay to be happy, Anna. Storm would hate it if we spent all our time moping over her."

He's right, and I can't believe I didn't see it before. I love Storm, miss her with all my being, but I can't believe I've let myself forget her—the eight-year-old who hated people to pity her because she was sick, the teenager who believed, more than anything, in following her heart and being herself. She loved life, and she loved love, and she was always more alive than anyone else in the room. And she would never forgive me if I used her as an excuse to push away love.

Wiping my tears away, not gently like Cameron had, but hard, rubbing my palms against my eyes, I get an idea. "I need to find a party store."

His surprise is palpable. "What?"

"You know," I say, staring at him, "a party store—I need to get a helium balloon."

He nods in understanding, already tapping on his phone screen. He brings up directions on the GPS and, without a word, pulls back onto the road. Nerves and excitement rush at me from all sides.

The drive takes five minutes, and when we pull into the parking lot, I jump from the car without waiting for him to come to a complete stop. The door hangs open behind me as I run toward the store. I pick the most Storm-like balloon I see, bright green and blue swirls with tiny white polka dots. At the checkout counter, I ask for a notepad and pen. The boy behind the counter, around fifteen years old and acne riddled, watches me curiously as I scribble my secret on the paper. I fold the note into a tiny square, shove it into the balloon, and ask him to fill it.

Cameron says nothing when I climb back into the passenger's seat, just looks at me expectantly. "Marina," is all I have to say, and he drives us there in silence.

I run along the docks, searching the boat names as I go, Cameron trailing behind me with Polaroid in hand. We race up and down the rows, and I'm just starting to panic, thinking I won't find it, when *Persephone* comes into view. I stop in front of the boat, standing in the middle of the dock. I hold the balloon high above my head and watch it dance at the end of its string, waiting to be set free, to soar into the blue sky.

I hear the shutter clap just as I let go of the string. Cameron steps beside me, wrapping an arm around my waist, but I don't look at him. I watch my balloon drifting upward, dipping and darting in the slight breeze, until I lose it against the bright blue of the sky. Then I turn into Cameron, looping my arms tightly around his neck and giving him a kiss. Above us, my secret floats into nothingness, set free at last.

Dear Storm,
You wrote to put a secret in a balloon and set it free, so here it goes: my deepest secret.
I was jealous of you. Not of your cancer and how sick you were, but of everything that it brought. The attention, how you were always just a bit more special than

the rest of us. I know you hated it, never wanted to be treated differently, but I couldn't help it. I was jealous. I always felt like I was second-string in our house.

I love him, Storm. We all do, I know. It's hard not to love Cameron Andrews. But with him, I am the most important person in the world, and I love him even more for it. Thank you for giving me Cameron, someone to love and someone who loves you as much as I do. I miss you desperately, and I will for my whole life. I'll never stop missing you. But I know now that I'll be okay. I'll live my life as fully as you always did.

And I will always love you.

Chapter 29

Once we hit the highway, the hum of the tires sings me to sleep. I snooze straight through the drive, only waking when Cameron shakes my shoulder and whispers, "We're here."

I blink away the blurriness in my eyes and watch the scenery pass by the car's window. An empty field gives way to a smattering of buildings, big box stores first, then clusters of identical brick houses lined up along curving roads.

The road bends into the city, and we pass tree-filled parks and a huge shopping mall. There's a tiny burger shack to our right, the line for the order window snaking down the block.

Cameron guides the car into the turn lane, and we stare straight at the entrance to the University of North Carolina at Wilmington. I can picture Storm here, walking between classes, sitting under one of the massive trees studying. We pull into the parking lot, and I send Aunt Morgan a quick message.

ME: We made it. Can you look in Storm's desk for her college paperwork?

AUNT MORGAN: I don't see anything. What exactly would it be?

ME: I dunno. Something that says what room she was assigned. Her roommate info and stuff.

AUNT MORGAN: Sorry, banana. All I'm seeing here is a form for her enrollment deposit.

I stare at my phone in disbelief. I remember when Storm got the envelope, her acceptance letter and scholarship offer, a shiny class brochure tucked in, too. The enrollment deposit form was in the envelope, way back in January. I watched Dad write the check. He handed it to Storm across the table one morning as we finished breakfast. Why is it still in her desk? Why didn't she send it in? This was her dream, everything she'd worked for since middle school.

"Aunt Morgan can't find what dorm Storm was supposed to be in. Did she tell you by chance?" I ask Cameron.

"Um, I don't think so." We are like an island in the empty sea of the parking lot. He rubs a hand across the back of his neck. "Does it really matter?" His words are clipped.

"What's up? Are you okay?"

"Yeah, why?"

"Well, could you tell your voice that?"

"Sorry. I'm just tired, I guess."

Rubbing his shoulder, I say, "You should have woken me up. I would have driven."

"Not a chance, lady. Last time you drove, the car fell apart."

I punch his shoulder. "Shut up! You said that wasn't my fault."

"I'm teasing. You looked peaceful." He pecks me on the cheek. "I don't mind driving, really. Let's walk around for a bit. I'll feel better soon."

We weave through campus, admiring the huge, beautiful buildings, their red bricks and white columns like something from a movie. When we see Dobo Hall, Cameron races up the steps and sits with his back against one of the white pillars. I follow, and when I reach him, he guides me into his lap, nuzzling his face into my hair.

"Better?" I say.

"I am now."

Storm had tacked a picture of Dobo Hall on the wall above her desk when she was a high school freshman. "This would have been where her classes were," I tell him. "All those marine biology ones. She would have practically lived in this building,"

"I know. She never shut up about it."

I hop up and hold a hand out to help Cameron to his feet. "Let's go find our room."

It doesn't take long to figure out that the dorms are closed for the summer. We run into locked doors everywhere we go, and I grow increasingly more frustrated at each barred entry.

"What are we going to do?" I sweep my hair over my shoulder, but Cameron stops my hands before I can start braiding it.

"Stay here. I'll figure something out. Be right back."

He runs off, leaving me standing in the middle of the open lawn. I watch him round the corner of the nearest building. To pass the time, I lie flat on my back, the grass cool beneath me, and watch the sparse clouds float by.

Something is wrong. I don't know what, but I've felt it since we pulled into town. It's like the pieces of this day don't quite fit, a puzzle forced together by a toddler. It may look all right from a distance, but up close you can see the wrongness of the thing. I open the messages on my phone, read back over my recent conversation with Aunt Morgan. Maybe I'm overreacting. Aunt Morgan finding that form doesn't mean anything. Maybe it's a duplicate and Storm already sent in the deposit. Maybe . . . I don't know, but there has to be some explanation other than Storm walking away from the dream she held since she was twelve years old. I text Aunt Morgan.

ME: Was there a check?

AUNT MORGAN: Where?

ME: In Storm's room. With the deposit form.

She doesn't respond for a while, my phone finally binging at the same time Cameron appears around the side of the building.

AUNT MORGAN: Yeah. It's here. Why?

I drop my phone to the grass. What were you thinking, Storm? This school was all she talked about, what she worked for all those years. She had a plan, a goal, and Storm never quit on her goals. Why, then, wouldn't she send in the deposit— wouldn't officially enroll?

"I got us a room," Cameron says as he approaches. When I don't move, he kneels. "Hey, you all right?"

No, I'm not all right, but I don't say it out loud. Instead, I force myself to smile at him. "Yeah." He doesn't look convinced.

I can't think about this now, don't want to deal with what it might mean—that I really didn't know her at all anymore. I need to focus, to remember why we are here. We're almost to the end of our journey. The list has only three things left on it—the dive-in movie, kiss in the rain, sleep in the dorms—and I can't believe we're so close. Shoving my phone into my pocket, I stand and clasp his hand. "Let's go see our room."

"Uh, we can't actually do that yet."

"Why?"

"Well, let's just say that it's not so kosher for us to be in there. But the guy I found working outside of the building said if we come back after he's off work, he'll let us in before going home."

"How much did that set you back?"

"You might have to flash him to get us through the door." He says it like it's nothing. I stop dead in my tracks.

"You told him what?"

"Relax, Anna. I'm kidding. I just told him what's going on. It's cool." He pulls me closer, tucking me under his arm as we start walking. "You sure you're okay?"

I don't know why I don't tell him about the unsent check. It's like talking about it would be admitting a truth: I didn't know my sister. Not toward the end of her life, at least. If I knew her, *really* knew her, wouldn't I have known something as big as this? So I don't say it, don't let myself believe it's true. Instead, I simply ask, "Where are we going?"

"Jerry told me—"

"Who's Jerry?"

"The dorm janitor. Keep up." He winks at me, and I can't help but rise on my tiptoes and kiss him, tripping us up. When we regain our balance, he continues, "Anyway, Jerry told me about this great burger place, P.T.'s. I'm starving."

Cameron navigates us to the burger stand I noticed on the way into campus, and we stand in the line, which is thankfully shorter than it had been before. We grab burgers and fries—heavenly—and sit at a little table in the corner of the porch.

In between bites, I say, "What are we going to do until we can get into the dorm?"

"Well"—Cameron stops to chew and swallow a massive bite of burger—"we're so close to Carolina Beach, I thought we could go find your dive-in and see what's playing this week."

I practically spring from my chair. "Yes, please! Let's go!"

"Calm down, Turbo. We can finish our food first."

We do, me wolfing down my burger and fries in record time, and Cameron moving slowly, savoring every bite. By the time he finishes, I'm about to explode.

"Geez, Anna, what's the rush?" he jokes.

We refill our sweet teas and head to the car. As we pull out of the parking spot I say, "I don't know if I can explain it, but it just feels like . . . everything has been leading up to this moment. This is the only thing on the list that I had a concrete plan for, and now we are almost there. It's surreal."

"Are you ready? To be done, I mean?"

Am I? I'm not sure, and suddenly, inexplicably, I'm nervous. "Not really, but I'm excited, too."

He squeezes my hand in agreement, and we head to Carolina Beach.

. · · · · .

The drive is beautiful. We make our way past the campus and out of town. Trees line the road for a few minutes, and then we climb a hill to a bridge. I gasp. The marshes lining the Intracoastal Waterway shine in the bright sun, gold and green with water sparkling among them. Birds flit above the water, and a boat trolls slowly beneath us. We cross, and a sign greets us at the other side of the bridge: WELCOME TO CAROLINA BEACH, HOME OF THE PLEASURE ISLAND SEAFOOD BLUES AND JAZZ FESTIVAL.

I can't believe we're actually here.

The park isn't hard to find. A sign directs us to the right, past the boardwalk entrance on the left. We stop the car in a small parking lot at the entrance of the park then walk in, neither of us saying a word.

Carolina Beach Lake Park is a world of its own. Lined by colorful beach houses, it's an oasis of grass, trees, and flowering plants. The lake at the far end is more of a pond, really—small but beautiful. We walk directly toward it, following a path around the perimeter until we're back where we started.

"There's nothing here," I say, staring at a family of ducks gliding in the water.

"Maybe they set up the dive-in right before it starts?" Cameron tosses a rock into the water, and we watch the ripples spread across the pond's placid surface.

A middle-aged man is walking toward us from the other side of the pond, a tiny fluff ball of a dog at the end of the rhinestone-encrusted leash. We wait for him to reach us. The dog immediately jumps on my shins, tail wagging, and I bend to pet it.

"I'm so sorry about that," the man says, tugging on the leash. "Come on, Clyde. Leave 'em alone."

"It's fine." I scratch the dog behind its ears. "He's cute."

"Excuse me," Cameron asks the man, "but do you know what the deal is with the dive-in?"

"The dive-in?" The man looks confused.

"Yeah, the movie thing," I clarify.

The man laughs. "Oh, I know what it is, darlin'. But they haven't shown movies here in years."

"They haven't?"

"Nah. Hurricane Irene tore up the screen a few years back, and the HOA decided it was too expensive to keep it up, so they stopped the movies. They play water volleyball once a week now instead."

"So it's gone," I whisper in disbelief. All these miles, anticipation, everything for the past week brought us to this. The only thing I had a concrete plan for. And it's gone. Just like her.

It's fitting, actually.

I'd been stupid to think I could complete a list. I can't remember a single summer when we finished one—why should this summer be any different? I guess I thought if I could do it, could actually tick off each item this one time, then it would be like I was giving her the thing she couldn't give herself. As if completing the list would keep Storm alive. But it hits me now that I can't complete the list: she's really gone. And I'm not ready for that reality.

Cameron thanks the man and leads me to a bench. As soon as we sit, my face is on his chest, tears flowing freely. It's the after-funeral day all over again, the pain of loss just as raw as it was then, as I let go of the last strings holding me to my sister. She's not here to guide me anymore. It's time to figure it out on my own.

I've never been so terrified.

We sit on the bench for minutes or hours, or days even. Cameron holds me as my heart breaks open. And then, I'm done, too tired even for tears. I stand abruptly. "Let's go."

"Do you want to walk around a bit more?"

I shake my head. "I just want to go home."

"Okay." He takes my hand, and we head toward the car. "I'll ask Jerry if he can let us in a bit early."

"No, not there. Home, home. It's over. I want to go home."

"Come on, Anna." We're at the car now, and I lean against the hot metal, Cameron hugging me close. He says, "Let's just go to the dorm. We can sleep on it, mark one more thing off the list. Then, in the morning, if you still really want to go back home, we can. Okay?"

I nod, and he stoops to kiss me. There's sadness in his kiss, and I can't tell if it's coming from him or me. Maybe it's both.

We stop at an ice-cream shop on the way back, Cameron ordering each of us tall cones of vanilla with gummy bears mixed in. The candy turns hard in the cold, making my jaw ache as I chew them. It takes the entire ride back to campus to make my way through the cone.

We park off campus, on one of the roads away from the dorms, so our car won't go noticed overnight, and then we head across the lawn toward our place for the night.

Jerry is nowhere to be seen. "You're sure this is the right building?" I ask.

"Yes. I'm sure. He said he'd be right here."

"Well, he's obviously not."

"Thanks for that astute observation." He shakes his head. "Sorry. I'm a jerk." He kisses my cheek and releases my hand. "Wait right here. I'll see if I can figure something out."

Dropping my bag to the ground, I sit with my back against the building and close my eyes. Suddenly, I want to cry again, but instead, I force deep breaths, trying to calm myself, to ease the anxiety brewing in my chest.

My phone bings. Saved by the bell.

CAMERON: 4th window to the right of center door.

ME: The yellow duck flies at midnight.

CAMERON: What?

ME: You first.

CAMERON: Please come to the 4th window to the right of the door.

Faintly in the distance, I hear the scraping of a window being lifted on its track. I heave myself off the ground, grabbing my bag, and run toward the sound. Cameron's there, inside a room, prying the screen off the window. He waves me in, grabbing my bag and helping me scramble over the ledge. As soon as I'm in the room, he presses the screen back on and closes the window.

"What the heck was that?"

"I got us in, that's what."

"How?"

He shrugs. "Found a service door."

"Cameron . . ."

The room is barren, just two twin beds, their mattresses naked, and two built-in desks. Cameron drops to one of the beds and pulls me down next to him. "Remember that year when Storm and I wanted to be PIs?"

"Vaguely."

"Well, we were totally into it. Learned to pick locks and everything."

I stare at him. "Seriously? We can get into huge trouble for this!"

He kisses my forehead. "Relax. I'm kidding. Jerry left the back door propped open. We're fine."

"Jerk."

"It was funny, and you know it."

"If you say so."

Cameron runs his fingers through my hair, working out the tangles, his breath moving slowly across the top of my head.

"Do you remember our first sleepover?" His voice is so quiet only the rumble in his chest gives the words away. I nod.

"I was four," I say, "and it was the first time I was allowed to sleep in the tent with you and Storm." It was a huge deal for me, the first time I was really included, a part of the group instead of just the little sister following them around. "I can't believe you remember that."

"Of course I do. I remember everything."

"Sap."

"Yup. Remember when you got scared of the wind?"

"Did not."

"Did too. Storm was sick, and we had to go inside early, remember?"

I nod.

"She wasn't actually sick," he says. "She faked it so we could go in and so you wouldn't be scared anymore."

I think back to that night. Mom had to come outside and move us into the house after midnight. We set up our sleeping bags on the living room floor, and Mom brought Storm a bucket, just in case she needed to vomit.

"She wasn't really sick?"

"No, she wasn't. She was always looking out for you. Always."

I trace a finger along his jaw, feeling the sandpapery stubble growing there. "I miss her."

"Me too."

When we come together this time, it isn't the frantic, desperate need to be together. This time, we reach our rhythm immediately, slower, sweeter. Coming from a need of comfort and connection. Coming from love.

Chapter 30

Cameron and I sleep tangled together on one of the twin beds, and even though my neck hurts and my lower back aches from the strange angle I've been in all night, I don't want to leave his embrace. I stay wrapped in his arms, my head resting on his chest, as I study the room in the pale morning light. The walls are white, painted cinder blocks. I wonder what the room looked like during the school year, with students living in it.

I can image these walls crammed with Storm's Polaroid pictures, neat little squares lined up side to side, black Sharpie phrases scribbled over them. Her side of the room would have been crisp and orderly, everything in its place, neat lines and patterns.

What would her roommate have been like? Storm filled out a survey about her likes and habits so the school could better match her with a roommate. Would the girl have been just like her, clean and neat? Or would the other side of the room have been chaos, a contrast to Storm's orderly nature?

"I don't get it," I say aloud suddenly.

"What?" Cameron has clearly been awake, too.

"Why Storm would put *this* on her list—sleeping in the dorm. She was coming here to live in the fall anyway. Why would she make this part of a summer list?"

Cameron remains quiet, but I notice his body go oddly stiff.

His heart races under my ear. I prop my head on my hand and stare at him.

"Oh, you know her secret," I tease, poking him in the side. "Come on, spill!"

He looks at me now, the pain on his face enough to break me in half. I hold my breath, my eyes pleading with him to say something. Reluctantly, he sits up, rolling me off of him. He pulls his pajama pants on, letting them hang low on his hips. He slips on his glasses and digs through his bag. I sit on the edge of the bed and watch as he extracts a small envelope from the bottom of the duffel.

It's battered and worn, as if it's been opened dozens of times. Cameron holds it protectively against his chest, and I can tell he doesn't want to show me what's inside. Fear overwhelms me. I have to know what's in there, but don't want to at the same time.

Finally, he extends the envelope to me. His voice is barely a whisper when he says, "I'm sorry." He sits on the opposite bed, and he feels worlds away.

My hands shake as I flip open the blank envelope. I pull out a few papers, and a small scrap flutters to the bed. I reach for it, but find myself paralyzed by the logo on the letterhead in my other hand. It's from the hospital.

Storm's oncologist.

The words blur in front of me, and I struggle to read the page, unable to focus through the panic rising in me. But I

get enough, individual words jumping at me, forming a dis-
jointed picture:

*Relapse . . . metastasis . . . migration . . . aggressive . . . brain . . .
palliative . . . noncurative*

6–9 months.

I stare at the numbers, not letting myself comprehend
what they are telling me. The page falls to the floor. The next
sheet is a sparse form, the blanks filled in with Storm's scrawl.
I hone in on a typed paragraph halfway down the page:

*Despite my physician's recommendation, I am declining to con-
sent to this medical treatment, test or procedure. The physician has
explained the following risks associated with not following through
with the recommended test/procedure/treatment.*

I can't read more. I scan to the bottom of the page, where
Storm's signature burns into me, the date two months before
the accident.

"What is this?" My voice shakes. The words bounce around
in my brain, the whole story there, but somehow unable to
come together in a way I can believe.

Cameron stares at me, his eyes glassy. "She gave it to me at
graduation." His voice is raw. "She was afraid your parents would
find it. She didn't want anyone to know. I didn't even open it
until later. I—I didn't know it'd be the last . . ." He doesn't finish,
but I know what is coming: *the last time I would see her.*

"How long have you known? Not this"—I wave the treatment refusal form in the air—"but that she was sick, I mean."

"Since March twelfth. I'm so sorry. She made me promise not to tell anyone. She begged me, and you know how Storm is."

"Was! How she *was*."

Cameron leans forward, moving to hug me, to comfort me, but I recoil from his outstretched hands. My movement rustles something on the bed. The scrap of paper, the one that fell out of the envelope. I pick it up. My fingers feel numb against the smooth paper.

It looks like it was torn hastily from a bigger page. Random print covers the back, words that make no sense. I flip it over. The front side of the paper has only two words, in Storm's handwriting.

I'm sorry.

"What—" But before I can ask, the realization slams into me, and my whole body grows cold, as numb as my fingers.

Cameron is talking, but I can't make out his words. The only thing I can think about, the only thing I know, is this: it wasn't an accident.

I'm on my feet now. It wasn't an accident. My sister chose to leave me, to disappear from my life. I race to the door. I don't know where I'm going, don't really care, but I can't be here stuck in this tiny room with Cameron and the proof of Storm's abandonment.

"Anna, wait—"

Suddenly, my voice rushes back, and I spin, lashing out. "You knew! You knew this whole time, and you still let me . . .

let me—" I sputter to a stop. Tears fight at my eyes, and I try to force them back. He doesn't deserve my tears, not after this. But they fall anyway.

"Let you what?" His voice cracks, and he stands statue-still, as if afraid he'll scare me off with any movement.

"You let me do all"—my arm waves in a broad circle, gesturing to the whole world—"this. To follow this stupid list. To give Storm the perfect summer when she didn't care enough to be here herself—to finish her own list!"

I crumple, falling to my knees, hysterics overtaking my body. Cameron's arms circle around me, tentative at first, then drawing me into his chest, his hand stroking my hair. He murmurs softly into my ear, words I can't understand, but the deep rumble in his chest is comforting.

I cry. I cry for Storm, who is gone. Even though I realize she did this to herself, to me, I miss her desperately. She left a whole life behind. In nine months, I'll be older than she ever was, and she won't be my big sister anymore.

Suddenly, I am so tired of crying, of feeling vulnerable. I rip myself away from Cameron. I get dressed, slipping a sundress over my head. Then I pack my bag.

Cameron's intake of breath is sharp, but I interrupt him before he can speak. "Please, Cam," I say, barely more than a whisper. "Just let me go." I walk out, the door clicking shut behind me, and I leave Cameron, the list, and this summer behind.

Chapter 31

I walk for hours until my legs ache and my feet are raw. I'm in a residential subdivision; ahead, the street dead-ends at a park, a wide lawn leading to colorful playground equipment and tennis courts. I sit on one of the swings and call Piper. It goes to voice mail.

"Where are you, Pip?" I groan and hang up. I've been calling her since I left the dorm, desperate for someone to talk to, but she's not answering calls or returning texts. Piper is never without her phone. I dial again. This time, it doesn't even ring before voice mail picks up. I sigh.

Another text alert dings on my phone. Cameron has called four times and sent countless text messages. I can't bring myself to read them. I swipe the notification from the screen and pull up Jovani's number.

"Hey, girl," he says, answering immediately.

"Hi, Jo." I'm flooded with relief at the sound of his voice. It's the first time I've heard it since I left.

"Anna? Are you okay?" I can hear Piper's voice in the background, and I wonder if he only answered because she wouldn't.

"No, not really."

"Hold on. I'm pulling over."

"You answered your phone while driving?"

"Relax, Mom. I'm stopped now. What's up?"

Swaying slowly on the swing, I tell Jovani my story, starting with the night of the horrible party, when I first found the list. I tell him about my plan with Dad and Aunt Morgan and convincing Cameron to come with me on this crazy trip. Nothing gets left out, and my face blazes as I recount—details excluded—rushing back to the B&B to be with Cameron. When I get to this morning's fight and what Cameron was hiding in that envelope, I choke over my words. The story exhausts me, and I slump against the swing chain once I'm finished.

"You really got a tattoo?" They're the first words he's said since I started, and the absurdity of the question, after everything I just told him, catches me off guard. I laugh. In the background, Piper echoes him. "She got a tattoo?"

"Yeah."

"You'll have to show me when you get home." He pauses, and I wait. It's one of the things I love most about Jovani, the way he never says something unless he really means it. He weighs his words carefully. "You love him?"

"I do."

"And he loves you?"

My chest flutters at the question. If there is one thing I could never doubt, it's that Cameron loves me. "Yes."

"Then you forgive him," Jovani says. Simple as that.

"But he—"

"I know what he did. It sucks. I'm not saying you should go running back to him right now. You are allowed to be mad at him. But find a way to forgive him. Don't throw away what you have over this one thing. Take some time and figure out how to get past it."

"What if I can't?"

"You can. That's not the question you need to be asking. The question really is, what if you won't?"

Can I forgive Cameron? I've never felt as betrayed as I do now—betrayed by the two people who love me the most. I think back on the summer. The devastation that's ripped me apart, and the trip that's started to piece me back together. Storm and Cameron, at the center of it all.

Yes, I know I can forgive him. Not now—now I'm too hurt, too angry. Someday, maybe tomorrow, maybe five years from now when we bump into each other in the aisles of the grocery store, I'll look at him and this will be forgiven, just another chapter in the story that shaped my life.

"Thank you, Jo. You always know what to say."

"It's a gift," he says. "So, what are you going to do?"

The words form in my mouth before I even know the idea has developed, and when I say them, I know they're true. "I'm coming home."

"What about Cameron?"

"I'll take the bus. The ride will give me time to think, away from him."

"Let me know when you get back. We can grab lunch, maybe watch a movie."

"That sounds, perfect," I say. "Thanks, Jo."

"Anytime. But can you do me a favor?"

"What?"

"Tell Cameron. Just send him a text if you don't want to talk, but let him know you are leaving."

"I will." I'm about to hang up, but something stops me, and I keep the phone to my ear. "Hey, Jo?"

"Yeah." His voice sounds far away.

"Why do you think we never worked out, you and me?"

He seems unsurprised by the question. "You don't love me."

I start to protest, but he talks over me. "I know you love me, Anna, and I love you. But we both know you never loved me the way you love him."

"I'm sorry."

He laughs loudly. "Don't be. We had fun."

"That we did."

"You okay?"

"Not yet, but I'm better."

"Good. I miss you, girl."

"You too." A pause. "I better call my aunt. I'll talk to you later. Tell Pip I said hi."

We hang up, but I don't call Aunt Morgan yet. Instead, I look up the number of a taxi company. I tell the man where I am and settle in to wait. There's another text from Cameron, but I'm still not ready to read it. I swipe it off the screen. Maybe later.

I push my feet against the ground, raising the swing higher, higher until I'm on my toes, nowhere else to rise. I let go, riding the swing on its subtle arc, a human pendulum. Pumping my legs the way Storm taught me when we were kids, I propel the swing to the limits of its chains.

Up here, soaring through the sky with my hair trailing behind me, it's easy to forget, to just let everything I learned this morning fade away. To pretend it never happened. I'm a child again, with no cares other than whether Mom and Dad will let me stay up late. Birds sing in the trees at the edge of the park; I squeeze my eyes shut and let the sounds of their song surround me.

I swing and swing until my legs are tired, and then I keep going, unwilling to come back to Earth quite yet. I could stay up here forever, away from the pain and heartbreak of real life.

But, all too soon, I hear the sound of gravel crunching beneath car tires, the unmistakable screech of brakes. The taxi driver waits for me to slow my swing, and I jump to the ground as soon as I'm sure I won't face-plant in the grass. The driver steps out of the car as I cross the lawn toward him.

"Are you Anna?" he asks.

"Yeah."

He grabs my bag from me and sets it in the trunk then rounds the car to open a back door for me. "Where are we headed?"

"Um, a bus station?"

"Like, Greyhound?"

I nod. "Yes, please," I say as I settle into the seat and close my eyes.

The taxi pulls away from the curb, and we wind through labyrinthine streets. The driver makes a few attempts at conversation, but when he's met with nothing but one-word replies and the occasional grunt, he abandons his efforts.

We arrive at the station sooner than seems possible. It's a small building, stark gray with only a sign in the window signifying that it's a bus station. Through a dirty window, I see a woman behind a counter, an ancient computer propped in front of her. Three vending machines stand against the outside wall, soldiers in a row waiting to serve.

I pay the driver and watch as he drives away. Dropping my bag on the ground next to a solitary wooden bench, I pull my phone from my purse and sit.

Aunt Morgan answers immediately. "Anna! Oh thank goodness. Where are you?"

Pulling the phone from my ear, I check the screen. I've missed twelve calls since I climbed onto the swing.

"What's going on?" I ask evenly.

"Why don't you tell me? Cameron called the house—"

"He did?"

"He's panicked! Told me you ran off and won't answer his calls or texts. Where are you?"

I wrap my hair around my wrist. "Did you know?" My voice is ice.

"What?"

"The truth, Morgan? Did you know?"

"I'm not sure . . . what do you mean?"

She sounds convincing, and my heart breaks at what I'm going to tell her. I'd been so sure that I was the only one left in the dark, that my whole family knew Storm was sick and had been lying to me, that I never considered that maybe she'd kept the truth from them, too. That maybe it was only Storm and Cameron who lied to me.

I'm not sure which version hurts more.

"Anna?" Aunt Morgan says apprehensively, when I don't answer for several moments.

"She was sick. Again."

"Who was—?"

"Storm! The cancer came back, worse this time. And she decided—" A sob heaves in my chest, snatching the words from between my lips before they have a chance to come out. I can't do it, can't say the rest out loud. Because saying it out loud is acknowledging the truth—that Storm hit that tree on purpose. Instead, I say, "And Cameron knew. This whole time. He knew, and he never said anything."

"Oh, Anna," she says. "I'm so sorry."

With the side of my hand, I wipe a tear away, hating that I'm crying again. I take a deep, shaky breath. "I'm coming home."

"Okay."

Suddenly, I'm reminded of why I love Aunt Morgan so intensely. She knows me better than I know myself sometimes, and she knows exactly when she can push me and when she should just let things be. She doesn't try to convince me to talk about it or to defend Storm and Cameron. She simply says, "Okay," and then, "Do you need any money?"

"I don't know," I admit. "I'm at the bus station, but I haven't checked to see how much a ticket will be. I'll go now and call you back if I need anything."

"Okay. Keep me posted. I love you, banana."

"You too."

It takes the ticket agent nearly fifteen minutes to beat her old computer into submission and to find a route that will take me from Wilmington to Muscatine with the fewest bus changes. She can get me as close as Cincinnati, where I'll have to catch a smaller shuttle to Muscatine. The cost of the ticket scrapes right to the bottom of my bank account, but I don't have to call Aunt Morgan for money. The woman hands my itinerary across the counter along with a receipt she grabs from a printer that's maybe even older than the computer. My bus leaves in ninety minutes.

Back outside and firmly situated on my bench, I find Cameron's number on my phone and send him a text.

ME: I'm going home. Taking the bus. I'm fine.

His reply comes immediately, and for the first time today, I read the words he sends.

CAMERON: Anna, please, just talk to me. I love you.

His face flashes across my mind, the pain that masked it as he pulled the envelope out of his bag. The hurt is brand-new all over again as I replay the papers he hid from me, the tiny scrap of paper Storm had written on. I echo her words to him now.

ME: I'm sorry.

I turn off my phone and shove it into my bag before settling in to wait for my bus. It's going to be a long ride home.

August

Chapter 32

Aunt Morgan sits next to me on the hard, unforgiving couch. Her knee bounces about six thousand times a minute, but I don't bother trying to steady it. Her outward emotion mirrors my inner one perfectly. The parentals will be back any minute. I keep glancing through the observation window, wondering when I'll see their plane dotting the sky.

I've been home a week, and I haven't told Aunt Morgan the whole truth yet. That little scrap of paper, Storm's apology, haunts me, taunting my efforts to go back to real life since the shuttle pulled into Muscatine and dropped me back into normalcy.

I haven't seen Cameron. Haven't talked to him, either. He came to the house the day he got home, dropping Storm's car in the driveway, but I stayed in my bedroom, ignoring the doorbell. He's tried a few times since, standing on the front porch, attempting to convince Aunt Morgan to let him in. Eventually, I heard her tell him to give me room, and his visits stopped, along with his texts and phone calls.

Jovani pushes for me to talk to Cam, but I can't bring myself to do it. After I got home, I tried to write an apology, but as soon as I typed the first two words, I was done. *I'm sorry.* The anger rushed back in, as fresh as it was when I first saw those same words in Storm's handwriting and learned that the boy I'd fallen in love with had been lying to me all summer.

Piper won't talk to me. I called her the day after I returned, but she didn't answer. I've texted, called, even went by her house. She's not answered anything. I stopped trying a couple days ago. I miss her fiercely, but she obviously needs time to get over it, and I'm trying to give her just that. I'm not sure how much longer I can wait, though. I need my best friend.

"It's here," Aunt Morgan says, knocking me with her knee.

The plane is impossibly huge in the sky, taking over the blue as it descends to the runway. Together, we walk to the window, joining the crowds waiting for their loved ones. The plane takes forever to pull up to the gate. We wait even longer. People pour off the jetway, looking weary. Some run and embrace their waiting families; more stream past us, down the stairs to the luggage carousel.

I see Dad first, his head peeking above the crowd, and then a family shifts, and Mom's standing there, smiling. She looks more relaxed than I've seen her since the accident. My parents clutch hands, moving as one unit, and suddenly I'm overwhelmed with how much I've missed them. I weave through the crowd until I'm standing in front of them, tears in my eyes.

Dad hugs me tight against his chest. In this instant, I'm six years old again, and my dad is the bravest man in the world. No one can comfort me or make me feel safe like he can. I let his steady breathing calm my nerves before I let go and hug Mom.

She's soft, a pillow I can fall onto and drift to sleep. She smells of vanilla and stagnant airplane air. I inhale deeply, finding her typical, mild citrus scent buried deep. "Welcome home," I say.

We wait for their luggage then pile into the SUV, Aunt Morgan at the wheel. "You all want to get some lunch?" she asks. "Or just head home?"

"Home, please," Mom says. "I'm exhausted."

The ride is filled with awkward small talk: How was the flight? You'll have to show us your pictures. Did anything exciting happen while we were gone? Both Aunt Morgan and I fall silent at that question, the weight of the summer infiltrating the air in the car, but Mom and Dad don't seem to notice.

When we pull into the driveway, I'm struck by how similar everything looks, a stark contrast to how different my world has become. The bags are unloaded, and the four of us file into the house in silence. Aunt Morgan clasps my hand, squeezes painfully hard. I know.

It's time.

"Mom, Dad, could you, uh, sit down for a minute?" My voice tips them off immediately and concern etches Dad's features. He looks at me, the question clear on his face, and I give the tiniest of nods. He leads Mom to the living room, and they sit as one unit on the love seat. I take my normal perch on the couch, grateful that Aunt Morgan is sitting next to me. For all her nerves and knee bouncing at the airport, she's steady now, strong and comforting against my rising anxiety.

The hem of my shirt rolls between my shaking fingers as I take a deep breath, stalling, looking for words that I know will never be enough. "First," I finally say, "I just want you to know I'm so, so happy you're back. I missed you."

My voice is oddly formal, as if I've prepared this speech. I wonder if I should have; it would be easier if I knew what I was supposed to say. Mom's knuckles are white beneath her vacation tan, her hands fisted together in her lap. She's scared, and I'm making her that way.

I rush to calm things, not that it's really possible, with what I'm about to say. But still, I try. "All right, here's the thing." My words are, thankfully, more me-sounding. "I don't want you to get mad at Aunt Morgan, okay? She was just trying to help me. . . ."

Dad's eyes are locked on mine, waiting for the rest, but I notice Mom's gaze wandering to her sister. She watches my aunt, waiting for an explanation, so I give her one before Aunt Morgan has to say a word.

I tell them about the list and the trip, giving them the *Reader's Digest* version of events, just enough so they know that I went and that Aunt Morgan let me. I'm surprised at the strength in my own voice, how calm I feel as I recite the events of the summer to them. Even when I get to the part where Cameron gave me the envelope, the story sounds like it's somehow not connected to me, like I'm merely providing a play-by-play of what happened to someone else. Someone not me.

The room falls silent when the story is finished. Dad is pale, ashen, and sick looking, more shocked than I thought he'd be. Mom's face is streaked with tears, but she doesn't make a sound. The quiet is oppressive, making me shrink into the corner of the couch. I had expected anger. Shock. Yelling. Grounding. Anything but this calm, silent acceptance.

"You knew, didn't you?" I whisper.

Mom stares silently at her hands. Dad clears his throat and says, "We suspected. She never told us, but the signs were there."

Signs? I think back to Storm's last months, the end of high school. What did I miss? How could I not have seen something this big? Even now, as I look back on those months, I can't remember anything different about my sister.

"Why didn't you *do* something?" I ask. Why didn't Dad tell me? I think back to our breakfast, me telling him about the list, hatching the plan to make this whole summer possible. He knew that whole time, and he said *nothing*.

"We couldn't. She was eighteen—an adult." Mom's voice is small, but crystal clear. "I tried to bring it up a couple times, but she changed the subject anytime I pressed her. She didn't want anyone to know, and I didn't want it to be true, so we didn't talk about it." More tears fall.

"Dad?" I stare at him, at his gaunt face and shiny eyes, and I see my own sadness reflected there. He looks like he's about to break apart, all relaxation from the vacation transformed into brittle, hard edges on his face. "What is it?" I whisper.

"I talked to Howard," he chokes out, his voice static, "to see if there was something we could do."

Mom's surprise is immediate. "You did?" she asks. "When?"

Aunt Morgan's gaze bounces between the two of them before she leans into me. "Who's Howard?" she whispers.

I shrug, but Dad answers for me. "Our lawyer." To Mom, he says, "The day before graduation. I knew something was wrong, that it'd gotten worse. And she"—he fists his hands in the sparse hair at the sides of his head, tugging on his scalp as his face crumples—"she wasn't doing anything. She didn't even care!"

"Roger?" Mom's voice shakes. Fear washes over her.

"I just wanted to see if there was something we could do. To force her to get the treatment. To make her see what she was doing to us." He crumples under the weight of his own words. "Maybe if I'd asked sooner, figured it out—I don't know, committed her? Made her do the treatment—maybe she'd still be here."

Tears stream down Mom's face. I can feel my own trailing down my cheeks, mirroring hers. She puts a hand on Dad's knee and squeezes his hand with the other. "You couldn't have stopped it, honey. You couldn't have—"

"I should've done something," he whispers.

His eyes meet mine for only a second, but it's enough. With one look, I know that he knows. The scrap of paper that haunts me every second of the day—he's never seen it, but he knows. And he blames himself. I wish I could take that away from him, to absorb his hurt, to let it live with my own so he doesn't have to feel it. But I can't. We will live with this hurt forever, the two of us, knowing that she chose to leave us.

And, just like I can't take his hurt away, I know I can protect Mom from feeling the same. The two of us, Dad and me—we can carry this burden so she doesn't have to. We will bury the knowledge deep, keep it locked away, and protect her. We can't give her Storm back, but we can give her this.

"Am I in trouble?" It's lame after the revelations we just shared, but it's all I can think to say.

"We're disappointed," Mom says, looking pointedly at me then at Aunt Morgan. "You should have told us."

I glance at Dad, taking in the way he stares at the carpet, and wonder if we'll ever tell Mom the truth and admit to our scheme, tell her how Dad was in on it from the start. Maybe it would be better if we did. For now, though, I lock it away with Storm's truth, another secret Dad and I will continue to guard. I ask, "Would you have let me go if I did?"

"Probably not," Mom says.

"Then I'm glad we didn't," Aunt Morgan says, her words sounding loudly in the room. The sentence hugs me, bringing me into Aunt Morgan's love, reminding me that no matter what happens next, she's on my side.

"That's fair." Dad is nodding, and a small smile plays across his face. He gives me a mischievous grin and asks, "Did you at least learn to drive your car?"

I don't realize what he's saying at first. The words hang between us, floundering over the living room rug, waiting for me to make the connection.

"You're giving me Storm's car?"

"We talked about it, and you're right. We can't keep you locked up, and we can't punish you for what happened to your sister. It's yours if you want it."

"I do. Thank you."

"That doesn't mean you're off the hook," Mom interjects. "We'll talk about your punishment tomorrow, when I'm less tired. Until then, you should probably go enjoy your last night of freedom."

"Thanks," I whisper, and, after giving them both hugs, I dash from the room. It's only an act of the travel gods that is letting me out of the house tonight, so I better use every bit of time I have. I need this last night of freedom to fix things with Piper.

Chapter 33

"Where's Pip?" I ask as I climb into the minivan.

Jovani shrugs and backs out of the driveway. "No idea. I went by her house, but she wasn't there. Maybe she'll just meet us at Shelly's?"

"Yeah, maybe." Piper didn't answer my call or texts, but Jovani talked to her earlier about Shelly's party, and she should be there. A knot forms deep in my gut. Inexplicably, I'm nervous to see my best friend. This is the longest we've ever gone without talking, and it scares me.

Shelly lives at the far end of town, in one of the shiny new houses perched on top of the hill. Pretentious eyesores, Dad called them while they were being built, dotting the formerly clear horizon. Jo and I ride in silence, letting the sounds of the road and the tinkle of the piano music that's always playing in the van keep us company. It's not until Jo eases off the highway near Shelly's house that he speaks again.

"How much trouble are you in?"

I sigh. "I don't know. Mom is too tired to be mad, so all punishment has been suspended until tomorrow. It'll be bad, though, I'm sure."

Nodding, Jovani echoes my sentiment. He would know—he's felt my mother's wrath more than most, getting the blunt end of a tantrum one night when he drove me home two hours past curfew. He's probably only still with us today because Mom isn't nearly as intuitive as her sister about what we were doing to make us late.

"Talked to Cameron yet?" Jo asks.

"No."

"Anna—"

"I know," I interrupt, "but I'm just not ready. I keep thinking I can go over there and make things right, but then I remember. He lied to me, Jo. Not just a little lie, but a major one. How do I forgive that?"

We pull up in front of Shelly's neighbor's house. Shelly's driveway is crammed with cars and more line the street. I unbuckle my seat belt, but Jovani doesn't move. "Can I say something?" he asks.

"Yeah?"

"I mean, can I say something you probably don't want to hear? And still be able to walk at the end of it?"

I hold up my hands in mock surrender. "I won't bite. Just say it."

"Cameron did the right thing."

Blood rushes to my face, pounds in my ears. Despite my promise not to react violently, I'm suddenly overcome with the intense desire to throttle him. "How can you say that?" I say with a cold, hard voice.

"Just hear me out, all right?" He takes a deep breath and squeezes the steering wheel with both hands. "Storm didn't want people to know she was sick again, right? So of course he couldn't say anything while she was alive—he was too good of a friend. And then, after she died? What good would it have done? He—"

"What good? I would have known! I wouldn't have the people I love lying to me."

"But you would!" For the first time, Jovani raises his voice to match my own decibel level. "If he told you right after she died, with everything so new and raw, it could have hurt you even worse. And you know what? You would still feel betrayed by him and Storm, because they lied to you when she was alive. Nothing would have changed that, because Storm didn't want it any different."

"And I know how Storm was," I whisper to myself.

Jo looks at me quizzically, but keeps talking. "So, he waited. He went with you on this crazy journey to work through what happened, and he waited to tell you the truth. Maybe he waited too long, but I can see why he did. I bet if you really think about it, you can see why, too."

That's the thing, though—I don't want to think about why Cameron did what he did. Because Jovani's right, and if I think long enough, I might understand Cam's motivation. And I don't want to understand. I want to be angry with him, to stay so mad that I see red when I think of that morning in the dorm. Being mad is much easier than the hurt and sadness I carried around for the first half of the summer. If I let go of the anger, there won't be anything left to stop the sorrow from overwhelming me again.

Without a word, I exit the car and follow the sidewalk to Shelly's front door. Jo rushes to keep up with me, but doesn't speak. He understands that the conversation is over.

Shelly greets us just inside the door, kissing Jovani fiercely then giving me a hug. "I missed you," she says. "Did you have fun on your trip?"

"Yeah, I did," I manage. "Is Pip here?"

"Living room," Shelly chirps before leading Jovani off to the kitchen. I head into the huge living room.

The couches and chairs are piled with bodies, everyone's attention turned to the front of the room, where Taylor and some guy I don't recognize—older, with scruffy black hair and a five-o'clock shadow—are singing a duet on a massive karaoke machine. I spot Piper at the end of the couch, her hair piled on top of her head in a chaos of a bun, her legs two white toothpicks sticking out of a dangerously short pair of shorts. I slip across the room and perch on the arm of the couch.

"Hey," I say when she doesn't seem to notice me.

She turns to me briefly, the smallest of smiles on her face. "Oh, hey," she says, nonchalant, then turns back to the front of the room. The duet is winding down, Taylor and the guy are staring into each other's eyes as they belt out the final notes. When the music stops, she kisses him on the cheek and they pass their microphones to a couple of girls sitting on the love seat, who flip through a songbook with laughter.

"What's up?" I say to Piper, pulling my knees to my chest. My toes hang off the edge of the armrest, and I curl them down, giving myself a tiny bit of extra balance.

"Oh, not much," she says, standing. "I need a drink." She breezes off without so much as a glance in my direction.

It feels like every eye in the room is focused on me. Rationally, I know that's stupid, that most of these people didn't notice Piper's dismissal, and those who did probably don't care, but the humiliation is real. Sliding off the edge of the couch, I follow her into the kitchen. It's empty except for Jovani and Shelly, who are leaning against the counter, making out. Piper digs through a cooler on the floor, and I stand just inside the doorway, staring at her.

Jovani and Shelly break apart just long enough to see who's joined them. Jo's eyes meet mine, and he raises an eyebrow in silent question. I give a miniscule head shake in response, and he and Shelly leave through the butler's pantry. Piper and I are alone.

She keeps digging through the cooler—apparently checking every can and bottle in there, refusing to turn around. I talk at the back of her head. "What's going on?"

"Nothing," she says over her shoulder. "I'm fine."

"Come on, Pip. You're not fine. Are you mad because I didn't tell you about the trip? I apologized for that. And I am *really* sorry. I don't know why I didn't tell you right away."

She turns around finally, a dark blue bottle in her hand.

Leaning against the side of the fridge, she twists the cap off and takes a long drink. "I'm not mad about that," she says.

"Okay, what are you mad about, then?"

She shrugs. "Nothing. I'm not mad."

"Stop. You've been avoiding me. Come on, Pip. What's going on?"

She takes another drink, longer this time. Lowering the bottle, she stares directly at me. "I leave for college in a few weeks. You were already gone, so it's just easier this way."

"Easier what way?"

"Easier if we aren't so attached. I thought leaving for college was going to be impossible, going without you. I've been dreading leaving you here. But then you just took off without even calling, and I realized that it won't be hard for you—just for me. So why don't we call it as it is? You don't need me, and I can find someone else at school. My roommate seems really nice." Her eyes fill with tears, and she looks away, her face hardening.

"That's not true," I whisper, and she scoffs. "I promise, Pip." I cross the room and stand directly in front of her. "I'm so sorry I didn't tell you about the trip. You know how messed up I've been since Storm . . . I should have called you, though." I touch her now, hesitantly, one hand on her shoulder. "I miss you, Pip, and I don't want things to be like this. You have no idea how much I'll miss you when you're gone. You'll be so sick of me visiting and crashing on your dorm floor."

"Promise?" Her voice is tiny.

"Promise. Your roommate better be okay with visitors, because I am going to be down there every chance I get. I'm not ready to let go of you."

She smiles, but still doesn't look at me. "You don't have to visit me every weekend," she says. "You should probably save a few for Cameron."

"What?"

"Come on, Anna, I'm not dumb. You're totally into him. And he is so crazy about you it's not even funny."

"How? . . ."

"I ran into him at Walmart yesterday. He asked how you're doing. Which seemed pretty weird to me since you were supposed to be super close."

"What did he say?"

"Nothing." She finally looks at me, her eyes bright. "What happened between you two?"

"Let's sit," I say. "This might take a while."

Chapter 34

Mom was true to her word. As soon as she woke up the next morning—which was way too early—she barged into my room, shaking me awake and presenting me with a chore list about a mile long. I worked all day, cleaning and organizing, weeding the neglected garden, and helping Dad restain the back fence. We finished the day with the sun, stopping only when it was too dark to see what we were doing. My muscles ached, and my skin was hot with the starts of a mega sunburn.

When we called it quits and went inside, Mom was waiting with dinner and the rest of my punishment: groundation for the rest of the summer, and I am only allowed out to join them at church on Sundays and to work at Dad's office, helping digitize paper files.

This morning marked a week since my punishment began. When I came down for breakfast, Mom was at the table, waiting.

"Morning," I said.

"Good morning, sweetie." I helped myself to the pile of bagels on the counter, smearing peanut butter and honey across mine. She poured me a glass of milk, and we sat.

"I've been thinking," she said.

"Oh yeah?"

"You're still grounded. But it'd be okay if your friends came over here. I know Cameron and Piper are going to college soon, and I think you should be able to spend some time with them before they leave."

"Really?" I forced my bite down and followed it with a drink of milk. My throat felt suddenly tight.

"Yes, really."

"Thank you so much." I rounded the table and hugged her from behind. Pressing a kiss to her cheek, I said, "You're the best."

"Don't you forget it," she said. "Now, go call your friends."

Now, Piper, Jovani, and I are smashed together on the couch, a bowl of Mom's caramel popcorn balanced on my lap and a teen slasher flick on the screen. It's our third movie of the afternoon, and we're dangerously close to taking root in the couch cushions. Piper is sleeping, her steady breathing almost lulling me off, too.

Jovani's phone lights up, and he bends forward to grab it off the table, nearly knocking the popcorn bowl from my lap in the process. "Shelly?" I ask.

"Nah." He swipes his screen then taps a few quick words out. He drops it to the couch and reaches across my shoulders, shaking Piper. "Hey, Pip, we gotta go."

"Mmhhuh?"

"It's time to leave."

"Wait!" I drop the popcorn bowl onto the coffee table and pause the movie. "Where are you two going?"

"Um . . ." Jovani is staring at his phone again, furiously

tapping at the screen. "We have . . . something . . ."

"We told Shelly we'd help her with . . . uh, something her mom has going on. Sorry, we thought the movies would be over by now." Piper looks at my ear, unable to make eye contact. She is possibly the worst liar under the sun.

"What's going on?"

Before they can answer, the doorbell rings, and they both freeze. It's only a second, just long enough for me to notice, before they are in full motion again.

"Guys?"

The doorbell rings again, and they both stare at the door, pointedly. I sigh. "Fine," I say. "Don't tell me." I head for the door and open it without bothering to peek out the window.

My heart stops when I see who's standing there.

"Hey," Cameron says, staring at the ground somewhere near my feet.

"What are you doing here?"

"We invited him." Piper steps up next to me, Jovani following on her heels.

"You did *what*?" But I can't bring anger into my voice.

"It's time," Jo says. He kisses me on the cheek and whispers in my ear, "Don't be too hard on him."

My two best friends leave, and I'm left standing in the foyer with the boy next door.

"Anna," Cameron says after a minute of silence, "I'm so sorry. I—"

Someone Else's Summer

"It's okay."

"No, it's not. I shouldn't have—"

"It *is* okay," I say, and as the words leave my mouth, I know they are true. I forgive him. I'm not sure when I did, but as I look at him now, I can't be mad at him anymore. And I don't want to be.

"Thank you." He steps toward me, moves like he's about to grab my hand, but changes his mind and stays just out of reach. "Come with me," he says. "I have something to show you."

"Can't." I look up the stairs, where Mom and Dad are in bed, watching their own movie. "Grounded for life. Mom didn't take so well to our little trip."

"I know." He steps closer. All it would take to touch him would be to reach a hand out, brush my fingers with his. I don't. "I talked to your dad. It's okay."

"You talked to Dad?" I hear Jo's car drive away from the house. "That was you texting Jovani, wasn't it?"

He nods. "Please, come," he says. "I promise it'll be worth it."

My body screams at me to take his hand and be led wherever he wants to take me. Standing this close to him, I miss him so much the ache is physical. But I stand rooted to the spot, suddenly nervous in a way Cameron has never made me feel before. What if I walk out that door, let myself trust him again, and it ends badly? I can't go through all of this again.

The door hangs open, the night air calling to me. I can't move.

"Anna, sweetie?" Mom calls from the top of the stairs. I freeze.

"Yeah?"

"Just go. It's all right."

I look at Cameron in disbelief then up the stairs to where Mom stands, out of view. "Um, okay," I say. I turn to Cameron, say it again. "Okay."

We don't go far. Cameron walks down my sidewalk, me alongside him. The air between us is charged with want and longing and fear. At the end of my sidewalk, he takes a left, crosses in front of the lawn, then heads up his own driveway. I stop next to his truck, ready to have him take me wherever we are going, but he continues to the back gate.

"You coming?"

I nod, confused, and walk to him. He reaches a hand out, hesitantly. Without giving myself time to think, I grab his, linking our fingers. He pushes the gate open.

His backyard has been transformed. Gone is the wide expanse of lawn and ever-present badminton net. In its place is a random network of kiddie pools set against one another in a lopsided spiderweb of puddles. Each pool has a float in it—Styrofoam noodles and blow-up whales and children's float rings. At the far end of the yard, against the wooden privacy fence, hangs a white sheet.

"What is this?"

Cameron's face is alive, lit with excitement. He guides me to a small table set up against the side of the garage then lets go of my hand. On the table, two bottles of Dr Pepper sit beside a bucket of popcorn and a box of Hot Tamales. A small, black projector is at the end of the table, hooked up to Cameron's laptop. He clicks through the screens on the computer, carefully shielding it from my view.

"Welcome," he says, turning around to face me, "to the Andrews' dive-in."

"The what?" I turn and take the scene in, slower this time, and the pieces fall into place, realization hitting me. A picture pops up on the screen against the fence, Cinderella's castle set against the Disney-blue background. Two lawn chairs stand in front of the biggest pool, and we walk to them, Cameron carrying the snacks with us. Settling into my chair, I drop my feet into the cool water of the pool and grab Cameron's hand again, squeezing fiercely.

"Thank you," I whisper.

His answer is overwhelmed by the opening notes of *The Lion King*, the animated sunset creeping up the screen. How many times did we watch this movie as kids—me, Storm, and Cameron lying in a row on the living room floor, drinking Dr Pepper and sucking down Hot Tamales? It was our go-to activity, the companion to rainy days or what we did when one of us was too sick to play outside.

"This is perfect," I say.

He squeezes my hand. "I'm really sorry I didn't tell you."

"I know."

"And I love you."

Tilting my chair into his, I lay my head on his shoulder. My hair falls over my face, and he brushes it behind my ear, his hand lingering on my jawline.

"I love you, too."

He kisses the top of my head, and we sit like that, the arm of my chair pressing into my ribs, but me too close to him to care, as the movie unfolds in front of us.

The popcorn goes untouched, the Dr Pepper forgotten. But we share the box of Hot Tamales. I suck on them like I used to as a kid, letting the sugar melt on my tongue, ignoring the urge to chew them until they've turned clear and flavorless. We eat them until my mouth is numb, and then I chew a couple more.

Simba is singing "I Just Can't Wait to Be King" when my chair starts to tilt. Cameron's legs shoot out, splashing in the pool as he tries to find purchase, but it's too late. We're falling faster than our balance allows, the metal chair arms clanging against each other. I let go of him, trying to sit up, and pitch the other way. Cameron hits the ground, hard, a deep moan pushing out of him, and I hang suspended just long enough to know I'm going down, too.

The water is cold, a shock against my skin and in harsh contrast to the warm August night. I'm soaked. Sitting on the ground, the water is up to my rib cage. I shiver. Then the laughter hits me, sudden and strong and uncontrollable.

"I'm glad you find my pain so funny," Cameron says, but his voice holds a laugh as well.

"Shut up. I fell, too."

He works his way out of his chair, standing slowly. He shakes his arms and shrugs, rolling his head from side to side. "Ouch," he says.

"Sorry. I didn't realize you actually got hurt."

"Wanna try that with a straight face?"

I shake my head. "Sorry, can't." Laughter overtakes me again.

Cameron holds a hand out for me. I grab his, but don't let him pull me to my feet. Instead, I jerk at his arm. He pitches forward, caught off guard, but stabilizes before falling in. "Nice try," he says.

"Come on." I tug again, gentler this time. "What's the fun of a dive-in if you don't actually get in?"

He lets me pull him down to the pool. He climbs in gently, releasing my hand so he can crawl on hands and knees across the shallow water, approaching me. I lean until my back is against the side of the pool, then stop, letting him come closer still. My heart gallops, my skin tingles, and I open my mouth, my eyes drifting shut in anticipation.

The kiss doesn't come. He hovers there, mouth inches from mine, so close I can almost taste him. Instead of closing the gap, he sits back in the water, and reclines against the far side of the pool. He drapes an arm across the inflated plastic, a clear invitation. I take it and settle in next to him, our heat warring with the cold of the water.

My toes are turning prunish when the first drop of rain falls. On screen, Simba is eating grubs with Pumbaa and Timon, trying to forget his own heartache. I think of Storm, watching this movie, yelling at the screen for the young lion to go back to his life. She could never understand why he stayed away, why he couldn't face the pride after his father's death. I can hear her, voice loud and high-pitched in my ear: "Get it together, Simba! You have a life! Go live it!"

I can live my life, I think. Even without her, I can live my life. I'll miss her, always, but I can't let her death be the thing that defines the rest of my days. I can pick up the pieces and go back—no, I can never go back. But I can go forward, build the rest of my future. I can love the way Storm always did, open and fearless, and I can live the way she wanted to, without hesitation. She'll be with me, forever, the one I want to tell my life to first, the one who will shape my future without a word. She would want me to move forward, not forgetting her, but not letting her death be the thing that holds me back, either. I know it—I've known it for weeks. Sitting in an inflatable kiddie pool in the arms of the boy next door, I'm finally ready to keep living.

A large drop of rain hits my face, then another. It sprinkles my shoulders and splatters my hair. The rain falls, faster and faster, until Cameron jumps up. I nearly slide the rest of the way into the pool.

"Sorry," he says. "I gotta cover my laptop." He jogs to the garage.

I follow and reach the garage door just as he comes out, holding a tarp. Together, we drape it over the table, cocooning his laptop and the projector in its protection, securing it with bungee cords. The screen goes black, the light of the movie trapped under the plastic. We don't bother unplugging the projector, though, and the movie keeps playing to an empty audience.

It's raining even harder, the type of August rainstorm that's neither warm nor cold, just fast and wet and intense. It'll last only a few minutes, I know—already the deluge is starting to lighten up, the heaviest squall lasting only a minute. We stand under the garage overhang against the wall, but the rain hits us all the same, the roof offering very little protection.

We don't move.

We're standing so close. It's dark and Cameron's face is in shadow, the pale light from the back deck reflecting off the rainwater, creating an image that is altogether familiar and surreal. Water drips from his hair, trailing alongside his nose to his upper lip.

He stares at me just as I stare at him, and I wonder what he sees in the half-light. His chest moves steadily with deep, controlled breaths. He comes closer. My head tilts up as my gaze follows his.

The whole of the summer is rushing back, me and Cameron together, a team checking off items on a list. In June, it'd seemed impossible, these tasks Storm left behind, but here we are, at the end of summer, with only one thing left to do. I'm not ready for it to be over, want to cling to the last bit of Storm I have left. I tilt my head to the sky and let the rain pummel me.

✓ 1. Watch the sunrise.
✓ 2. Take pictures of EVERYTHING.
✓ 3. Get a tattoo.
✓ 4. Go inside a lighthouse.
✓ 5. ~~Meet my soulmate.~~ Fall in love.
✓ 6. Go skinny dipping.
   7. Kiss in the rain.
✓ 8. Put a secret in a balloon & let it fly away.
✓ 9. Road trip!
✓ 10. Crash a wedding.
✓ 11. Go to a dive-in movie.
✓ 12. Speak in a British accent all day.
✓ 13. Sleep in the UNCW dorms.
✓ 14. Go parasailing.
   15. Be brave with my life.

Be brave with my life. This summer, I started. I faced my fear of heights and jumped off the cliff. I rode the parachute to the end of the rope, floated above the ocean, Cameron at my side. Heights—one fear faced. But there is so much more, so many things I can do.

The list will never be done. As long as I am alive, moving forward, I will have Storm with me, her words etched on the last page of the journal and inked on my ribs, reminding me to be brave with my life. It's not something I can do in one summer, or one year, or one decade. #15: Be brave with my life, is a number I can never check off, and there is something intensely comforting in that knowledge.

I look at Cameron. He's watching me, face soft, apprehensive. With one step, I'm standing against him, my hand grasping his T-shirt. I pull him to me.

"Number seven?" he whispers.

I nod. "Number seven, and so much more," I say.

My mouth meets his, a kiss that's a promise. A promise to be brave with my life and with my heart. A promise of a thousand kisses to come. We stand there, arms wrapped around each other, lips connected, as the rain slows to a drizzle, the storm moving on as quickly as it came, and then we kiss a bit longer, until Cameron breaks away from me and disappears into the garage.

He's gone only a moment, returning with the familiar old Polaroid in one hand, the list in the other. He hands the book to me, and I take it, but don't open it. It's the story of a summer, of a life, of a death. I'll treasure it, look back on it in the future with fondness, remembering the list that changed everything. For now, I hold it tight, the cover sealed. I'm not ready to look back yet—don't want to remember. I want to live now, here with Cameron, looking forward together. I tuck the book under the edge of the tarp, safe on the table, then take the camera from his hands.

We stand together, like we have for so many pictures this summer, with the pools and makeshift movie screen behind us. I hold the camera at arm's length, and when Cameron leans down to kiss me, I click the shutter.

Together, we set our chairs upright. Then we lower into them, side by side, and watch as the photo develops.

Acknowledgments

To Ashley Maker, without whom Anna and Cameron's story would still be sitting on my hard drive. Thank you so much for your endless encouragement, for reading drafts so fresh I didn't even run spell-check, and for knowing my characters better than I do sometimes. You always know the exact right ways to make my books better, and you always give me the little nudges I need to *do something* with them. All the CPLove.

A massive THANK YOU to everyone behind Pitch Madness. Brenda Drake, for all the time you put into running such amazing contests, a million sparkly rainbows. Summer Heacock and Dee Romito, the fearless leaders of Team Rainbow Road, for pulling my little book out of the slush pile and giving it a chance, "thank you" isn't enough. Here, have a unicorn. And to my fellow teammates, for all the encouragement. You all are the best. #TeamRainbowRoad for life.

My amazing agent, Liza Fleissig: I'm pretty sure you love this book even more than I do. Your enthusiasm from day one has been spectacular, and I can't imagine being in better hands. You are a champion.

Julie Matysik, editor extraordinaire, what would this book be without you? Thank you for loving my characters and my story. And even more for showing me where I went wrong and shaping this book into something so much better. T.L. Bonaddio, how did you manage to capture so much of my book in one amazing cover? What you've done is beautiful. The team at Running Press has been great to work with—thank you all for taking such good care of me. Special thanks to Kristin Kiser, Adrienne Szpyrka, Amber Morris, Susan Hom, Cassie Drumm, and Emily Epstein White.

My Montana Mythcreants writing group: you guys are the best. It is so great to have a group to hang with while I write, to keep me motivated, to laugh when things are hard. Thank you for all your support! And to the Great Falls Hastings Cafe staff. Every word of this book was written at your tables, and you were always so welcoming. I miss you.

Finally, and most important, to my family. Without your support, this never would have happened. Kelvin, most patient husband ever, thank you for dealing with the messy house and unwashed laundry and late nights. You are the best. And Connor, my favorite little man, you put up with so much while I was working on this book, and you never complained. How did I get so lucky? I love you, my boys.

Q&A
WITH Rachel Bateman

Q: What was the catalyst for writing *Someone Else's Summer*? How did you come up with the idea for the road trip? The bucket list?

A: First thing's first: I *love* summer. We're talking major, let's-run-away-together love. So when the days get shorter and colder, I tend to write stories set during exciting, beautiful summers. And something I love just as much as summer? A good road trip. So those two things naturally fell together for me.

The idea of a bucket list is something that's been with me for a long time. Growing up, I loved making lists. (Who am I kidding? I still love making lists.) Every summer, I'd make extensive lists of all the things I wanted to do. Of course, by about week one of summer break, the list was forgotten, so it never got done, but the idea is one that stuck.

I was driving to my yearly lake vacation when the idea for *Someone Else's Summer* hit me. I was thinking back on all those abandoned summer lists when the thought of a girl trying to complete a list came to me . . . but what if she didn't write the list? How different would things be if she didn't get a say in what was actually on her list? So much of writing comes from that one question: what if?

The rest, as they say, is history.

....

Q: Did you pull from your own life experiences to develop your characters or their stories?

A: As an author, I am constantly pulling from my own life and experiences, even when I don't realize it. We all see the world through our own unique lens, our view being shaped by the experiences we've had. That said, there were some specific parts of my life that made it into *Someone Else's Summer*:

My name is Rachel. My older sister is Rani. Growing up, I was always kind of miffed that my parents were so creative in naming their first kid, but then I got such a *normal* name. When I started writing, Storm was already such a force in my imagination that I decided to play with that dynamic. (My parents were also total hippies. They might disagree, but I've seen their wedding pictures. . . .)

Much like Storm, I decided at a young age to study oceanography at UNC-Wilmington. Also like Storm, I ended up not doing that, but (obviously) for different reasons.

The summer after I graduated high school, my best friend and I decided to road trip from Montana to North Carolina. After our first long day of driving, we had to stop for the night. It was raining so hard we could barely see the end of the car. But there was a problem: it was Sturgis Bike Week, and we were smack dab in the middle of South Dakota. We searched for rooms for*ever* until we finally found one that was remarkably like the sketchy one Anna and Cameron stay in (including the man in the lobby taking responsibility for us to stay).

The amazing burger joint in Wilmington, North Carolina? It's a real place. If you ever find yourself in the area, make sure you grab some food at P.T.'s.

....

Q: Did you write with a specific audience in mind?

A: I did. From Day One, I knew I was writing this book for teenage girls. As a culture, sometimes we tend to hate things teenage girls love for no other reason than that teenage girls love them. How ridiculous is that? With *Someone Else's Summer*, I was writing what *I* wanted to read, but I always had teenage girls in the back of my mind, and I tried to write something they would love.

....

Q: Were you surprised at how the characters developed, or was it all planned?

A: Both, actually. I am a meticulous outliner, so I had pages and pages of notes on the story and characters before I ever started writing. I felt like I knew Anna, Cameron, and Storm so well. Not a lot changed with them throughout the writing process.

But, still, things have a way of cropping up and surprising me while I am writing. That's one of my favorite things about being an author! Sabine, Nina, and Court, the trio Anna and Cameron meet at the food truck in Virgo Beach, were meant to be one-scene throwaway characters. But as I wrote them, they really came alive on the page, and I knew I needed more of them. So I rearranged my entire outline to give Anna and Cameron more time in Virgo Beach. And to give Sabine, Nina, and Court some more page time. Readers have told me those scenes were their favorites, so I'm thrilled to go with the flow when those wonderful surprises happen.

Piper is another character who surprised me as I was writing. The more I got to know her, the more I knew some people would absolutely hate her. And they do! The most frequent complaint I get about this book is, "Ugh, but Piper is *terrible*." Truthfully, I love Piper, because I understand her so completely. She doesn't mean to seem heartless and uncaring. She's actually a real softie who just doesn't know how to deal with Anna's grief . . . so she doesn't. It makes her seem like she's not a great friend, but she's trying. Nobody is perfect; Piper's imperfections are just a bit more in-your-face than others'.

....

Someone Else's Summer

Q: What were the most heart-wrenching issues in the book that you grappled with while writing, and how did you balance Anna's grief with the fun of the road trip?

A: This was a careful balancing act for me. I knew going into the book that I wanted it to be uplifting and light on the surface, but with this heavier core of loss and grief. There were times when I worried Anna and Cameron would seem insensitive as they went on their journey. But then I thought about what grief is really like: it can be all-consuming, but sometimes it fades into the background and, before you know it, you're having fun and enjoying life again, if only for a moment. Grief ebbs and flows, and it can catch you off-guard, both by its intensity and its lack of intensity. Once I had that realization, the balance came more naturally.

The hardest, most heart-wrenching thing for me to write had to be Anna's relationship with her mother. Or, really, lack thereof. Here I was, writing this girl who needed her mother more than ever, and I couldn't give her that. Readers don't get to see it, because we pick up the story at Storm's funeral, but in my mind, I knew that Anna and her mother actually had a good relationship before the grief got to be too much for her mother.

....

Q: How did you approach writing the father-daughter relationship in *Someone Else's Summer*, especially writing in a genre with such established conventions around parents' involvement with their protagonist children?

A: In my first draft, Anna's father was just as mentally checked out as her mother, which made it really easy for Anna and Cameron to head out on their trip. But it didn't make for a very strong character, or for a realistic story. The thing about young adult books is: they are about these awesome teenagers and their adventures, and the teens need some sense of autonomy to make things work. Because of that, we often have absentee parents in some way or another. (Like Anna's mom, they mentally check out; they are neglectful; they are dead; you name it, as long as they aren't around.)

But the most compelling parents in young adult literature are the ones who are an active part of their teen's life. I knew I needed to show that Anna does have a good relationship with at least one of her parents still. Her mother couldn't be there for her, but her dad could handle it. The scene with the two of them in the diner started as a quick writing exercise to see how they would interact with each other. Before I knew it, I had them hatching this plan together, Roger fully in Anna's corner trying to support her in whatever she needed to work through her grief. I fell in love with the character of Roger a bit that day, and I think that shows through the rest of the book.

....

Q: One of my favorite things about the book was Anna and Aunt Morgan's relationship. What inspired you to write that?

A: I come from a very big family with lots of aunts and uncles. I love them all so much, but one aunt in particular has always been really special to me. My Aunt Cindy was the only one of my aunts who didn't have kids of her own, and I think because of that, she was the favorite of all of her nieces. Her attention never had to be divided by her own children, so it could be fully on you when you were at her house. We used to go to Aunt Cindy's for sleepovers, and we just loved to dig in her closet and play dress-up with all her clothes and high heels.

I knew I wanted to give Anna someone she could talk to when she didn't have Storm anymore and her mother was too absorbed in her own grief to be there for Anna. Because of my Aunt Cindy, it came pretty naturally for Anna to have an aunt she is close to, kind of like a younger, cooler version of her mom. (Sorry, Mom!)

....

Q: One of the bucket list items that resonates most with Anna is to be brave with her life. Why do you think it's important for teenagers and young adults to be brave?

A: The teen years are an interesting time in life. We are finally old enough to be making serious decisions for ourselves, but at the same time it can feel like everything is already planned for us. Whether it's pressure from parents or friends or society, it can be hard to really embrace what we want, rather than what is wanted for us.

It takes a lot of bravery to figure out who you are and what you want. And it takes a ton of bravery to make mistakes along the way. What's so great about life is that we naturally have that bravery in us—just watch a little kid for a while. They are not afraid to try new things and make mistakes in order to get what they want.

A lot of pressure is put on teenagers today to do things "right." When a young child makes a mistake, it's just part of life, but for some reason when a teenager makes a mistake, suddenly that's a problem. And when mistakes are problems, we tend to play it safe so we won't make more. I don't know exactly when the shift happens or when we start playing it safe, but I think it's so important for us to hold on to that part that is willing to screw up occasionally. Because that's true bravery—to figure out what you want and to go for it, even if it means falling on your face a time or two along the way.

....

Q: How do you feel knowing you inspired so many people with your book?

A: I am seriously in awe of how people have responded to Anna, Cameron, and their journey. My readers have been so enthusiastic and fantastic in sharing their own stories and experiences with me. A lovely reader in Italy (hi, Jess!) was so inspired by the book that she wrote part of Storm's list on her wall to remind her to be brave. That absolutely blows my mind.

Sometimes I really have to step back and look at the tweets and Instagram posts and just think, *Whoa, I wrote that. It was really me.* Life can be weirdly beautiful sometimes.

....

Q: You wrote *Someone Else's Summer* during National Novel Writing Month, and now you're a NaNoWriMo Municipal Liaison. What about NaNoWriMo do you love so much?

A: NaNoWriMo is such an exciting time for so many authors. By having the goal of writing 50,000 words in a month (the official NaNoWriMo goal; I try to write a full book during that month), you are forced to turn off that little voice in your head that is constantly saying, "This isn't working, you've got it all wrong, oh my gosh this book sucks why are you even writing it?" When you write as fast as NaNo pushes you to, you simply don't have time for those thoughts. In my experience, some of the best, most creative, and purest writing comes from the push of NaNoWriMo.

On top of that, there's a community to NaNoWriMo that makes things so much fun. The forums are full of writers swapping ideas and cheering each other on, hosting word wars, and commiserating when things get tough. The people at NaNoWriMo have really built a community, and I love it.

....

Q: Are you working on anything new right now?

A: I feel like I'm always working on something new! I love trying new things with my writing. Sometimes that gives me something really exciting; sometimes I end up with a giant flop. Diving into something new is always an adventure.

I had a baby right before *Someone Else's Summer* was published, so I took some time off from writing to enjoy hanging out with him. Now, I'm feeling my way back into what my next project should be. Stay tuned!

....

Q: What, exactly, was the deal with the sushi that time?

A: My sister Rani is amazing. (The ego that was already boosted by that dedication just grew more.) While I was writing *Someone Else's Summer,* she would come visit me pretty regularly, often with food. Seriously, I didn't starve during my mad-dash drafting thanks to her generosity.

One night, while I was working on edits, I was craving sushi something fierce, but I didn't want to stop working to go get some. So I sent Rani a text message saying I'd dedicate the book to her if she'd pretty please bring me some sushi. She didn't know that I'd decided to dedicate it to her long before, so I thought I could get some sushi with a bit of a false bribe.

She didn't go for it. I never got my sushi, but she got her dedication.